WICKED DARLINGS

ALSO BY JORDYN TAYLOR

The Paper Girl of Paris
Don't Breathe a Word
The Revenge Game

WICKED DARLINGS

JORDYN TAYLOR

DELACORTE PRESS

This is a work of fiction. Names, characters, places, and incidents either are the product of the author's imagination or are used fictitiously. Any resemblance to actual persons, living or dead, events, or locales is entirely coincidental.

Text copyright © 2025 by Jordyn Taylor
Jacket photo copyright © 2025 by Brian Powell/Stocksy

All rights reserved. Published in the United States by Delacorte Press, an imprint of Random House Children's Books, a division of Penguin Random House LLC, New York.

Delacorte Press is a registered trademark and the colophon is a trademark of Penguin Random House LLC.

GetUnderlined.com

Educators and librarians, for a variety of teaching tools, visit us at RHTeachersLibrarians.com

Library of Congress Cataloging-in-Publication Data is available upon request.
ISBN 978-0-593-70985-6 (trade) — ISBN 978-0-593-70987-0 (ebook) — ISBN 979-8-217-02777-4 (international ed.)

The text of this book is set in 10.75-point Chronicle Text.
Interior design by Ken Crossland

Printed in the United States of America
10 9 8 7 6 5 4 3 2 1
First Edition

Random House Children's Books supports the First Amendment and celebrates the right to read.

Penguin Random House values and supports copyright. Copyright fuels creativity, encourages diverse voices, promotes free speech, and creates a vibrant culture. Thank you for buying an authorized edition of this book and for complying with copyright laws by not reproducing, scanning, or distributing any part of it in any form without permission. You are supporting writers and allowing Penguin Random House to continue to publish books for every reader. Please note that no part of this book may be used or reproduced in any manner for the purpose of training artificial intelligence technologies or systems.

For Russell.
I'm lucky to be your sister.

WICKED DARLINGS

CHAPTER 1

I would have hated this party if my sister were alive. Leah would have strolled out in the cutest bikini imaginable, showing off her sculpted muscles from soccer and her glowing skin that by some scientific miracle only tanned and never burned. She would have replaced my Top 40 playlist with something obscure but catchy that got everyone gushing over her music taste. She would have introduced some fun new drinking game, and told wild stories from her first year of college. She would have been funny, and magnetic, and smart, and beautiful, and perfect.

And everyone would have forgotten that I was the one who invited them.

I couldn't *not* plan a party when I found out my parents would be in Canada for some cousin's daughter's bat mitzvah the weekend before graduation. For the first time ever, I wouldn't have to wrestle with Leah for the spotlight; I could just bask in its glow, knowing my friends had come to see me, and me alone. I went all out. I messaged everyone in my grade. I ordered a cornhole set and a giant pool floatie shaped like a unicorn. This morning, I spent hours hanging string lights, cleaning the pool, and blowing up so many shiny Mylar balloons that I legitimately almost passed out.

But holy hell, was it worth it. Because here I am, encircled by friends who knew Leah, but now they're all chanting my name: Noa. Today, I'm not the other Falk sister; I'm *the* Falk sister. And I'm sorry, but it's awesome.

On the count of three, I knock back the shot of dragon fruit vodka my friend Charlotte just shoved into my hand. Ugh. It tastes like lipstick and bleach had a baby, but whatever. People are cheering, and that takes the edge off the burning in my esophagus. I hold out my little plastic cup so Charlotte can top me up.

"Oi! Noa!" Someone with a sexy British accent shouts my name from the pool. It's Alistair, the exchange student I've been casually hooking up with for the past few months. He shakes his wet curls out of his eyes. "Come be my chicken fight partner."

"One sec!" I down the second shot—dear God, this is literal poison—and bounce over to the pool, where I take off my linen shirt and shimmy out of my denim cutoffs.

"Wow." Alistair's eyes travel up and down my red one-piece bathing suit. I'm a shorter, paler, much-less-athletically-inclined version of my sister, but Alistair doesn't know that. He's never met Leah, since she died last summer, and he came to New Jersey in the fall. I have to admit, I like it that way, and I'm going to miss him after he flies back to England tomorrow. I sweep my shoulder-length dark-brown hair into a bun and slip into the water. Alistair dives beneath the surface, swims through my legs, and lifts me up on his shoulders.

"Is now a good time to say I've enjoyed being between your legs?" he jokes.

"AL!" I swat his arm, but he can obviously hear the glee in my voice. When Leah was alive, guys would only take interest in me after she rejected them first, and a few girls only kissed me for a shot at becoming her friend.

Our first matchup is against a pair of girls on the softball team, each with biceps the size of grapefruits.

"Al, we're screwed."

"No, we're not. C'mon. You've got this."

We are, in fact, screwed. It takes Sarabeth approximately six seconds to knock my shrimpy body backward off Alistair's shoulders. I come up for air, laughing. "Told you." I splash him. "That was a total fail."

"I bet we could win at something," he says. He nods toward the grass, where Millie and Reza, this year's prom king and queen, are tossing beanbags back and forth. "What about the game I can never remember the name of?"

"Cornhole?"

"That's the one." Alistair smirks. "You *did* say I have to try this time-honored American tradition before I leave."

I did say that while I was ordering the cornhole set the other day, but I didn't envision us playing it with Millie Santiago, who, aside from being prom queen and valedictorian, is also the unofficial president of the Dead Sisters Club. I'd rather let Charlotte pour dragon fruit vodka straight down my throat than play cornhole with Millie, but it's too late to make up an excuse.

Alistair's already pushed himself out of the pool, and he's waving to the couple, asking if we can join. Millie's overjoyed at the suggestion, because *of course* she is. She's the only person here who I wish liked me less.

Bouncing on the balls of her bare feet, Millie gestures with her arms for me and Alistair to split up. "Let's do me and Rez versus you guys," Millie says. "Noa, you come stand with me."

Fabulous. But I'm not about to be a bad host. "Okay," I say as I drag myself out of the water.

We launch into a practice round so Alistair can learn the rules. When he immediately sinks a beanbag through our hole, I jump up and down and cheer. Millie flips her long black hair over her shoulder and lobs a beanbag over. As soon as it flies out of her hand, she asks me a question under her breath. "How are you, Noa?" Emphasis on the *are,* like she knows something other people don't.

Millie's older sister, Gabby, died by suicide when we were sophomores. Before that, Gabby had dealt with terrible depression for years. After Leah took her own life last summer, Millie rushed to my side to support me, having gone through the same thing herself. She started inviting me to eat lunch with her at least once a week; then she asked me to join her at family fun runs and bake sales and dance-a-thons for mental health awareness. She was a *good* sister, clearly. I had to tell her I was way too busy with college applications and newspaper stuff to hang out, because the truth was way too complicated to explain.

"I'm good," I tell Millie.

Alistair's beanbag thuds onto the edge of our board. "You're doing so well!" Millie shouts. As I line up my shot, Millie lowers her voice again. "But how are you *really,* Noa?"

"I'm fine," I mutter to Millie. "Seriously."

I throw the beanbag way too hard. It flies over the boys' board and smacks Alistair in the hip. "Ow!" he yelps. "Hitting your teammate isn't extra points, as far as I understand."

"Sorry!"

"You know you can be real with me," Millie murmurs.

"I *am* being real with you."

She gives me a pitiful look as we collect the beanbags for the next round. "After Gabby passed away, I found it so hard to enjoy stuff like this," she says gently. "I might have told you this before." *Only forty billion times, but let's make it forty billion and one.* "This voice in my head would be like, *It's not fair that I get to be here and my sister doesn't.* You know? NICE ONE, BABE!" Reza's beanbag just skidded onto the board and knocked Alistair's through the hole. Play-fighting, Al elbows Reza, and Reza shoves him back. They laugh like they don't have a care in the world, and my chest aches with envy. I wish I could just exist without constantly having to calculate how much I should loathe myself. "Just know that if you're feeling that way—hypothetically, of course," Millie continues with a wink, and it makes me want to hurl a beanbag at her forehead, "my therapist, Gloria—who's amazing, by the way—says it's totally normal, but we also have to challenge that belief. And you want to know how we challenge it?"

Not especially. "How?"

"By having fun."

Millie winds up for her next shot. She doesn't realize I *was* having fun until she had to go and remind me what a monster I am. Her next beanbag makes a perfect arc through the air and whooshes through the opposite hole.

"OH, YAY! WE WIN!" She skips across the grass and throws her arms around Reza's neck. She kisses him on the lips, then asks, "You guys wanna play again?"

"Actually, I really need the bathroom," I say. "You don't have to wait for me." Before Millie can say anything else, I turn on my heel and march into the house, through the kitchen, and into the foyer. Oh no. I'm relieved to be away from Millie, but not to be standing face to face with the gallery wall of family photos.

Since I was the younger sister, my parents always signed me up for whatever activities Leah was already doing. There we are, ages nine and seven, at Miss Sugar Plum's Ballet School. I was never as flexible or as graceful as Leah, which meant I was always shoved in the back, while she took center stage. There's another photo from when we were fourteen and twelve and I was forced to join the soccer team that Leah was already captaining. That was the year I chopped off my hair in a desperate bid to assert my own identity. The pixie cut required way too much pomade to look even half decent, and I regretted it almost immediately.

In high school, I finally forged my own path. I stage-managed the school play. I joined yearbook. And I started reporting for the school newspaper, my favorite activity of all. By the end of ninth grade, I knew I wanted to be a journalist. Not only did I have a passion for it, but Leah *didn't*, which felt almost as, if not just as, important. Journalism was my dream, and mine alone.

Until it wasn't.

It was May of last year, and Leah came home from her first year of college with an announcement: she'd scored a last-minute internship offer from the *Gotham Sentinel*, a historic

Manhattan newspaper with a rich and powerful readership. Her job would be to go to wealthy people's parties and write about them: what happened, who was there, who *wasn't* there, and why. From June to August, she would basically be a full-time society reporter at a famous publication.

I dropped my fork with a piece of chicken still speared on the end, got up from the dinner table, and stormed out of the room. It didn't matter that Leah's beat at the *Sentinel* would be different from the investigative reporting I wanted to do. By accepting that internship offer, she'd gone ahead and claimed my dream as her own.

Leah followed me out of the kitchen and chased me up the stairs. "Why can't you just be happy for me?" she pleaded.

I whirled around in my bedroom doorway. "Why would I be happy? You just stole my whole *thing,* Leah!"

"I didn't steal anything!" she cried. "You've told me a billion times how great a career in journalism would be."

"Yeah, because I wanted you to know it was *mine.*"

"Why can't it be mine too?"

"BECAUSE EVERYTHING IS YOURS, LEAH!"

She stood there, blinking slowly, like I'd slapped her across the face. "What do you mean, everything is mine?"

"You really are oblivious, aren't you?"

"Oblivious to what?" she asked.

"How good you've always had it." Did we live on different planets? Leah was clearly our parents' favorite. They drove up to Skidmore to watch her soccer games, they called to ask how she did on every test. Mom had maybe read a few things I'd written for the school paper, but there was no way Dad had. Did he even know I wrote for the paper to begin with? Unlikely. I was a random afterthought. A shadow.

"Oh, sure, it's *great* being me," Leah snapped sarcastically.

I couldn't believe the words coming out of her mouth. "If you can't see how lucky you are, then you are so fucking clueless, Leah."

She narrowed her eyes at me. "You're the one who's clueless, Noa."

"Oh yeah? Well, I know one thing."

"What?"

"I'm done with you."

"You're *done* with me?"

"Done."

"What does that even mean?"

"It means I don't want to see you again for as long as I live."

And then I slammed the door in my sister's face.

Later that night, I passed Leah in the hallway on my way to brush my teeth. Her mascara had bled around her eyes—from crying, or from washing her face without using a makeup wipe first? I didn't care. I did, however, realize it would be hard not to see my only sister again for the rest of my life. At least she'd be in the city all summer, and then back at Skidmore for the fall. I wouldn't have to see her in any meaningful way until Thanksgiving, at the earliest.

For the next week, I avoided her around the house. For dinner, I went to friends' places, or ate cereal in my room. When Leah left our house in New Jersey for her sublet in Hell's Kitchen for the summer, I didn't say goodbye. I knelt on my bed and watched out the window as she and my parents pulled out of the driveway, and I thought, *Finally. She's gone.*

That August, early on a Saturday morning, we got a call from the police that Leah's roommate, Janie, had come home from her bartending shift and found my sister's lifeless body on the floor of her bedroom. Leah had apparently returned from covering a party for work and overdosed on a painkiller called oxycodone.

The earth fell out from under us. We didn't understand. Leah hadn't been dealing with depression—at least, not as far as we knew—and she didn't leave a note explaining anything. My parents got a court order that gave them access to her phone. I'm not sure exactly what they found on there, but once they'd dug through it, they said it was clear the pressure of her workload at the *Sentinel* had become too much for her to handle.

That explained the text she'd sent me the day before she'd gone to that Friday-night party.

LEAH

Hey, N. I miss you. I know you're probably still mad at me, but I could really, really use your help right now. I can explain more in person or over the phone, but I've never been this anxious in my life. There's this party I'm supposed to cover tomorrow, and I was wondering if you could come with me. I'll send you money for a train ticket and you can sleep in my bed. It would mean so much to me, you have no idea. Let me know. I love you.

She was right: I *was* still mad. All summer, she'd been proudly posting links to the articles she was writing. She'd even shipped physical copies of the paper home to Jersey so we could all see just how great she was—and I could have salt shoved in my gaping wound. I refused to read any of her stories. And when she texted me that day, saying she'd never been more anxious in her life...

I thought, *Good. Serves you right for stealing my dream.*

And I ignored her.

I can't look at these family photos anymore. Might as well go to the bathroom. Slamming the door behind me, I stare into the mirror at my pale face, my soggy topknot, and my slate-gray eyes, cold and hard. I look away before the tears come.

The sound of my name in Alistair's voice snaps me out of my funk. He's standing there, waiting for me, when I get back to the kitchen. Like me, he's still wearing just a bathing suit, and I can't stop staring at his sculpted shoulders, dusted with freckles. This guy is hot, and nice, and in possession of a British accent. Best of all, he came inside looking for *me*.

Alistair's hands find my waist, and he pulls me in for a kiss. "Missed you," he says.

"I was gone for like two minutes."

He kisses me again. "Well, I'm leaving tomorrow, and I want to make the most of every minute before I go." Alistair's eyes dart toward the stairs.

I'm out of my head and back into my body, and my body wants to take him up to my bedroom. Grabbing his hand, I lead him out of the kitchen, careful not to glance at any photos on the way. I don't want Leah's face guilting me for ignoring her desperate text last summer, or for the complicated truth I can never confess to Millie, or anyone, for that matter...

... which is that ever since my sister died, a part of me has felt free.

CHAPTER 2

When Al and I rejoin the party, the backyard's bathed in that magic golden-hour light, and one of the pop songs of the summer is blaring from the Bluetooth speaker. People sit at the edge of the pool with their feet in the water, dance in the grass, and cuddle together on patio chairs. When college starts in the fall, we'll scatter like dried leaves in the wind. I can tell no one wants to think about this chapter in our lives being over.

Personally, I don't want to think about this *night* being over. But a little after one a.m., the party starts to wind down. I wince as each guest says goodbye—with the exception, maybe, of Millie, who I'm perfectly fine showing to the door.

"You're sure you don't want to stay over?" I ask Al, sliding my arms around his waist and looking up at him with my best attempt at doe eyes. My parents wouldn't be cool with it, but like with me throwing this party while they're out of town, what they don't know won't hurt them.

"Oh, don't get me wrong, I *want* to stay over—especially when you look at me like that." Al kisses the tip of my nose. "But I told you, I'm not done packing, and my flight leaves from Newark at—"

"Eight. I know."

Al pulls out his phone and calls an Uber.

"Is he close?"

"Six minutes."

We wander out to the front steps, where we kiss one last time and promise to hit each other up if we're ever in each other's cities. When the headlights appear at the end of the block, Alistair sighs. "I really am sorry I can't stay over."

"It's okay." It's not, really. Now the only person staying over is Charlotte, and she's passed out cold in the guest room after taking who knows how many shots of that dragon fruit toxic waste. Char's up for anything, always on the hunt for a party, and a great person to hang with when I'm desperate for a distraction. Except when she goes a little too hard—like now.

With mounting dread, I watch as Alistair climbs into the Uber. The spotlight that's been shining on me all day starts to dim, and as the Uber disappears around the corner, the light shuts off altogether. I'm shivering in the dark, alone.

I shut the door, sealing myself in the quiet house. Our town is nothing like the city, where I'll be moving in a few months to start my first year at NYU. I've spent some time in Brooklyn with my best friend, Zayn, who's a year older than me and just finished their first year at Pratt. No matter what time it is, you can always hear cars honking, strangers yelling, and dogs barking out on the street. That's one of the great things about New York: there's always something to distract you from all the things you hate about yourself.

Like the fact that I enjoyed that party more than I would have if Leah were still alive. The shame sets in like clockwork, and this time, there's no Alistair calling my name to jolt me out of my thoughts. At the top of the stairs, I ease open the guest room door and poke my head through the gap—maybe if Charlotte's awake we can debrief on the party until we both drift off—but to my dismay, she's fast asleep under the paisley quilt. Ugh.

In the bathroom, I peel off my still-damp bathing suit, sling it over the shower curtain rod, step into the tub, and turn on the faucet. Under the piping-hot water, I scrub my skin with a furious intensity, washing away the chlorine, and the sweat, and the sunscreen, and whatever else is clinging to me. Everything but the shame. It's buried so deep that I don't even know how to reach it. I wash my hair twice, because it gives me something to do, and then I brush and floss my teeth. The whole time, I try not to break down in sobs.

As I walk down the hall to my bedroom, I pass the door that used to be Leah's. Pink glittery block letters still spell out her name. They twinkle, even in the dark, like my sister is calling out to me from wherever we go when we die. *You heartless bitch,* she's probably saying—only Leah never cursed, because my parents hate foul language, and again, Leah was perfect.

I can't hold back anymore. As I collapse into bed, the tears come on strong, streaming sideways down my cheeks and getting lost in my hair. What kind of selfish monster thinks, *Gee, hosting parties is way more fun now that my sister is dead*?

Oh, I know: the same kind of selfish monster who gets a text from her sister saying she's never been so anxious in her life, and ignores it. As further evidence of how little I apparently care about Leah, I've never even looked through her phone to see exactly what had been stressing her out so much last summer.

With a decisive sniff, I throw off the covers and pad down the hall to the door with the sparkly pink letters. I haven't been in here since Leah died, and we keep the door closed at all times. I turn the knob, step inside, and flick on the light.

Leah's bedroom is just the way I remembered it: the cozy window seat and queen-size bed that made me ache with envy from my smaller, plainer room; the pink walls collaged with sports ribbons and photos of her countless friends. I can still faintly smell her strawberries-and-cream perfume. Once she started wearing it, all the other girls at school did, too. I told her I hated the smell, but secretly I loved it. I was just frustrated I hadn't discovered it first. Whenever Leah "claimed" something, I would force myself to consider it off-limits, because there was no way I could jump on board without reinforcing the idea that I was her mini-me. It's the same thing that happened when she told us about the *Sentinel* internship.

My eyes land on the big cardboard box in the middle of the floor. Mom and Dad brought it back after they cleaned out Leah's apartment in Hell's Kitchen. Kneeling on the pink shag rug, I nudge open the cardboard flaps. I pull out a copy of the *Gotham Sentinel* and read one of the front-page headlines.

THE AMP-TONS

Weekend travelers refuse to let noise complaints stand in the way of their Hamptons-bound helicopters.

Also on the front page: a story about where to find red diamonds, the rarest and most expensive diamond color of all (I didn't know diamonds came in other colors besides . . . clear?); a profile of some Wall Street executive nicknamed "The 90-Billion-Dollar Woman"; and a review of a Japanese restaurant with a thousand-dollar omakase menu. I try to picture that meal next to the two-roll delivery combo I always get from the sushi place in town, but I can't begin to imagine what a thousand dollars' worth of raw fish would even look like. Shaking my head, I set the paper to the side and keep picking through the box of Leah's belongings, searching for her signature sparkly phone case.

It isn't in here. Where would Mom and Dad have put her phone after they finished looking through it? I check Leah's desk, dresser, closet, and bedside drawer. No luck.

Maybe it's in my parents' room. I tiptoe down the hall—not that I think Charlotte's going to hear me, but just to be safe—and go inside. First, I check the drawer next to Mom's side of the bed, but it's just lip balm, hand lotion, and a stack of books about healing after loss. Dad's drawer is a mess of coins, a random key, some old chargers, and a bottle of prescription sleeping pills that's now empty. I go to the walk-in closet and open all the drawers, but I can't find it. What the hell did they do with Leah's phone? There's no way they got rid of it.

I'm about to abandon the closet when I notice the metal safe, tucked in the corner beside the shoe rack. I crouch and fiddle with the door, but it's locked—obviously. On the front, there's a small golden keyhole.

The random key.

I hurry back to Dad's bedside table and pluck the key out of the drawer. It's definitely small enough to fit in that slot. Back in the closet, I drop to my knees and shove the key in the hole.

It fits.

I turn the key and open the safe door.

Inside, I see my parents' social security cards, a wad of emergency cash, a wooden box containing the diamond jewelry Mom inherited from her grandmother, and some other random stuff. I shove it all to the side so I can see to the back of the safe. Aha! There, stuffed in the back behind everything else, is Leah's sparkly phone case. Why the hell have my parents been keeping her phone under literal lock and key?

I tap the screen, but it's dead. I have the same kind of phone, so I carry it back to my room and plug in my charger, watching as the screen lights up with a dead battery warning. After a few minutes, Leah's lock screen appears: a black-and-white photo of the Empire State Building. I guess her phone still has service since we're all on the same family plan.

I swipe to make the passcode screen appear. When my parents got that court order granting them access to her phone, I'm guessing they would have changed the passcode to something of their choice. I've seen Dad unlock his own phone; his passcode is 5-5-5-5-5-5. Our family's Wi-Fi password is "WiFiPassword," and Mom keeps the code to her laptop on a sticky note next to the trackpad: "Password123." All of which is to say, it doesn't take me long to get into Leah's phone. After a couple of failed attempts, tapping 1-2-3-4-5-6 does the trick. It's amazing my parents haven't been hacked yet.

If Leah was stressed about work stuff, the evidence would probably be in her email. I open her mail app. This must be her personal address; after ten months of disuse, it's filled with unopened messages from brands she used to like and newsletters she used to subscribe to. I try to toggle over to her *Sentinel* inbox, but a message pops up that the address leah.falk@gothamsentinel.com is no longer active. I go back to her personal account, where I scroll past hundreds of messages—the dates creeping closer and closer to last summer—until I come across something that doesn't look like spam. It's an email from a person named Noelle Rice, sent two weeks after Leah's death:

Subject: Pitch from a journalist

From: Noelle Rice
To: Leah Falk

Hi Leah,

I'm so sorry for the delay in getting back to you—I've been swamped. I'm curious to learn more about your pitch. Want to give me a call? I'm at (212) 555-3829. (By the way, your job at the *Sentinel* sounds interesting! I'd love to hear more about that, too.)

Sincerely,
Noelle

Hmm, that's odd. Why would Leah be pitching a story to a different publication from the one she was working for—

especially given how stressed she was with *one* job? I scroll down to read my sister's initial outreach to Noelle Rice.

Subject: Pitch from a journalist

From: Leah Falk
To: Noelle Rice

Hi Noelle,

My name is Leah Falk. I'm currently a reporter at the *Gotham Sentinel,* where I cover the social lives of Manhattan's most powerful people. However, I have a pitch that I believe is better suited for the *New York Times'* social justice coverage, and I was wondering if you might be open to hearing more about it over the phone or in person.

Please let me know. Thank you so much for your time.

Best,
Leah Falk

My stomach drops. An editor at the *New York Times,* a place I would kill to work at someday, was interested in one of Leah's ideas. Jealousy smolders like hot coal in my chest—the exact opposite reason I'm supposed to be looking through her phone right now. *Come on, Noa. Stay on task.* I glance at the time stamp on Leah's email to Noelle. She sent it the day before she died.

Maybe there's something in her messaging app that will tell me about her stress. I open it and instantly feel like I've swallowed a stone. There's that desperate text Leah sent me, asking me to come to the party with her. That was five hours before she reached out to Noelle.

Just below my name is another name I recognize: Emmeline Gilbane, editor-in-chief of the *Gotham Sentinel*. I follow a bunch of famous journalists on social media, and she's one of them. I tap Emmeline's name.

LEAH
> Good morning, Emmeline. This is Leah Falk. I wanted to text you (instead of email) because I'm dealing with a difficult personal matter and would really appreciate your help. I hope this is okay.

EMMELINE
> What's the matter?

LEAH
> At the event last night, one of my sources behaved extremely inappropriately toward me in a physical sense. The same person is going to be at the Sunday Service grand opening tomorrow, and I was hoping you might be able to have someone else cover the event. I'm sorry about the late notice, but I don't feel safe being there.

EMMELINE

I'm sorry, Leah.

It is too late to find a replacement. In any case, maintaining professional boundaries with sources is a crucial part of this job, and you must learn that.

My sister finally responded around two hours later.

LEAH

Okay. I'll be there.

My anger swells as I read their exchange, until I feel like I'm going to scream. Why didn't Emmeline give one single fuck that someone had violated my sister?

But as I read the messages a second time, my anger turns to confusion. My parents have always insisted that the pressure of the internship pushed Leah to take her own life, but these messages tell a different story. In the days leading up to her death, Leah wasn't just stressed about her *workload;* she was stressed because someone had "behaved extremely inappropriately" toward her on Wednesday, and she was worried they'd do it again at the grand opening of a place called Sunday Service on Friday. (I Google Sunday Service; it's a restaurant in Manhattan with four dollar signs.) Leah's roommate found her body in the wee hours of Saturday morning.

I furrow my brow. Leah once told me she tried not to move her forehead because she didn't want to get wrinkles. Won't be the case for me. Squinting at the screen, I wonder if my parents saw this exchange with Emmeline when they went through

Leah's phone. They may not be the most tech-savvy people on Earth, but these texts are literally right at the top of her messages. Then again, grief does weird things to your brain. My parents were despondent after Leah died. Maybe they really did miss these messages. Or maybe they read them, but they were way too out of it to process what they might have meant.

I pop the case off Leah's phone, bring it back to my parents' bedroom, and place it in the back of the safe, sparkles up. This way, if they open the safe for any other reason, it'll look like the phone is still there. I lock the safe and return the key to Dad's bedside drawer. Back in my room, I pick up Leah's phone again, wishing I had done this months ago. I think there was more to Leah's death than work stress, and I might be the only one who knows.

CHAPTER 3

The knock at my bedroom door makes me gasp.

"Hey, girl!"

It's Charlotte. Her makeup's smudged and her dirty-blond ponytail has slipped down the side of her head, but her eyes are bright with newfound energy.

"You're up? How?"

She shrugs. "Sometimes I need a quick nap, but I can always rally." She glances over her shoulder, into the hall. "Anyone else still here?"

"Nah, it's just us."

"Aww, man, I missed the end of the party." She shrugs again. "Oh well. Now we can debrief!" Charlotte scurries to my bed and plops down next to me on the mattress. Do we have to do this now? I want to keep looking through Leah's messages, but not with Charlotte here. I stuff the phone under my pillow. Char doesn't seem to notice; she's staring at her own phone, tapping through people's Instagram Stories from the party.

"*Whoa,* look at this video of Sarabeth and Delia. Do you think they hooked up?"

"I dunno. Maybe." I couldn't care less about debriefing.

"I hope so. They're both in my drama class and they've been into each other for-*ever*. Oh my God." She snort-laughs. "You have to watch this video of Mara trying to teach James her cheerleading moves. He's actually surprisingly flexible."

"Wow." I fake a giant yawn and stretch my arms over my head.

"Oh no! You're not tired, are you?"

"Actually, I'm wiped. You mind if we go to sleep? I have to get up early and clean up before my parents get home." That part is true, but I also want to go back to Leah's phone.

"*Fiiine,*" Charlotte concedes, "but I'm sleeping in here with you. I hate being alone." Before I've even had a chance to reply, she's wriggled under the covers.

In the morning, Charlotte offers to stay to help remove all evidence of yesterday's party from the backyard, but I insist I can handle it on my own.

"You're sure?" she asks at the edge of the pool, where a cluster of empty hard-seltzer cans floats at our feet. They're lapping against the opening to the pool filter, too big to fit through the gap. There's an empty pizza box wedged sideways in the bushes (why?), and an actual slice of pizza lying cheese-down on one of the recliners (gross).

"Yeah, I'm good. Thanks, though." *Please, I just want to be alone so I can think.*

Charlotte looks relieved to not have to handle any deckchair pizza. She hugs me and heads out. "See you at graduation!"

Oh yeah—the ceremony's tomorrow morning. I literally

almost forgot. After Charlotte leaves, I spend an hour and a half tidying the backyard until there's officially no trace of yesterday's pool party. At this point, I barely remember the party myself. All I've been able to think about is Leah, and what my parents *really* know about her death. Were they just totally out of it when they went through Leah's phone, or is it possible they've been hiding this information from me?

At the sound of my parents' car doors in the driveway, I leave my bedroom and go to the top of the stairs to say hi.

"How was Toronto?" I ask all casually, like I didn't find Leah's phone locked in a safe in their closet last night. It's hard to keep the skepticism out of my voice. If they *are* hiding things from me, how can I trust anything they have to say? Were they even *at* a bat mitzvah in Toronto?

"Good," Mom says evenly. "It was nice to see my cousins." She perches on the bench in the foyer to unclip her wedge sandals, then places them neatly on the floor of the coat closet. By the delicate, birdlike way she flits around the home, you wouldn't guess that she's a sales executive at a digital media company, with a big team reporting in to her. Or, it used to be big. "I forgot how quick the flight is—you're up and down," Mom adds. "And the tickets are *so* affordable."

"But customs at Pearson was an absolute shitshow," Dad grumbles as he kicks off his slip-on loafers. It's probably *less* surprising that he's a college professor, given how much he likes telling people what to do. "Explain to me how you can have hundreds of people in line, and only three agents working."

Mom pats his shoulder. "We made it, though."

"Barely. That's the last time we're going there for a *while*."

"Yeah." Mom's voice is small. In our family, she's a sparrow, and Dad's a hawk. Dad's parents both died in a car accident when he was in high school, which meant he grew up really fast; suddenly, he was a "father" to two younger siblings when he was still a kid himself. He's always called the shots in my parents' relationship, but in the past year, he's gotten more aggressive, like Leah's death stripped away whatever small amount of softness he used to have. He's more irritable, too. A few months ago, the university gave him a verbal warning after he grabbed a student's water bottle off their desk and whipped it across the room. Dad said he just couldn't take the crunching of the plastic while he tried to deliver a lecture.

"And how was the bat mitzvah?" I ask my parents.

"She botched her portion," Dad grunts.

"She didn't *botch* it," Mom says gently.

"She botched it."

Mom turns to me. "She stumbled over one part, but it was only for a second."

My cheeks go hot. I stumbled over a part of my portion too. I was nervous, and my throat got all tight out of nowhere. I remember glancing up from the Torah, bracing myself for Dad to be disappointed in me. Instead, he was checking his phone. Disappointment would have been better. Mom gave me a little nod, though, and I took a deep breath and kept going until the end.

"What did you get up to while we were gone?" Mom asks.

If my parents really *are* hiding something, then now's not the time to grill them. I have to be strategic with how I bring it up. I cross my arms and shrug. "Charlotte stayed over last night. But otherwise, not much."

—

After graduation the next day, my parents take me for lunch at Gino's, the Italian place in town. The French bistro a few streets over used to be our go-to for special occasions, but lately, my parents have been trying to save money. I don't mind, because Gino's is still amazing, and in any case, my priority isn't going on some transformative culinary journey.

When Leah was still alive, I couldn't wait to be done with high school so I could move to the city and start my own life without her. Now I'm sitting here in my billowy black robe, my tasseled cap resting beside me on the red vinyl banquette, and the only thing I want to talk about is my sister.

When Leah left for college, our family dinners became unbearably awkward, like we were members of the same friend group who'd never hung out just the three of us before. For the first few nights, I thought Dad might finally take an interest in me, but I should have known better. Since he couldn't talk *to* Leah, he now talked *about* Leah: what classes she was taking; what kind of food she might be eating in the dining hall; what photos she'd posted on Instagram lately. After she died, our dinners were mostly silent, if we even sat down to eat together at all.

At Gino's, we sip our drinks and fidget with the paper straw wrappers. I wish I could just blurt out the questions that are on my mind. *So, about those texts on Leah's phone you never mentioned: Did you not see them? Did you not think they were important? Or is there something you don't want me to know?* The tricky thing is, if my parents *are* hiding something, I doubt they'll just admit it. They'll be way less guarded with their answers if they don't know what my angle is.

"Sorry if I seem a little quiet," I venture.

Mom twists her straw wrapper around her index finger. "Is something wrong?"

"I've just been thinking about Leah."

"Oh, Noa." Mom pats my hand.

"Leah won—what—four, five awards at her graduation?" Dad muses.

"I think it was five," Mom answers quickly, before turning back to me with a sad smile. "I know it's hard not having her here on big days like this."

"It's partly that." I can't let them know I'm steering the conversation, so I chew my bottom lip, feigning innocence. "But there's also something else."

"It could have even been six," Dad murmurs, looking out the window.

Mom raises her eyebrows to show me she's still listening.

"Well, you hear about how fast-paced and intense it is living in the city," I go on. "I guess I think about how overwhelmed Leah got in just a few months, and, well, it freaks me out. Like, what if the same thing happens to me?"

That gets Dad's attention. His head swivels back to the table. "What do you mean by 'the same thing' happening to you?"

I swallow hard. "Like, maybe *I'll* get super anxious and overwhelmed from all my work, and then, one night, it'll all be too much for me to handle, and I'll find a bottle of pills, and—"

Mom cuts me off. "Noa, sweetie, that's not going to happen to you."

"How do you know?"

"I just do."

"But it's exactly what happened to Leah." Dad looks at Mom with a why-did-you-have-to-ask-her-about-her-feelings face.

Mom looks at the door to the kitchen, like she's hoping the server returns with our plates of pasta. When neither of them speaks, I tap the nail of my middle finger against the table. "What's up with you guys? You're acting weird."

Dad turns to me, his eyes narrowed. "Why are *you* suddenly so interested in Leah?"

"So now it's weird that I want to talk about my own sister?"

Mom pushes out her bottom lip in a sympathetic frown. "In Dad's defense, Noa... when we mention Leah, you usually don't want to hear it—which makes me so sad, because she was your sister, and she loved you."

My tapping finger comes to a rest. Guilt squeezes my heart. Then Dad deals a crushing final blow. "To be honest, Noa? Sometimes I don't even know if you miss her."

I slump against the back of the booth. "Obviously, I miss her. God."

Neither of my parents says anything, and we lapse into awkward silence. Some of my classmates and their families are here too, and they're all having a way better time than we are. The Santiago family cheers as they all clink their glasses—Millie beaming at the head of the long, rectangular table. I accidentally catch her eye, and she waves. She seems to notice the miserable vibes at the Falk table, because she mouths "HAVE FUN!"

I flash Millie a double thumbs-up and turn to look out the window while my parents pull out their phones. I really *do* miss Leah. Maybe I didn't when I hosted that party, but I swear, I *do*— at least, sometimes. Leah and I occasionally had fun when it was just the two of us: searching for seashells on the beach on vacation; exploring the ravine behind our house while our parents made dinner; driving aimlessly at night under a sea of stars after

Leah got her license. In those precious hours, we could strip off our practiced identities and just *be*. We got along, when nothing else mattered besides being together in those moments.

We eat our meals in silence. The penne alla vodka I usually crave goes down like tasteless mush. As my classmates' laughter echoes under the vaulted brick ceiling, I think about what to do next. If my parents aren't willing to talk about Leah's death, I need to find people who are—people who knew her last summer. I think we're all relieved when Mom pays the check, and we hustle out of the lively atmosphere at Gino's, where we clearly don't belong.

As soon as I get home, I text Zayn, asking them to call me whenever they get a break from work.

Zayn was my editor at the paper for most of high school. Starting when I was in ninth grade, we'd spend long evenings staring at screens together: moving clauses back and forth, mulling over *just* the right word choice. It wasn't long before we realized that in addition to loving good stories, we were also both queer, and a friendship was born. I was always nervous to get too close to anyone for fear they might be using me to get close to my dazzling, popular sister, but Zayn wasn't like that. They didn't even realize I *had* a sister until I mentioned Leah offhandedly while we were editing a story on her soccer team's latest win.

Twenty minutes later, I get a FaceTime from Zayn. I pick it up on the first ring. "Hey. How are you?"

Zayn sits on the stoop of the brownstone next to the coffee shop where they work when they're not in class or producing their podcast. They have bronze skin, loose dark-brown curls cut in a high fade, and small gold hoops in both their earlobes.

Zayn needles me with sharp brown eyes that are always so perceptive, even through FaceTime. "I'm fine. Work sucks, but I'm done in an hour. What's wrong?" Zayn doesn't believe in small talk, and they sometimes get frustrated when people don't tell stories using the inverted pyramid structure. All of which is to say: they can be kind of intense, but I love them.

"Would it be all right if I came to stay with you earlier than we planned?" I ask. I was supposed to visit Zayn for a week or so next month.

"I'll have to check with Ivy and Killian, but I'm sure it's fine," Zayn answers quickly. They wrinkle their brow. "Noa, you still haven't told me what's wrong."

"I think my parents might be hiding something about Leah."

"What?" Zayn's eyebrows shoot up behind the curls spilling over their forehead.

"You know how my parents said Leah killed herself because she was overwhelmed by her workload?" They nod. "Well, get this. The other night, I found her phone in my parents' safe, and I went through it, and it turns out, there was a source who—who attacked her, or something. And she was scared to see this same person on the night she died, but her evil boss made her go to the party anyway." I leave out the part where I ignored Leah's plea for me to join her. Zayn doesn't know about that, nor do I plan to tell them.

"Did your parents not see that stuff on her phone?" Zayn asks.

"I mean, it's theoretically possible that they missed it, or, like, they saw it but weren't able to process it, but I dunno. It seems weird that they were hiding the phone in their safe, don't you think? When the rest of Leah's stuff is just sitting out in her room?"

Zayn looks confused. "Why were you going through your parents' safe?"

"Oh, I was looking for some documents I needed for NYU registration stuff," I mumble, looking away. Zayn knows about the pool party I hosted on Saturday, but I haven't told them *anything* about the occasional rush of adrenaline I get from being the center of attention now that Leah's gone. Zayn cocks an eyebrow. Before they can ask another prying question, I say, "Anyway, at lunch today, I said something about Leah taking those pills 'cause she was overwhelmed with work stress, and my parents got all weird."

"Weird how?"

"Like, they didn't want to confirm or deny it, so they just didn't say . . . anything."

Zayn thinks for a second. "Okay, I'm with you. It sounds like they're hiding something."

Fear seeps through my veins like ice. It's one thing for me to be suspicious, but Zayn agreeing with me makes everything feel more real. "Right? And I'm guessing there are people in the city who know more than my parents are willing to tell me. There must be people who know what happened between her and this source, or who saw her or talked to her at that last party she covered for the *Sentinel*. If I go through all her articles, and her notes, I feel like I can find them."

"You're probably right," Zayn says. "When were you thinking of coming in?"

I bite my bottom lip. "How's tomorrow?"

When I hang up with Zayn, I grab my suitcase from the closet. In addition to my regular clothes, I pack the fanciest stuff I own: the slinky midnight-blue dress I wore to prom with Alistair; the strapless black tulle gown I wore to my cousin's black-tie wedding; every nice piece of jewelry I got for my bat mitzvah, minus the necklace that says *Noa*. If I manage to track down people who knew Leah last summer, I might have an easier time getting information out of them if they don't know I'm her sister.

As I kneel on the top of the suitcase and wrestle with the zipper, I remember Dad's comment from earlier. *Sometimes I don't even know if you miss her.* Would someone who didn't miss Leah be packing a suitcase to go to New York to investigate her death? No. They'd be like my parents, hiding evidence in a safe and possibly spreading lies about what really happened to her.

When I'm done packing, I take out Leah's phone to start my research. Some old-school reporters still swear by voice recorders to store their interviews, but everyone I know just uses their phone. I go to Leah's Voice Notes, and sure enough, there's a bunch of recordings here. They're all from last summer, and each is labeled with a name and place. The most recent one catches my eye.

SYLVIE AVALON—SUNDAY SERVICE

My heart skips a beat. Whoever this Sylvie Avalon is, she talked to my sister the night she died.

CHAPTER 4

My alarm goes off an hour before my parents get up for work. Dad's teaching summer school classes this year, possibly to improve his standing with his supervisors after the water-bottle-throwing incident. I put on denim cutoffs and a tank top, brush my teeth, and haul my suitcase down the stairs. I'm out the door within fifteen minutes of getting out of bed.

I craft a text to my parents from my seat on New Jersey Transit.

ME
> Hey guys! Zayn needed my help with something last-minute, so I decided to visit them earlier than planned. Not sure exactly when I'll be back, but I'll keep you posted! 😊

Mom tells me to have fun, be safe, and say hi to Zayn. Dad says nothing—just gives the message a thumbs-up. With a sigh,

I rest my temple against the cool window. The spiky spine of Manhattan is just visible in the distance against the baby-blue sky.

At Penn Station, I haul my suitcase down to the subway so I can finish making my way to Brooklyn. The platform is hotter than a sauna, and I stop to tie my hair in a topknot while I wait for the train.

"You look good with your hair like that."

I turn toward the sound of the voice. A middle-aged man slouches against the nearest pillar, leering at me from underneath the brim of a Yankees cap.

He pouts. "C'mon, you can't even give me a smile?"

Once, Charlotte and I got catcalled by some drunk loser sitting outside one of the bars in our town. Rounding on him, Charlotte shrieked, "Let's do it! Let's hook up: right here, right now." The guy froze with his jaw hanging open, like she'd scared the life out of him. That's when I learned that guys like Mr. Yankees Cap aren't trying to make a connection. They're trying to flex their power.

Rolling my eyes, I snatch the handle of my suitcase and walk to the opposite end of the platform. By the time I glance over my shoulder to make sure the guy didn't follow me, he's already moved on to pestering a group of thirtysomethings in bachelorette party attire who look like they were out all night. Men can be depressingly predictable.

When the A train arrives, I take it one stop to 14th Street, where I transfer to a Brooklyn-bound L. Fourteen stops later, I get off in a neighborhood called Bushwick. With sweat dripping down my spine, I drag my suitcase along the bumpy sidewalk, past warehouses and corrugated steel walls covered in street art.

Zayn's new building is a renovated factory that takes up half the block. They moved here a few weeks ago with two friends from their first year at Pratt. I jam my finger onto the button for Loft 4A. At the sound of the buzz, I open the door.

The lobby smells like incense and spices. A large bulletin board has a flyer for a rooftop solstice party featuring live drumming and poetry readings; another handmade sign offers a tarot card reading or an astrology consultation in exchange for help assembling Ikea furniture.

Three flights of stairs later, I'm panting in a wide hallway with uneven hardwood floors and exposed pipes on the ceiling. There's a folding table with a teetering stack of novels on it, and a sticky note hanging off the edge saying *Take a book, leave a book* in neat handwriting that I recognize as Zayn's.

My heart still pounding from pulling my suitcase up the stairs, I rap on the door that says 4A.

"Coming!" Zayn opens the door and wraps me in their willowy arms, but they release me almost immediately. "Eww. You're very sweaty."

"It's good to see you too."

"Yeah, yeah. Come on in." Zayn leads me through the door and down a corridor with reusable shopping bags and umbrellas hanging on hooks.

"Thanks again for letting me come so early."

They look back over their shoulder like they can't believe what they're hearing. "Um, obviously. Your parents are being shady as fuck." We emerge from the corridor into a cavelike kitchen with a low ceiling and exposed brick walls. A butcher-block island sits in the center of the room. "Welcome to La Forêt."

"La Forêt? Like, 'the forest'?"

Zayn shrugs. "We decided it sounded sexier than 'Loft 4A,' so that's what we call it now. I'll give you the tour. It has some quirks, but so does every apartment in New York, unless you're, like, a billionaire."

They lead me into a bright living area with soaring high ceilings and a giant arched window. Succulents of all shapes and sizes crowd the edges of the space. In the center of the room, there's a coffee table surrounded by squashy, mismatched furniture.

"Are Ivy and Killian home?" I ask.

"No. Ivy's interning at this cool art gallery for the summer, and Killian's allegedly working on his play at a coffee shop, but I'm pretty sure he *actually* went there to flirt with the dude who makes his lattes."

Zayn helps me carry my suitcase up a narrow staircase to a platform over the kitchen with a railed edge. There aren't individual rooms up here so much as there are three . . . I don't know . . . sleeping "areas" sectioned off in creative ways. A bunch of curtains hang from the pipes: some of them velvet, some of them beaded. Big pieces of furniture, such as armoires and bookshelves, divide the personal areas in places where the curtains don't reach.

"We have a blow-up mattress, so we were thinking we could put you in there." They gesture at a pocket of space between two curtains.

I shrug. "Works for me." I lay down my suitcase and open the zipper. The black tulle springs up like a jack-in-the-box. "Wanna see what I've found so far about Leah?"

"Show me." They plop down on their bed, next to a desk with

a microphone, ring light, and some other fancy recording equipment. Zayn hosts a popular podcast where they interview people about their journeys in understanding and expressing their gender identity. I grab Leah's phone and join them on the bed, where I tell them about the interview I found from the Sunday Service grand opening.

"It's with this girl Sylvie Avalon, whose family owns the Avalon Hospitality Group. It's this network of fancy restaurants and hotels, including Sunday Service. Here, listen." I tap Play on the Voice Note.

LEAH: Hey, can I ask you a few quick questions for the Sentinel?

SYLVIE: Of course. Come, sit down.

LEAH: Did we wander into some kind of satanic ritual, or is it just me?

SYLVIE: [Laughs.] Isn't it so sexy, though? I'm obsessed with it. Can you believe all these candles are real?

LEAH: I heard some of the former congregation was actually pretty upset with what they did to the space.

SYLVIE: Well, I don't know anything about that. Why are you asking me?

LEAH: I'm a journalist. I'm trying to learn about all sides of the story.

SYLVIE: [Laughs.] Okay, Miss Journalist, but you haven't even asked me about this amazing food and this incredible drink! My mind is blown. This is the beef tartare; this is a goat cheese tart; and see these little latkes with smoked salmon and caviar? They're going to change your life. And I'm drinking an extra-dirty vodka martini. The olives are smoked, and I'm telling you, it takes the classic cocktail to a whole new level.

LEAH: Wow. That's some high praise. But your family owns the restaurant, right?

SYLVIE: Leah, come on.

LEAH: What?

SYLVIE: Why are you being like this?

LEAH: Like what?

SYLVIE: If you're going to be like that, this interview is over.

  The talking stops and the ambient sounds of the restaurant take over. The recording goes on for another minute or so, but there's nothing more from Leah or Sylvie. My guess is Sylvie got up and walked off, and Leah was so stunned that she forgot to hit the Stop button right away.

"Damn," Zayn says. "Your sister was asking good questions."

"I know," I murmur, a little annoyed. Leah didn't just steal my passion; she was good at it, too. "But more importantly, we know Sylvie was at the party that night," I point out.

"Can I see a picture of this Sylvie person?" Zayn asks.

I open Instagram on Leah's phone and pull up Sylvie's profile, which I found yesterday. She's twenty-one and a student at Columbia, according to her bio. Tall, curvy, and strikingly beautiful, she has shiny chestnut-brown hair and the dewy, pinkish skin of someone who drinks more than the recommended amount of water every day, or at least uses wildly expensive skincare products with French names. Her photos are all stylized shots of her and her friends at Avalon properties around the world: splashing in the ocean in Crete; sipping Aperol spritzes in a courtyard in Rome; taking in the sunset and the silhouetted skyline from a Manhattan hotel rooftop.

"Not only was Sylvie at the grand opening, but she and Leah legit knew each other last summer. Look." I go into Leah's DMs, search for Sylvie's name, click into their chat history, and scroll back to the very beginning.

> **Sylvie:** Hey Leah! I'm Sylvie. My mom said she met you at that speakeasy open house thing last night, and that she instantly knew we'd get along. She also said you might want to check out some of our restaurants! Lmk if you ever need a dining buddy—I can show you all the best things on the menu ;)

Leah: Hey Sylvie! It's great to meet you! Your mom said the same thing to me 😄. I guess we're destined to be friends? She also told me all about your family's restaurants, and yes, I'd love to check them out. Just so I know, would the expectation be that I'd write about them for the Sentinel?

Sylvie: A story in the Sentinel is always amazing, but there's truly no pressure! I just thought it would be fun to hang out, since my mom couldn't stop gushing about you.

Leah: OMG, you guys are too sweet. Sure, let's do it! When are you free?

When I first read these messages last night, I could feel my sister's excitement coming through the screen. I could see her thumbs typing at warp speed, the way she used to text her friends while she watched her Netflix reality dating shows. Here was Sylvie Avalon, a stunning Manhattan socialite, taking an interest in Leah, who was living in a five-story Hell's Kitchen walk-up. It would have felt, to Leah, like being plucked from obscurity and teleported to a whole new plane of existence.

Two weeks after their first messages, Leah and Sylvie were communicating like friends: an emoji reaction to a Story here, a few memes exchanged there. They must have gotten dinner together by that point. In and around the friendly chatter, Sylvie invited Leah to hang out even more: there was a gala for the charitable arm of the Avalon Hospitality Group; a rooftop Fourth of July party at one of the family's hotels; a tour of one of their restaurant's wine cellars, complete with a sommelier-guided wine tasting ("They won't card you, haha," Sylvie added). Every time, my sister said yes.

"She did get weirdly cozy with her sources," I point out, almost triumphantly. I know better than to cross that line. Building genuine friendships with sources can be risky for reporters because it can compromise their ability to report on something objectively.

"Maybe the rules were more lax at the *Sentinel* than at other publications," Zayn wonders.

I keep scrolling to show them the final messages Sylvie and Leah sent each other.

> **Sylvie:** Heyyy. This is SO random, but the daughter of the GM at one of our hotels is a DJ, and she's doing a set at this bar called the Haven on Wednesday night. You wanna come? The usual crew will be there.
>
> **Leah:** Hey! What time does it start? I'm meeting a friend for dinner and not sure if I can make it.
>
> **Sylvie:** It doesn't start until 11 so you're def good! And they literally never card at the Haven, so you're good there too, haha.
>
> **Leah:** Kk! I'll be there

Zayn's eyes go wide. "Wednesday night? Is that . . ."

"The night Leah said a source 'behaved extremely inappropriately' with her—yes." I wave the phone in the air. "Sylvie was there, too. She's gotta know *something*."

"You just have to find her," Zayn says, taking Leah's phone.

"WAIT!" I grab their hand a split second before they open Sylvie's Stories. "Don't touch that. It would be weird if she saw Leah's account viewing her Stories." Granted, Sylvie has thousands of followers, so I doubt she'd notice, but you never know. Sometimes, when you're curious to see whether a certain person viewed your Stories, you *do* end up working through that list with a fine-toothed comb. "Can we look at her Stories from your phone? Just to be safe? I also have Falk in my username."

Zayn opens Sylvie's Stories on their phone. There's a mirror selfie from the spa yesterday afternoon, followed by a shot of a dozen oysters at a downtown seafood restaurant called Mist, and then a video of her pedicured feet in platform sandals walking through Central Park this morning. "Well, there's one piece of good news," they say. "It shouldn't be hard to find her. Seems like she's constantly posting her location."

"I'll have to follow along from your phone."

"I gotta head into work," Zayn says, "but I'll keep checking her Stories and send you screenshots of whatever she posts."

"You're the best. Thank you."

Zayn stands up and grabs their bike helmet off a hook. "Are you gonna go out? I can leave you the keys."

I shake my head. "Nah, I'm gonna stay here and do more research."

"Okay. Help yourself to anything in the fridge or the pantry."

"Thanks."

"And just a heads-up: if you hear any weird scratching noises coming from inside the walls, don't worry. It's just rats."

"*Just* rats?"

"IMO, better than cockroaches. Roaches are like little aliens. But rats are like, I dunno. Small cats."

I shake my head solemnly. "New York has changed you."

Zayn smirks.

True to their word, Zayn keeps me updated on Sylvie's whereabouts for the rest of the afternoon. Unfortunately, she's been at home most of the day, trying on outfits in her massive walk-in closet. Ugh. Can this girl go out and do something already?

Around five o'clock, Zayn sends me a string of siren emojis.

ZAYN

🚨🚨🚨🚨🚨🚨🚨🚨🚨🚨🚨🚨🚨🚨🚨

CODE RED: SYLVIE'S GETTING DRINKS AT SUNDAY SERVICE!!!

INTERNSHIP LOG

LEAH FALK

June 3

Skidmore wants us to keep a log of everything we do in our internships so we can write an essay about the whole experience and then get credit for it. So, here we go! To stay on-brand, I'm using one of the reporter's notebooks I found in the Sentinel's newsroom.

    My first two days at the Sentinel were amazing! I fact-checked a couple of stories for print, and got my first-ever byline on the website! It was a 250-word news post about a luxury spa offering something called a "placenta facial" (I have questions), and it was essentially a write-up of a press release, but, you know, gotta start somewhere! The wellness editor told me my copy was super clean and my writing was surprisingly graceful. (Why "surprisingly"? I'm not exactly sure what he meant by that, but I'll take it.)

CHAPTER 5

I've never gotten ready so quickly in my life. I throw on a little black dress and strap on a pair of platform sandals that straddle the line between "dressy" and "I can still walk." Then I hightail it to the subway, hoping I can make it to the Upper East Side before Sylvie's moved on from Sunday Service. And that's assuming her latest Story is in real time. For all I know, she took that photo of a dirty martini some other day, and only got around to posting it now, with *cocktail hour* written in curly cursive font.

Please be there. Right now, Sylvie's my most promising lead. At Union Square, I join the crowd flooding off the L train and switch to an uptown 4, which rockets me to Lexington Avenue and 59th Street in just two stops. Thank God for express trains. I climb the stairs onto a sidewalk crawling with pedestrians, which makes sense when I realize we're right in front of Bloomingdale's. There's a cacophony of car horns squawking and city buses screeching up to the curb.

Things get quieter as I follow 59th Street to the west, away from Bloomingdale's. I hurry down a tree-lined block with expensive-looking home-design stores on the ground level, their window displays showing off golden candelabras, three-tier chandeliers, canopy beds, and claw-foot tubs. I go a few blocks north on Park Avenue, with its regal-looking doorman buildings straight out of old New York, until I find myself in front of a very old church—or, that's what it looks like from the outside.

Sunday Service is housed in an imposing building made of dark-brown stone with a green copper steeple. Sculptures decorate the soaring façade, from religious figures in flowing robes to gargoyles squatting on various ledges. Directly in front of me, a set of stairs leads up to a heavy wooden door under a sculpted archway. I remember what Leah said in her interview with Sylvie: that the former congregation was pissed with what the Avalons did to the old church.

There aren't windows to offer glimpses of what's happening inside. As I stand on the sidewalk looking up, the doors open to let out two middle-aged men in crisp suits, and a loud burst of clubby music. When the doors shut behind them, everything becomes quiet again.

Here goes nothing. I march up the stairs and yank open one of the doors, making my way into the restaurant.

Whoa.

No wonder the former congregants were mad: their church was basically taken over by the devil.

It's nearly pitch-black in here, the restaurant lit almost entirely by candlelight. There must be hundreds—thousands—of flames burning inside hurricane glass candleholders positioned around the cavernous space. In the central area where the pews must have been, there's now a circular bar surrounded by dining tables. There's a DJ up on the stage, and behind him, a towering sculpture of twisted metal lit up from below. As my eyes travel up the altar—if you can even call it that at this point—I see that the balconies are still in use too, with servers running drinks up the carved spiral staircases on either side of the room. It's so dark and so loud that I almost feel like a ghost. No one can see me, and no one can hear me. A person could get away with anything in here.

The thought makes my stomach turn over. It nudges me to the edge of an abyss I've been scared to approach, but I've known it was there. Of course I have, from the night I found Leah's phone. She didn't leave a note or have a history of depression, and on the night she died, she was scared for her own safety. As I tiptoe farther into the underworld of Sunday Service, it isn't the first time I've considered that Leah's death might not have been suicide.

I approach the hostess behind the front desk, who gives me an icy smile as she tilts her head to the side. "How can I help you?"

"Er, are there any seats available at the bar?" That's where it looked like Sylvie was sitting in her "cocktail hour" photo.

The hostess glances over her shoulder. "Unfortunately, no, but I can seat you in the North Lounge. Does that work?"

I don't know what the North Lounge means, but if there's no other option, I'll take it. "Yeah, that works."

The hostess grabs a menu before leading me around the dining tables and up one of the spiral staircases to the balcony on the left side of the room. It's a dark strip of space with a long banquette lining the wall, so guests can sit side by side in the shadows and look out over the railing. It's a great spot if you want privacy with a date, but it's not good for my chances of casually striking up a conversation with Sylvie.

The woman guides me to the table on the end. "Someone will be right with you to take your order," she says.

I flash her a pinched smile. "Thanks."

The hostess leaves, but before I sit down, I peer over the railing—and there she is. There's a cluster of candles right in front of her on the bar, so I can make her out better than most guests in the restaurant. Sylvie's so stunning she almost glitters, with her dewy skin and shiny chestnut hair. She wears a sleeveless V-neck dress that hugs her soft curves and shows off the diamond pendant nestled against the top of her chest. I think I saw on her Instagram that she's an ambassador for Van Cleef & Arpels. Casual.

I also recognize the guy to her left, after reading about her family all afternoon. That's Duke Avalon, Sylvie's twin brother. He's a giant: easily six-foot-five, with broad shoulders and beefy arms pushing at the fabric of his sharp white button-down. I noticed on Instagram that despite his sheer size, his baby face makes him look younger than twenty-one: big green eyes, rosy cheeks, plump lips, and chestnut hair curling around his ears like a cherub in an old painting.

On Sylvie's other side sits a skinny girl with long blond hair and slightly sunburnt skin. Her strapless floral dress reveals the tan lines from the bathing suit straps she must have been wearing earlier.

"Excuse me, miss? Are you waiting for someone else?" A server who looks like he doubles as a model cocks an eyebrow at me.

"Oh! Um, no. It's just me." I take my seat and open the menu.

"Can I start you off with something to drink?" I have Leah's fake ID on me, but the cocktails here are $25; the entrees are all $60 and up.

"Er, can I do a ginger ale, please?"

He nods and disappears. Now I just have to wait and hope a seat opens up at the bar. A few minutes later, the waiter returns with my drink. "Can I take the rest of your order?" he asks. I may have access to a few thousand bucks from my bat mitzvah, but I'm not dropping $60 on a main, or even $30 on an appetizer, if I'm not sitting next to Sylvie.

"Can I have a few more minutes? Sorry!"

He gives me a skeptical look, like he's wondering what the hell else I was doing while he was getting my drink, if not looking at the menu. "Certainly," he says.

Once he's gone, I get up and go to the railing again. The two women eating dessert at the table next to me must be wondering why I can't sit still. As I survey the bar, a bolt of excitement shoots through me. The hostess is showing a couple at the bar to a table that just opened up nearby. Suddenly, there are two open barstools; they're not exactly close to Sylvie, but it would be a whole lot better than sitting up here, practically in the rafters.

I grab my ginger ale and rush along the balcony. It's so dark up here that I nearly collide with my server at the top of the stairs. "Where are you going?" he asks.

"Down to the bar. I'm actually not very hungry, and I don't want to take over this table. Is that all right?"

He makes no effort to hide his eye roll. "Fine, but you'll have to pay for your drink first."

I'm going to lose my seat at the bar! I wrench open my purse, grab my wallet, and fumble inside for a $10 bill. "Is this enough?"

This man might want to kill me. "Do you need any change?"

"No. All yours." I shove the bill into his hand and race down the spiral staircase, sighing with relief when I see the seats are still open. I weave around tables as fast as I can without spilling my ginger ale, refusing to slow down until my butt is on a velvet-cushioned stool.

If the bar were a ship, Sylvie and I would be sitting on opposite sides of the prow, facing each other. She's aimlessly scrolling on her phone, while the blond girl looks on, totally enraptured. Duke squeezes his toothpick between his thumb and forefinger, apparently playing a game of nibbling the olive in his martini as slowly as humanly possible. I wonder how I'm going to get any of their attention.

"Mind if I see some ID, miss?"

I blink at the bartender, who smiles politely under his waxy sculpted mustache. "Oh, this is just ginger ale."

"Okay, but you need to be legal drinking age to sit at the bar."

I grab my wallet again and fish out Leah's fake ID. I noticed it the other night when I was going through the cardboard box in her room, and I decided to go in and grab it before I left the house this morning. I figured it might come in handy, since I don't have a fake of my own—and I guess I was right. I slide the card across the bar like it's no big deal. My heart pounds as the bartender picks it up and inspects it under a lamp. He looks at it long and hard, tilting it this way and that. The fake has Leah's actual photo on it; she and I don't look that different, do we? The picture was taken a few years ago, before she started highlighting her hair, so it was the same dark brown as mine. And it was blow-dried that day, so you wouldn't know she usually wore her hair in its natural beachy waves, whereas I tend to wear mine straight. As the bartender walks back over, I hold my breath.

He hands the card back to me. "Thanks. Let me know when I can get you something else."

Exhaling with relief, I go back to watching Sylvie, who's still swiping away at her phone. If you ask me, she looks bored. She doesn't care that she's at one of the nicest restaurants in Manhattan, drinking a twenty-five-dollar cocktail. She's probably desensitized to things that would be super exciting to 99 percent of the world. What's she doing right now: watching TikTok without sound? And Duke's trying to see how long he can make an olive last. To get Sylvie's attention, I have to entertain her. And to entertain her, I have to do something she's never seen before. Something surprising, in a good way.

The check from the people who were sitting here before us still rests on the bar by my elbow. I slip my hand into the check presenter and swipe the pen they used to sign the receipt. Then I reach over the bar for a gold cocktail napkin and draw a grid with nine squares. In the box on the top left, I make an *X*. At the bottom of the napkin, I write: *Your move.*

CHAPTER 6

That's right: I'm going to play tic-tac-toe with Sylvie and Duke Avalon. I'll admit it's a weird tactic, but I think it might work. I chug the rest of my ginger ale, flag down the bartender, and ask for another one. "And, before you go"—I hold up the napkin—"would you mind dropping this off with my friends? Sylvie and Duke?"

The bartender stares at me blankly, and I think he might refuse. But then he plucks the paper from my fingers.

I have to say I'm proud that on my first night in the city, I managed to be sitting at the same bar with Sylvie Avalon, Leah's friend from last summer. I'm so nervous I can hardly watch as the bartender approaches the trio, holding my cocktail napkin in the air. When he points in my direction, all three sets of eyes land on me. I hit them with a sly smirk. In the glow of the candlelight, there's no mistaking Sylvie's and Duke's grins as the bartender sets the napkin down in front of them.

The blond girl looks confused, if not a little offended. She reaches for the napkin first, like a bodyguard inspecting a suspicious package. But no sooner has she grabbed it than Duke reaches across Sylvie's body to snatch it out of the friend's hand. He peers at it closely, his boyish grin getting wider by the second.

Sylvie leans over to look too. She strokes her chin for a few seconds, then says something to Duke as she points to a spot on the napkin. With her other hand, she fishes around under the bar and returns with a pen, which she passes to her brother.

Oh my God. I did it.

When the bartender goes back to them with a round of fresh martinis, Duke hands him the napkin and nods toward me. His eyes follow the bartender as he makes his way over with my new ginger ale and the updated tic-tac-toe board. Even Sylvie, who's gone back to scrolling, glances up every few seconds to watch the game's progression.

They put their O in the middle square: a smart move. Tic-tac-toe is almost impossible to win if your opponent goes first and takes a corner, but your best chance of forcing a tie is if you put your O exactly where they did. I send the napkin back with my next move.

On and on we go, Sylvie eventually abandoning her phone to focus fully on the game. She seems to be the mastermind when it comes to making moves, but Duke helps by writing fake-threatening messages around the edge of the napkin, like *You're going down!!!* and *Hope you like to lose!!!*

Finally, the exasperated-looking bartender brings the napkin back to me with the twins' final move: an O in the top-right corner. The square on the bottom left is the only remaining space, and it'll force a draw.

That's when I notice the latest message scrawled across the bottom: *Did you really think you could beat us?*

When I look across the bar, Duke is leaning back with his hands behind his head, and Sylvie's twirling the pen around a lock of her hair. Both of them are staring at me. I pick up my drink, eyeing the two seats that just opened up next to Duke. My plan is to make friends with Sylvie—and the other two, if it helps me get close to her. Today is just the beginning; once Sylvie and I are buddies, it shouldn't be *that* hard to get her talking about a good friend who died of an overdose less than a year ago.

I just hope they weren't good enough friends that Sylvie spots our resemblance. Our eyes were the same shade of gray, and we both had the same petite nose. Thank God Leah dyed her hair and wore it wavy. She was taller and built like an athlete; she was lean where I have curves, her muscles hardened from soccer and dance. This afternoon, I also double-checked that I'm not in any photos on Leah's Instagram, so there's no way Sylvie would recognize me from there.

Rolling up to the other side of the bar, I put on the same sly smirk as before. "I guess I was wrong. I *did* think I could beat you."

Sylvie's laugh is sweet and smooth, like honey. "Big mistake, Tic-Tac-Toe Fairy."

"If you're the Tic-Tac-Toe Fairy, does that mean we get three wishes for winning?" Duke asks. There's a sliver of space between his top front teeth that ups his boyish charm even more.

"Hmm." I pretend to think about it for a second. "Isn't it genies who give out wishes? And, to be fair, you didn't *win*."

"How about one wish?" Duke counters.

"All right, I guess I can give you that."

Duke nods to the two empty stools right next to him. "I wish for you to sit with us. I'm Duke, by the way."

"Hailey." It's my middle name: easy to remember, even when I'm on the spot.

"I'm Sylvie," says Sylvie Avalon. My heart pounds as I shake her buttery-soft manicured hand. "And this is my dear friend Jocelyn Poole." She gestures to the blond girl, who gives me a resigned wave. She seems a little disappointed to be losing some of the twins' attention. *Sorry, Joc. Looks like you'll have to share.*

With the way the bar curves, we can all see each other, even though we're sitting in a row. Sylvie peers at me. "You look familiar. What's your last name?"

My pulse thuds. "Star," I answer quickly—Mom's maiden name.

"Star? Sick name," Duke says.

"Actually, the story's kinda fucked up." I hop onto the stool next to Duke. "My great-great-grandparents' original last name was Shklovsky, but the immigration people made them change it to something more 'American-sounding' when they came here in the early nineteen hundreds. So, yeah: I'm technically supposed to be Hailey Shklovsky." It's a true story: Zaidy—Mom's dad—explained it to me the last time we visited him and Bubbie in Florida. More importantly, it successfully distracts Sylvie from my resemblance to whomever she thought I looked like.

"Are you just chilling here by yourself?" Sylvie asks.

I roll my eyes. "Ugh. I was actually supposed to have a date, but the guy bailed on me at *literally* the last minute. I was already here, so I was like, you know what? I look cute. I'm gonna hang out and have a drink. And maybe meet some other cool people." I gesture at the three of them.

"Wow, fuck that guy," Duke says. "You're better off with us." He slings an arm over the back of my stool. I know I'm not here to actually make friends with these people, but I have to admit, the attention is a treat. It's that same warm feeling I had at my pool party—like standing in the glow of a spotlight and not having to share the stage.

"What brings *you* guys here?" I ask them.

Sylvie laughs. Jocelyn copies her with a knowing giggle.

"What's so funny?"

Duke snorts. "You're so full of yourself, Sylv."

His sister raises her eyebrows at me. "Oh! Sorry. I thought you were joking. People usually recognize us from Instagram." Sylvie twirls her hair. "Our family owns the restaurant, so we're here like all the time."

"We came like three times last week," Jocelyn chimes in.

"Wow. You don't get bored of it?"

"No." Sylvie shrugs. "Although, to be fair, it only opened last summer."

"We were all there at the grand opening," Jocelyn brags. God bless this obnoxious girl, because the grand opening is exactly what I wanted to ask about next, and now I don't have to.

At the mention of the grand opening, Duke coughs on a sip of martini, spraying his sister's bare shoulder in the process.

"Eww, Duke!" Sylvie snaps.

Laughing, Duke wipes his mouth with a napkin, then dabs Sylvie's shoulder. "Sorry. I was just remembering how blasted we got that night."

Sylvie visibly relaxes. A rueful smile spreads across her face. "We maybe had a few too many."

"You had like a billion," Duke says. "Joc, didn't you say she told you to get up on the bar and dance at some point?"

"She did," Jocelyn confirms.

"And you did it," Sylvie adds. "Duke, you missed the whole thing."

"I blacked out," Duke tells me. There's a note of pride in his voice.

Sylvie pokes him with the toothpick from her martini. "You puked in the potted plants outside."

Duke snatches the toothpick out of her hand and pokes her back. "Thanks, Sylv. Make me sound like a total degenerate in front of the cute girl I just met."

I can't help it: my chest flutters.

"Anyway, should we order some food? I'm fuckin' starving. *Tommy!*" He snaps his fingers and looks around.

"And you think *I'm* the one making you look like a degenerate," Sylvie chides.

Duke snickers and lowers his arm. "I'm just joking."

"Who's Tommy?" I ask.

"Tommy Sunday," Jocelyn answers, her face brightening. "The chef. He's *amazing.* It was his idea to name it Sunday Service, 'cause it's a restaurant that used to be a church, and his name's Sunday. So smart, right?"

Sylvie rolls her eyes. "Jocelyn's in culinary school," she explains. "We're trying to get her an externship with Tommy."

Meanwhile, Duke has been putting in a pretty sizable-sounding order with the bartender. Remembering the prices here, I put a hand on his arm. "I-I'm not super hungry," I stammer.

Duke waves me off. "Don't worry." And then, seeing my face, he whispers in my ear, "It's comped." The bartender asks if he wants to add caviar to the salmon dish. "Yeah, yeah, throw it on there," Duke says. Apparently, the richer you are, the more you get for free.

Our food comes out at VIP speed. There's beef tartare; little pancakes with caviar on top; heirloom tomatoes with burrata and prosciutto. The grand finale is a seafood tower with shrimp, lobster, crab legs, and oysters, delivered to the bar by a middle-aged white man in a chef's jacket. He reminds me of a lion, with a wide nose and long, sandy hair pulled back in a bun.

"Oh my God, Tommy!" Jocelyn gushes. "This looks *phenomenal*."

Tommy Sunday doesn't even glance at Jocelyn as he sets the seafood tower between the twins. "I gave you guys the most jumbo of the jumbo shrimp." He notices me sitting next to Duke and raises his eyebrows. "Guess it was a good call, since you're four tonight. Who do we have here?"

"A celebrity," Duke says. "One of the top-ranked tic-tac-toe players in the world." Tommy chuckles uncertainly. He isn't in on the joke, but he also doesn't ask for clarification—and Duke doesn't offer any. He just shoots me a sexy smirk. "Tommy, this is Hailey Star. Hailey, this is Tommy Sunday."

"First time here?" Tommy asks.

"Yeah," I reply. "This place is awesome. I'll definitely be back."

"Well, you're welcome whenever you want. Any friends of the Avalons are friends of mine." And with that, I'm officially a friend of the Avalons. My heart swells with pride as Tommy comes over with an arm outstretched. I guess we're about to hug. "Great to meet you, Hailey."

His arm circles my body, and—wait, what's he doing? I try not to noticeably stiffen as his fingertips graze the side of my left breast, but I'm *very* aware of their presence, tracing a delicate figure eight across fabric that suddenly feels way too thin. No sooner has he touched me than he steps back and busies himself with tucking two loose strands of hair behind his ears. He's smooth, and I can picture him doing this countless times before, with who knows how many creeped-out girls. Then a light bulb goes off in my head. Tommy Sunday was obviously at the restaurant's grand opening last summer. What if he was the person who behaved extremely inappropriately with Leah?

Tommy hugs Duke and Sylvie next. Jocelyn extends an arm, like she's expecting a hug too, but all she gets is a quick pat on the back. "Gotta run," Tommy says. "My sous chef called in sick at the last minute, so we're slammed."

"Oh no." Sylvie groans sympathetically.

"Yeah. I'm gonna kill that fuckin' guy if he does this again. Lemme know if there's anything else you want."

"You know we will," Duke replies.

Jocelyn lets out a nervous laugh, like she's hoping no one noticed how the chef brushed her off a few seconds ago. "Thanks, Tommy," she says.

"You got it." Before striding back to the kitchen, he waves—and *winks at me*. My skin prickles unpleasantly in the place where Tommy touched me, and again I'm nearing the edge of the abyss, contemplating the terrifying things that might lie in its depths.

"That dude's the best," Duke says, reaching for one of the jumbo shrimp and eating the whole thing in one bite. "His food is like next-level. Here, Hailey, try one of these." He passes me the plate with the smoked salmon and caviar pancakes. I'm not hungry at all anymore, but I need to bond with the Avalons if I'm going to learn more about Leah, and that means joining them in this decadent feast. A curtain drops in my head, blocking the dark thoughts and pushing me back to the present.

I slide one of the salmon things onto my fork and take a bite. "Oh my God, this is *amazing*."

"Right?" Duke gushes.

It tastes fine. I bite down on a fish egg and it bursts in my mouth like a pimple. Squeamish, I set the other half of the pancake on my plate.

Sylvie asks if I'm in school. Luckily, I visited Zayn enough times this past year to convince her I'm a student at Pratt.

"What's your major?"

"Writing." That's what Zayn's doing.

"Oh yeah? You want to be an author?"

"A journalist, actually."

I bite my tongue, but it's too late. The answer just slipped out, as naturally as an exhale. What if one of them makes the connection between me and Leah *now*? But to my relief, Sylvie's face lights up. "Oh, we love journalists!"

"You do?"

"Our mom is head of public relations for Avalon Hospitality Group, and I help her with publicity stuff," Sylvie says. "We constantly rely on good journalists to tell our story. You should meet her—our mom. Gracie. She has so many contacts in the media world. Maybe you could come to some of our events and write reviews!"

My head is spinning with shock at how perfectly this is all coming together, my fingertips itching to grasp the possibilities on the horizon. I can figure out what happened to Leah *and* potentially get real journalism work out of this.

"Hailey should be my date to Mom's gala on Friday," Duke says.

"Oh my God, totally," Sylvie gushes. "I think Emmeline's going to be there."

My breath catches in my throat. "Emmeline?"

"Emmeline Gilbane," Sylvie says. "The editor-in-chief of the *Gotham Sentinel*."

INTERNSHIP LOG

LEAH FALK

June 6

OMG, I've been here less than a week, and I just turned in a draft of what will be my first-ever story in print! Last night, I was sent to cover this supercool event (which is what the piece is about). It was this 1920s-themed open house in the most gorgeous home I've ever been in. This might sound so naïve, but I didn't realize the whole Gossip Girl world was... actually real! Like, some people in Manhattan really are that rich. That's the coolest part of this internship, I think: how you can enter these other worlds that you otherwise couldn't access, or even know about. It's like lucid dreaming.

I was SO nervous before the party, having to walk in there without knowing anyone and try to find people to talk to for the story. But it turned out to be shockingly easy?! Right away, this one super-nice woman started talking to me, and she agreed to let me interview her. She turned out to be a publicist who knew, like, everyone at the party, and she introduced me to a bunch of other people to interview. Everyone was so nice to me. It was like I was holding court. This one guy said his girlfriend runs a *company that rents out designer clothes, and he'd be happy to hook me up with whatever I want! Also, the publicist lady said I could come for dinner at any of the restaurants she represents. I looked them up, and they're all super fancy. I feel like Cinderella!*

CHAPTER 7

After about an hour, Sylvie looks at the time and realizes she, Duke, and Jocelyn have to get to a friend's birthday party. "Let's stay in touch about Friday," Sylvie says. She taps something on her phone and thrusts it into my hands. "Here, give me your number."

I add "Hailey Star" as a new contact. Hopefully she doesn't search my number and see that it's registered to Noa Falk—but that would be super weird.

"Are you on Instagram?" Duke asks.

I am, but Hailey isn't. "No," I say with a shrug, and keep it at that. They say over-explanation is a sign of insecurity.

Duke smirks. "Mysterious. I like it." He shoves his phone in his back pocket. "I'll get your number from Sylvie." He pulls me into a one-armed hug. Sylvie does too. Jocelyn gives me a little wave and a tight-lipped smile that looks more like a wince. She doesn't say anything about getting my number.

The twins wave goodbye to the bartender, and like Duke said, there's no mention of a bill. I don't need to be a math genius to know that everything they just ordered for *sure* cost hundreds of dollars. A few minutes later, before I get up to leave, I flag down the bartender.

"Hey! What can I getcha?" He's way friendlier now than when I first sat down at the other side of the bar.

I unzip my wallet. "I never paid for that ginger ale I ordered over there."

The bartender waves his hand in the air. "You're good."

"Really?"

But he's already darted away to help another customer. Wow . . . being a friend of the Avalons clearly has its perks. I pull out a handful of singles and leave them on the counter as a tip. For less than twenty bucks total, this night was more than worth it.

My phone buzzes on my walk back to the subway. It's a text from an unknown number:

> Hey, it's Duke ;)

I stop in my tracks to text him back, a smile creeping over my face.

ME
> Hey! So fun meeting you tonight 😊

DUKE
> Excited for Friday

ME
> Me too!!

Is it weird that I'm suddenly thinking about what it might be like to kiss Duke? It's only been three days since I said goodbye to Alistair. No, that's no big deal. Yes, he was my prom date, and yes, we hooked up all semester, but we were never anything serious. Even if we had been, it's not like there's an official rule for how long you're supposed to wait before moving on to someone new. If there's anything weird about me picturing myself tilting my face up to meet Duke's lips, it's that I'm supposed to be focusing on Leah.

"I *am* focusing on Leah." I actually say the words out loud, like I have something to prove to the mannequins in the windows of Bloomingdale's.

I catch a downtown 4 train at 59th Street. Only after the doors shut behind me do I realize I've boarded a subway car where the air-conditioning doesn't work. Ugh—it's stifling in here, and the air smells faintly sour, like plain yogurt. The man next to me has visible beads of sweat on his bald head; another guy in a dress shirt has pit stains that practically go down to his waist. After spending all that time with the Avalons at Sunday Service, this train ride is a glaring reminder that I am so not from their world. A woman smacks me in the arm with the paperback novel she's using as a fan. God, I feel like such a *commoner*.

Back at the loft, a new face greets me at the door.

"Hey!" she says. "I'm Ivy."

I've seen Ivy Okamoto in Zayn's Instagram Stories, but this is my first time meeting her in person. She has straight shoulder-length hair that's black on one side and bleach-blond on the other, and a delicate silver septum ring at the base of her nose. She's beautiful in a way that knocks me off balance.

"I-I'm Noa," I stammer. Somehow, it was easier to give my fake name to the twins than my real one to Ivy. We shake hands. "I've heard so much about you from Zayn."

She grins. "Likewise! I keep saying to them, 'When am I gonna get to meet this girl?'"

"Well, here I am."

Ivy laughs as I strike a little pose, then steps aside to let me through the door. "I'm sorry to hear about this stuff with your sister," she says. "You must be totally freaked out."

My face burns. After I switched to an air-conditioned subway car, I spent the ride to Bushwick fantasizing more about this gala on Friday than figuring out what happened to Leah. Dad's words slice through me again. *Sometimes I don't even know if you miss her.*

"Er, yeah," I tell Ivy. "I *am* totally freaked out." I'm not sure how convincing I sound, because no sooner have the words left my mouth than somebody shouts Ivy's name from the kitchen, diverting her attention.

"We need your help!" the voice screams.

Ivy rolls her eyes. "I leave the two of them for one minute..."

I follow her down the corridor and into the kitchen, where Zayn leans over the stove next to a slim guy with scraggly blond hair. This must be their other roommate, Killian Byrne. He looks at Ivy with wide, frantic eyes. "The mushrooms look done, but we don't know how much miso to add. Does this look right?" He holds up a serving spoon with a small mountain of light-brown paste.

"Jesus." Ivy rushes over and grabs the spoon. "You need like one-fifth of that."

"I told you." Zayn nudges their elbow into Killian, who backs away with his hands in the air.

"This is what I get for trying to help!" he exclaims.

"You can cut the avocados," Ivy tells him. "And say hi to Noa." She gestures at me.

"Hey! I'm Killian."

"Noa."

Killian opens an avocado and starts to coax out the pit, but he loses control, and the round pit goes skidding across the island, nearly tumbling onto the floor before I catch it and hold it in place. "We got some action-fast reflexes over here," he says, impressed.

"How'd it go tonight?" Zayn asks. "You were gone for a while."

"It went *great*." I grab a stool as Ivy serves up three miso mushroom rice bowls.

"You want one?" she asks me. "It's like the ultimate Japanese comfort food—at least, in my house."

"Thank you, but I'm super full." I turn to Zayn. "I met Sylvie and her brother, Duke, and they basically ordered the full menu. For *free*."

The three roommates join me at the island, where Ivy leans over her steaming bowl, closes her eyes, inhales, and smiles softly. While they eat their dinner, I tell them about mine: how I managed to get the attention of Sylvie, Duke, and Jocelyn, all of whom were there on the night Leah died. They're impressed when I tell them I scored an invite to the gala on Friday, and disgusted when I tell them about my unsettling interaction with Tommy Sunday.

"It happened so fast, for a second I thought it was an accidental boob graze," I say.

"That doesn't sound like an accident to me," Ivy says. "I bet he knew *exactly* what he was doing."

"I think he did too." I shudder at the memory of Tommy's eyes when he called me a "friend of the Avalons." They roved over my body like I was a slab of meat he was eyeing for a steak. "That's why I'm wondering if he was the person who attacked Leah." I explain to Ivy and Killian the texts I found on Leah's phone.

"The theory seems legit to me," Zayn says.

"Agreed," Ivy adds.

"Whoever crossed a line with Leah, it was someone she referred to as a source," I point out. I pull out my phone and open Google to see if Leah ever interviewed Tommy Sunday for the *Sentinel*. I type in "site: gothamsentinel.com Leah Falk Tommy Sunday," and gasp at the first link that comes up.

A PEA GROWS IN BROOKLYN

At the 11th annual fundraiser for his urban farming initiative, chef Tommy Sunday announces big plans for little legumes.

BY LEAH FALK

"Hang on," I tell the roommates. "We can literally listen to their interview." I hop off my stool and sprint upstairs, nearly tripping over the slanted top step. I grab Leah's phone out of my backpack, slumped on the floor next to my deflated air mattress, and race back down to the kitchen. I open her Voice Notes app and find the recording labeled *TOMMY SUNDAY—CITY CROP FUNDRAISER*.

I hit Play.

The first few minutes are pretty bland. Tommy has a charity called City Crop, which funds urban farming initiatives in underserved communities. He's clearly press-trained when it comes to talking about the organization, his answers coming out with practiced ease. He sounds like he's parroting whatever's on the City Crop website. But it's toward the end, when Leah asks a question about the nitty-gritty mechanics of urban farming, that all of us exchange horrified looks.

TOMMY: You should come check out one of our sites sometime. You know, it's one thing to hear me ramble on about what we can do, but it's another thing to see it in person.

LEAH: That would be cool.

TOMMY: I could give you a private tour. You could ask whatever questions you needed to.

LEAH: Oh, um . . . yeah! Okay. Thanks.

TOMMY: We wouldn't have any time constraints, like here. After, I could even take you for dinner at one of our partner restaurants that uses our produce. That way, you can see how the whole system works. What do you think?

LEAH: Well, I'd have to pitch it to my editor.

TOMMY: C'mon. Is that a no?

LEAH: [Laughs.] It's not a no! It's an "I have to ask."

TOMMY: Okay. Ask your editor and let me know. I'll take you up to our site in Harlem.

LEAH: Okay, cool! So, um, is there anything else our readers should know about City Crop?

TOMMY: Well, Leah, one more thing people need to know about urban farming is . . .

Leah wraps up the interview soon after that. I can practically *hear* her squirming with discomfort, from the false, high pitch of her voice to the forced laughs. My sister obviously didn't want a private tour or dinner with Tommy, and I can't blame her.

"Um, Tommy Sunday is a definite creep," Ivy declares. "He's gotta be the person your sister was scared to see that night. I know *I'd* be scared to see him."

"How are you gonna know for sure?" Killian asks.

I pause to consider the question. "The next step is finding out whether Tommy was also at this bar called the Haven on

Wednesday. I read her DMs with Sylvie, and that's where Leah was on the night the source first crossed the line with her." I look up the Haven on Google Maps. It has a 3.1-star rating. I swipe through the photos. "This place looks pretty terrible."

"Oh, the Haven is like the grossest bar in New York City," Killian says.

"You've been?"

He grimaces. "Too many times. I grew up in the city. The Haven is one of those places where high school kids go to party because they don't card anyone. A toddler could get a tequila shot at the Haven. It's a shitshow."

"You think a guy like Tommy Sunday would want to go there?" Zayn asks.

"I think a guy like Tommy Sunday would go wherever there are women with a pulse," I mutter.

Ivy nods.

I open Instagram and find Tommy Sunday's profile. Then I pull up the list of accounts he's following. "He follows Leah," I announce.

"See if he posted anything the day Leah was at the Haven," Zayn says.

"Okay." I'm starting to feel sick. Tommy's a fairly frequent poster, so it takes me a while to scroll back to last summer. Finally, a photo of him sabering a bottle of champagne catches my eye; according to the caption, it's from the Sunday Service opening. I scroll to the next post. "Oh my God! This one's from that Wednesday."

I put the phone down on the island so we can all see the photo. It's a picture of Tommy standing on a dock and holding a giant live lobster in each hand. I read the caption out loud: "'Sourcing the best of the best for the Sunday Service grand opening on Friday.'" I look at the location tag. "He took this in Bridgehampton. How far is that from here?"

Ivy looks it up on her phone. "It's like two and a half hours by car."

"So he could have been back in the city by Wednesday evening, when Leah was at the Haven." That's when I remember the front-page *Sentinel* story in the box in Leah's bedroom. My pulse spikes. "Some people even take helicopters to and from the Hamptons. He could have been back in like forty minutes."

I lean forward and dig my fingertips into my temples, appalled by the story that's gradually coming to life: Tommy Sunday coming home from the Hamptons in time to meet Sylvie and her friends at the Haven, maybe because he knew the pretty young *Sentinel* reporter who interviewed him at his fundraiser would be there; Tommy cornering Leah and doing something "extremely inappropriate," whatever that entailed; Leah, trying to get out of seeing him again at his restaurant's grand opening; then . . . what, exactly? Did something happen between them that pushed her to take her own life?

Deep in my gut, I know that's not what happened. I know it the way you can sense someone's hand in front of your face, even with your eyes closed.

Ivy gently touches my forearm. "Are you all right, Noa?"

I'm at the edge of the abyss, and for the first time, I peer straight down into its depths. The air whooshes from my lungs, and my voice comes out as a whisper. "What if Tommy Sunday killed my sister?"

CHAPTER 8

The words harden into stone and settle onto my chest, where they stay for the rest of the night, suffocating me. It's hard to go more than a few minutes without remembering Tommy's fingers grazing the barely-there fabric of my dress, and wondering what the chef might have done to Leah.

There's free Wi-Fi at Sweet Bean, the coffee shop where Zayn works, so the next day, I post up at the bar for the duration of their shift. It's a cozy little spot with bookshelves lining the walls and vintage furniture. The air smells like sugar and butter, and there's a resident cat named Stefan, who may or may not be a health code violation, but nobody seems to mind. The iced coffee is also exceptionally strong, which I desperately need, having spent a good portion of the night tossing and turning on my air mattress with disturbing images racing through my mind.

"I have an iced almond-milk latte and a gluten-free carrot muffin for Alia!" Zayn shouts as they deposit someone's order on the counter. "What are you working on?" they ask me in a quieter voice.

"Finding out what Leah's relationships were like with the rest of the Avalons." I take out her phone and open my laptop to do some more research, starting with my sister's Instagram DMs. She chatted with Duke on here too, their chat history going back almost as far as her history with Sylvie.

With a lurch in my stomach, I notice Duke messaged Leah the morning of her death—although it was totally random. He'd sent Leah her own grid post from earlier in the week: a shot of flowers in Central Park. "I missed this one when you posted it," he'd written. "Such a great shot." Sweet, baby-faced Duke. Leah saw, but never replied to his innocent message; by that time, she was already preoccupied with the stress of her assignment later that night.

I scroll back in time to read the rest of their messages—only I can't, because they seem to have communicated almost exclusively in disappearing photos. Occasionally, Leah replied to one with a heart or a laughing emoji, but it's hard to get a sense of their relationship. That doesn't matter, though: they were clearly friends, which means that if I get close to Duke, I might be able to get him talking about her.

Then there's the twins' mom, Gracie Avalon. In Sylvie's very first DM to Leah, she said my sister had met Gracie at a "speakeasy open house" thing. On my laptop, I search "Leah Falk Gracie Avalon speakeasy open house" and click the *Gotham Sentinel* article at the top of the results page.

BACKDOOR LISTING

Need to sell your $50 million townhome? Turn it into a Prohibition-era speakeasy.

BY LEAH FALK

The bartenders were dressed in suspenders and serving up sidecars and Sazeracs on Thursday evening. But this building on East 72nd Street wasn't home to yet another new speakeasy-style cocktail bar on the Upper East Side: it was a dazzling townhome listed for $48 million.

Out-of-the-box open houses are standard practice for selling luxury homes these days, and Suzie Santorini, executive vice president of Celestial Real Estate, spared no expense when it came to showing off the historic residence on Central Park East (built in 1928—hence, the theme). Brokers, buyers, and a who's who of the socialite set wore beads, feathers, and sequins as they explored the six bedrooms, 12 bathrooms, and two terraces spread across six lavish stories.

"This home still has so many original details, it's actually been recommended as a national landmark," Santorini said, pointing to the carved wooden fireplace. "There was no question we had to go with a speakeasy theme to really grab people's attention."

Lounging in front of the fireplace, French 75

in hand, was Gracie Avalon, director of publicity for the Avalon Hospitality Group and self-proclaimed "dear, dear friend" of Santorini.

"She's a marketing genius, and I say that as a publicist myself," Avalon said. "If I'm not careful, she'll have me leaving here with a second home in the neighborhood!"

I look at the date of the story and open Leah's Voice Notes app. GRACIE AVALON—OPEN HOUSE is the first interview my sister ever recorded. I put in my earbuds and hit Play.

LEAH: Awesome. So, um . . . Well, first, can I get your name?

GRACIE: Of course. It's Gracie Avalon. G-R-A-C-I-E A-V-A-L-O-N.

LEAH: Thank you so much, Ms.—oh my God. I'm so sorry. You literally just told me your name, and I'm blanking. This is so embarrassing.

GRACIE: Don't be embarrassed, my darling! It's Gracie Avalon, and you can call me Gracie.

LEAH: Gracie. Thank you.

GRACIE: Did you start at the Sentinel recently?

LEAH: Just this week. I'm interning for the summer,

and . . . this is actually my first in-person assignment.

GRACIE: Well! I'm honored to be included. And congratulations, Leah. You know, Emmeline Gilbane is a dear, dear friend of mine, and I know how selective she is with her interns. You must be quite talented.

LEAH: Oh, wow. Thank you. Uh, please don't tell Emmeline that I forgot your name.

GRACIE: [Laughs.] It can be our secret. Okay! You got this. Hit me with the questions.

LEAH: Okay! So, I guess we should start with . . . what brings you here tonight?

GRACIE: Well, Suzie Santorini is another dear, dear friend of mine. I'm here to support her, first and foremost. And secondly, I can't resist a good French Seventy-five.

LEAH: So, I take it you're a fan of the whole speakeasy theme?

GRACIE: I'm absolutely obsessed! Suzie, she's a marketing genius, and I say that as a publicist myself. If I'm not careful, she'll have me leaving here with a second home in the neighborhood!

LEAH: I love your costume, by the way.

GRACIE: Thank you! I just love flappers, don't you? Not just the whole look, but everything they stood for: these women going out and dancing and smoking and wearing their hair short . . . just being free.

LEAH: We love to see it!

GRACIE: Yes, we do!

LEAH: Well, thank you so much for talking to me, Gracie. It was really nice to meet you.

GRACIE: I'm sure this won't be the last time we run into each other, my darling. Feel free to come say hello whenever you see me out. I know how intimidating it can be to approach strangers at these things. I can make introductions, or—whatever you need!

LEAH: That's so nice of you. Thank you.

GRACIE: No need to thank me! I always want to help other independent young women. Also, my darling, I mentioned to you that I'm a publicist. I represent my family's business, the Avalon Hospitality Group. Have you heard of it?

LEAH: No, I don't think so!

GRACIE: Oh my goodness. We *have* to get you out to one of our restaurants for dinner sometime! You can't live in New York and not have eaten at an Avalon restaurant. We have some of the best chefs in the world working for us. What's your favorite kind of food?

LEAH: Um, I love everything! Maybe . . . Italian?

GRACIE: Ah! [Claps.] Say no more. You have to come by Il Tavolo. It's the best pasta you've ever had in your life. Do you like spaghetti carbonara?

LEAH: I love it.

GRACIE: The one at Il Tavolo is to die for.

LEAH: [Laughs.] I've been eating a lot of frozen Trader Joe's meals, so that sounds amazing.

GRACIE: I'll have my daughter, Sylvie, come too. She's in college, like you. You two would get along great. You're both so ambitious! Here, give me your number, and I'll set something up.

LEAH: Wow, that would be amazing. I don't know very many people my age in the city, either.

GRACIE: Leah, I am so happy we ran into each other.

By the end of the interview, I can hear my sister relaxing. Gracie's outgoingness and generosity must have put her at ease. From the sounds of it, this conversation was just the beginning of Gracie and Leah's relationship. The twins' mom is someone else I'll have to charm, and where better than at the charity gala, which takes place in her own home?

A notification pops up on my own phone, one I've been eagerly waiting for since I got to the city. I swipe to read the DM from @janiewallace46, and when I do, I jump off my stool.

"Are you okay?" Zayn asks.

"I gotta go," I tell them. "Leah's roommate from last summer just got back to me. She said she's around for a few hours if I want to come by."

"Oh! Get outta here."

"I'll see you later!" I grab what's left of my iced coffee and hightail it for the door.

I take the subway to Hell's Kitchen and find my way to the corner of 52nd Street and 11th Avenue, to a five-story redbrick building with paint chipping from the cornices on the windows and roof. A few windows have flower boxes; another has a child's messy crayon drawing taped to the glass. I jog up the steps and press the buzzer for apartment 5C. The lock clicks, and I open the door of the building where Leah died.

The hallway is narrow, the floor slanted, and the walls slightly tilted like a funhouse. It smells like bacon and eggs and something else. Dog food, maybe. I start to climb the stairs. The apartment is on the top floor of a walk-up—i.e., an apartment building with no elevator—and by the final flight of stairs, my heart feels like it's going to blast through my rib cage. I used to get like this when I tried to keep up with Leah during soccer practice. I bet she had no problem summitting these stairs.

I'm greeted by a Black woman in her mid-twenties with short, hot-pink curls. I recognize her from the funeral, where she stood over by the wall of the synagogue, crying softly, with her arms wrapped around her torso. Janie was Leah's roommate last summer—the person who found her unresponsive in her bedroom and called 911. She gives me a sad smile and opens her arms for a hug. "Hey, Noa."

"Hey."

"You doing okay?"

"I've been better. Thanks for letting me come by."

"No problem. Come on in." She steps to the side and ushers me in. "I forget: were you ever here last summer?"

"No," I answer guiltily. "First time."

"Well, don't mind the fact that the shower is in the kitchen."

Walking through the door of 5C, I find myself in a windowless kitchen-slash-common-room with a fridge, a sink, and a stove all jammed together with no counter space in between. Next to the fridge, as Janie promised, is an ancient-looking bathtub the color of Pepto Bismol. I remember what Zayn told me: that every apartment in New York has *some* weird quirk, unless you're mega-rich.

Janie shows me the room that used to be Leah's. There's a double bed pushed against one wall, and a dresser and garment rack on the other. Sunlight beams onto the desk under the window, which has a sliver of a Hudson River view. I do my best to picture Leah writing there, and not lying dead on the floor, where Janie found her. It doesn't work. There's a lump in my throat and pressure behind my eyes, and the next thing I know, I'm crying in a stranger's bedroom.

Janie rubs my back. "You want to sit down out here?" I nod, and she leads me to the love seat in the living area. While I sit down, Janie pours me a glass of water from a Brita filter and places it gently on the coffee table. The cup has little yellow daises on it.

I take a big gulp. "Sorry, Janie. I didn't mean to come here and just cry all over you."

"Hey, it's totally understandable." She glances at the time on the microwave before she joins me on the love seat. I know she has to leave for her bartending job in a bit. "So, what can I help you with?" When I messaged Janie, all I said was that I had a few questions about Leah, and I'd love to find time to meet up.

"Well, I've been trying to understand why my sister . . . did what she did. I was just wondering if . . . I don't know . . . you knew anything that might help explain things."

"Oh, Noa, you poor thing." Janie squeezes my knee. "To be honest, we didn't actually talk all that much last summer. Leah was out all the time doing internship stuff, and I was busy with work and summer classes. We had a ships-in-the-night kinda relationship. If she was struggling, I just didn't have any idea." She frowns. "I wish I'd paid more attention during the times we *did* hang out."

"Remind me . . . you weren't here when Leah came home from the party that Friday night, right?"

Janie shakes her head. "I was closing at the bar that night. I didn't get home till three a.m., and that's when I . . ." She glances at the bedroom that used to be Leah's. "When I found her."

Something about her story seems off to me. "What made you go into her room at three in the morning?" I ask curiously.

"I didn't randomly go in," Janie says a little defensively. "The door was open. I saw her as soon as I walked through the living room."

"Oh. That makes sense." Janie glances at the clock again. I take another sip of my water. "Do you remember any details of... I don't know... how she looked? Or what was around her?"

Janie scratches her chin. "She was still in a nice dress—I remember that. I rushed to check on her, and when I realized she was unconscious, I ran to get my phone, but I tripped over her water bottle and almost busted my ankle. I remember thinking, *Oh God, she must have used that to wash it all down.*" Janie grimaces. "Sorry—is this too much detail? Let me know."

"No, please, go on."

"That's kind of all I remember. I went into shock after that. I'm sorry—I wish I could be more helpful."

"You said you guys hung out a couple of times. Did she ever talk about any issues she was having at work?"

Janie raises her eyebrows. "Issues at work? No. As far as I could tell, she *loved* that job at the *Sentinel*." Out in the hall, a neighbor unlocks their door. A dog barks, and a baby starts to wail. "Sorry," Janie says, "these walls are like paper."

"That's okay. So, you got the sense she was loving her internship?"

Janie smiles to herself. "Oh yeah, *big* time. I remember she'd come home from these fancy events and be like, 'Oh my God, I feel like Cinderella!' Meanwhile, I was working at a bar near Times Square serving cocktails named after Broadway shows. I was low-key *so* envious."

Janie chuckles, and I do too, only a little red flag goes up in my head. Janie just admitted she was envious of Leah last summer. "Did you ever go to any events with her?"

"Nah. She said she couldn't bring plus-ones. Had to ask, though." Janie smirks. "Anyway, to answer your question: I didn't get the sense she had any issues at work. If anything, writing for the *Sentinel* was the best thing that had ever happened to your sister."

CHAPTER 9

On Friday evening, back at the loft, I shower, blow-dry my hair, and slip into the midnight-blue dress I wore to prom. It's a slinky floor-length gown with an open back and a thigh-high slit in the skirt.

"Hey, Ivy?" There's no way to knock up here on the second level, so I awkwardly poke the green velvet curtain that delineates the edge of her space. "Mind helping me with my dress for a sec?"

"Come in!" she says.

I pull back the curtain to find her sitting cross-legged on her bed, her back against the exposed brick wall, and her eyebrows wrinkled in concentration as she stares at her laptop screen. When she looks up, her eyes go wide, and she blinks like she's surprised to find me standing there.

"Noa! You look amazing."

Her earnest tone makes my cheeks flush, and I spin around

in case I'm noticeably turning red. "Thank you! I love this dress, but the strings at the back are impossible to tie without help. They're supposed to crisscross and end in a bow...." I wiggle the ties in an attempt to demonstrate.

"I got you! Don't worry." Her mattress creaks, and then I feel Ivy's hands on mine, easing the ties from my fingertips. "I love a corset back," she muses. "How's that? Too loose?"

"Maybe a little."

"I didn't want to hurt you." She tightens the strings. "How about now?"

"Perfect."

She ties the bow, and I turn back around. Ivy raises her eyebrows. "Okay, damn. You look hot."

I press my palms to my cheeks. "You're making me blush."

"It's the truth." Ivy shrugs and goes back to her bed. She's wearing a black leotard tucked into baggy gray sweatpants. They ride low on her hips, revealing half-moons of bare skin beneath her hip bones.

When I catch myself staring, I avert my gaze to my dress and pretend to brush off a nonexistent bit of fluff. "Well, thanks for your help."

"Thank *you*. My brain needed a little break." She hauls her computer back onto her lap. "This is so freaking hard."

"What is it?"

"You know the gallery where I'm interning this summer?" I nod. "They have this exhibition coming up, and they invited me to show some of my photos."

"Oh my God, Ivy, that's huge. Congrats."

"Thanks. It's the first time I've ever shown my stuff in like a real gallery." She lets out an aggravated sigh. "But that's why I'm ripping my hair out trying to decide exactly which shots I want to include."

"Don't rip your hair out!" Then I add, "It's too pretty." Was that the cheesiest comment of all time? Possibly. It just came out. I think Ivy's leotard cast some kind of spell on me.

She looks up at me, and her smile makes my cheeks burn even more than when she told me I looked hot. After a couple of seconds, Ivy closes her eyes and shakes her head. "Sorry. Here I am complaining about my gallery show when you're dealing with something a million times worse."

"Hey, it's okay." I nod at her laptop. "That sounds legitimately stressful."

Ivy sighs. "It'll be all right."

"Good luck," I tell her. I turn to leave, pulling the velvet curtain to the side.

"Good luck to you too," Ivy says.

I use the bathroom before I go, and while I sit on the toilet, I Google the Avalons' Upper East Side penthouse and click on the real estate site that pops up. Holy shit. It says they bought the place for $70 million. "The luxury condo building is one of the tallest in Manhattan, with unbeatable views of Central Park and the surrounding city," the article says. If Zayn's theory about New York City apartments is true, then the Avalons' penthouse must be among the least quirky homes in the city.

"Look at this," I tell Zayn and Killian, who are chilling in the kitchen when I come out of the bathroom.

"Whoa," Killian says. "These people are like next-level loaded."

Zayn pokes him. "Didn't *you* grow up in a doorman building?"

"Yeah, but not like that!" Killian says defensively. "I mean, we weren't struggling by any stretch of the imagination. But like, my family has a vacation home in Rhode Island; people with condos like *that* probably own—I dunno—multiple islands."

"Or hospitality empires," I add, trying to wrap my head around the sheer magnitude of the Avalons' wealth. My town in New Jersey has two main socioeconomic groups: you're either rich and go to the private school a few towns over, or you're comfortable, like my family, and go to the local public school. Maybe it takes being rich to realize there are so many different levels of being rich.

I take the subway to the stop near Bloomingdale's again, and follow my GPS west. One block before the Avalons', I duck into an alley beside a Botox clinic and pull my heels out of my purse. I would have broken an ankle if I'd tried to commute in them. I place them on the ground side by side. Gripping a crack in the concrete wall for support, I transfer my feet from my comfy slides into my heels, careful not to let my skin touch the grimy sidewalk.

"AHHH!" A cockroach the size of a Medjool date crawls out of the crack in the wall and skitters across my fucking fingers. Fuck, fuck, fuck, that's disgusting. I yank my hand away, scoop up my slides, shove them in my purse, and stumble back out to the street. Up ahead, a black SUV glides onto the Avalons' block and stops in front of their building. The door opens, and out climb two glamorously dressed women who probably haven't seen a cockroach in their lives.

I teeter the rest of the way to the Avalons' building, which reminds me of a giant icicle rising from the earth. It has a marble base that supports a soaring tower of glass, tapered toward the top as the units per floor get fewer and fewer. I pass through a pair of thick Grecian columns, where two doormen proceed to usher me through double doors into a lobby lit by glittering chandeliers.

"Good evening," says the man at the front desk. He's dressed in a sharp black suit. "How may I help you?"

"I'm here for Mrs. Avalon's event in the penthouse suite?"

"Your name?"

"Hailey Star."

He types something into a computer and nods. "Thank you, Miss Star. The elevators are just through those columns. You'll want the bank on your right. Have a wonderful evening."

"Thank you."

My shoes clicking across the gleaming marble, I text Duke to let him know I'm here. I board the elevator and press the button for the ninetieth floor. My stomach drops, and I grasp the handrail as I rocket toward the penthouse. My ears pop from the pressure change as I get to the top. The only other time I've had this happen in an elevator is when my school took a field trip to One World Observatory, and the elevators whisked us up 102 stories in less than a minute.

With a *ding,* the elevator doors glide open. I'm not in a hallway; *I'm in the Avalons' actual home.* I step into a marble foyer with a three-tiered water feature in the center. I hear piano music, and beyond the fountain, I can see into a sprawling great room with at least a hundred people in dresses and suits, and what looks like a jaw-dropping view of the city.

Duke comes bounding up the steps to the foyer in a royal-blue dinner jacket and black pants that must have been custom-tailored to fit his giant frame. "Hailey! You made it!" He spreads his arms wide, first as a welcoming gesture, then to wrap me in a hug. He really does seem like a giant teddy bear.

Duke steps back to hold me at arm's length. "Wow." He smiles. "You look great."

"So do you."

"Really? I always feel so stiff and uncomfortable when I'm dressed like this." He tugs at his black bow tie. "I don't know how people breathe in these things. Anyway, come on in. I'll show you around. A bunch of us are hanging out upstairs in Sylvie's room, but you should probably meet my mom first. Sylvie told her you were coming, and that you wanna go into journalism and stuff."

"Oh, wow. That would be awesome." I can't help it: my heart thuds with excitement. The evening furls out before me like an endless red carpet—a pathway to infinite possibilities.

"No problem. C'mon." Duke spins around. Then, with a running start, he leaps down the three marble steps onto the hardwood floor below, stopping his trajectory just before he careens into an older man in a tux holding a very full champagne glass.

"I have a heart attack every time I watch you do that, my darling."

A woman with a sleek chestnut-brown blowout, dressed in a periwinkle boatneck gown, puts a manicured hand on Duke's shoulder. I recognize Gracie Avalon from the photo on her Wikipedia page, where her bio read:

Gracie Avalon is an American publicist and philanthropist. She is the daughter-in-law of Avalon Hospitality Group founder Rex Avalon and the widow of the prominent hotelier Bradford Avalon. Avalon is an advocate for prostate cancer awareness and research.

She also has the same green eyes as the twins. They crinkle ever so slightly at the corners when she smiles at her son.

"If you always have a heart attack, then you should try not to watch me do it again," Duke jokes.

The man with the champagne glass sniffs disapprovingly. He has neatly combed white hair, a white goatee, and the clean, pinkish skin of an executive who spends their days in a fancy boardroom. I recognize Rex Avalon—the twins' grandfather and Gracie's father-in-law—from his headshot on the Avalon Hospitality Group's website. He's the company's founder and CEO.

"Bradford would never have stood for behavior like that," Rex snaps. He doesn't direct the comment at Duke, but at Gracie. "He would have smacked him upside the head, and rightfully so."

Gracie maintains a stiff upper lip. "Well, I'd rather not smack anyone," she replies. "Least of all my own son."

"A future leader of the family business and he's jumping around like an animal at an important event." Rex shakes his head. "Tighten the reins, Grace. It can't all be sunshine and rainbows over here."

Duke looks at his feet. "Sorry, Grandpa. It was my fault."

"Don't let it happen again," Rex says.

Gracie pouts. "Go easy on him, Rex. It's a party!"

Rex glares at Gracie. "If you won't take a hard line, I will."

Instead of responding, Gracie takes a deep breath and plasters on a grin as she drags her gaze from Rex to me. Her nails make indentations in the shoulder of her son's dinner jacket. "So sorry about that. Duke, darling, who do we have here?"

Duke introduces me—or, rather, Hailey Star—to his mom and grandfather. Rex envelops my hand in a firm shake, but Gracie brings me in for a hug. "It's lovely to meet you, dear. You're our new journalist friend, aren't you?"

"Aspiring journalist," I humbly correct her.

"If you're a junior in college, surely you've done reporting before, even for a school publication?"

"Oh! Yeah, tons."

Gracie waves her hand. "Then drop the *aspiring,* honey. You're doing journalism, so you're a journalist!"

My face splits into a grin. I'm starting to like Gracie Avalon as much as my sister did.

"When Emmeline gets here, I'll have to introduce you," she goes on. "Do you know her? Emmeline Gilbane? She's the editor-in-chief of the *Gotham Sentinel.*"

It's a struggle to keep up the smile once I hear Emmeline's name. Nevertheless, Leah's boss from last summer is a good person for me to know. "That would be amazing, Mrs. Avalon. Thank you so much."

"Oh my gosh, of course!" she replies. "And please, call me Gracie."

Duke touches my elbow. "We're gonna go hang upstairs for a bit, but we'll come back down in a little while to talk to Emmeline."

"Fabulous!" Gracie replies.

I smile at Rex. "It was nice to meet you, too, Mr. Avalon."

Rex nods curtly without returning the smile.

Before we head upstairs, Duke leads me over to the floor-to-ceiling windows spanning the length of the room. My stomach plummets ever faster than it did on the elevator ride. Central Park is the size of my hand; the other buildings, mere specks. It's like seeing the city from an airplane.

Duke looks over his shoulder. "Is my grandpa looking? No? Okay, good. Check out this thing I like to do." As he approaches the window, I realize it's slanted ever so slightly, as though it's peeling away from the building at the top. With his toes against the base of the glass, he leans forward so his entire body rests on it—all six-and-a-half feet of him. "It's kinda like you're flying," he says. "You get to look down at like ten million people. C'mon, try it."

My stomach's still in free-fall mode. There is no way I'm leaning on that slanted glass, ninety stories off the ground. "I'm a little afraid of heights," I confess, crossing my arms and stepping back.

"Aww, Hails, you'll be okay. Trust me." He stands up straight, looks over his shoulder, and smiles at me. "I'll be right next to you."

The back of my neck prickles with sweat, and I'm pretty sure there's no blood left in my head, but when Duke reaches his hand out, I can't *not* take it. I'm so grateful to be here and I don't want to jeopardize the bond we're building. I'm sure this glass passed some sort of rigorous safety testing, right? Duke pulls me, gently, toward the window.

"Ready?"

My throat is sealed shut, so I nod. The glass is cool against my forehead. I squeeze Duke's hand as I lean the whole of my weight against the window.

"Are your eyes open?" he asks.

"No."

"C'mon, you got this. I'll count you down."

"I'm scared!"

"Three... two... one... *open*."

I do as I'm told—and I gasp. "Oh my God. It really is like you're flying!"

"Right?!"

"Oh my God. Oh my God!" The roller-coaster ride from terrified to relieved to amazed has me feeling almost giddy.

"*Duke!*" The roar of Rex Avalon's voice makes us both jump back from the window.

"Oh shit!" Duke, still holding my hand, tugs me away from the window. It's impossible not to giggle as we sprint up the hardwood spiral staircase, away from his angry grandfather and the rest of the crowd. "My grandpa can be such a dick," he says, leading me along a mezzanine overlooking the gala. "But that's also why he's so successful."

I follow him down a hallway and through an open bedroom door. It's a spacious room with a king-size canopy bed, and six elegantly dressed bodies are draped across it. The whole group is laughing en masse, like one connected organism.

Sylvie and Jocelyn lift their heads from the pile, and Sylvie flashes us a relaxed smile. "Don't you two look cute! Did Hailey meet Mom?"

"Yeah, and Grandpa." Duke and Sylvie share a knowing eye roll. "Mom said she'll introduce Hailey to Emmeline whenever she gets here."

"Amaaaaze."

"Who's this, Duke?" asks a girl in a silky gold dress that pops against her medium-brown skin. She's lying in the lap of a white guy with long, curly hair pulled back in a bun.

"This is Hailey," Duke says, before introducing me to the rest of the group: Lina is the girl in the gold dress; Mateo is the guy she's snuggling with; Divya is the girl sprawled out on her back, her head on Jocelyn's outstretched legs; and Owen's the guy sitting beside Sylvie against the upholstered headboard, his hand clasped around the neck of a Dom Pérignon champagne bottle. Owen offers it to me as I climb onto the bed, and I take a quick swig before passing it back to him. I settle myself at the foot of the mattress, with my back to one of the bedposts. Duke takes a spot against the footboard, so he's next to me, but not quite touching.

"Okay, my turn," Jocelyn announces, evidently picking up a conversation from before. "Never have I ever . . . had sex on a private jet."

Lina shrieks with laughter. "Mateo, you better put a finger down."

He laughs, snatching the champagne bottle from Owen. "Yeah, yeah, I'm on it."

"Where did that happen?" Divya asks.

"The Greek Islands," Lina replies. "Can't remember which ones we went to that time." She cocks an eyebrow at Duke. "Hey, didn't you and some girl once . . . ?"

Duke rolls his eyes as he tucks his thumb under the rest of his fingers. "Fine. You got me."

"Classic," Owen says.

Duke glances at me apologetically. "For the record, I was trying not to bring up a past hookup like two seconds into our date."

The word *date* gives me butterflies. Then I feel hot with shame for getting butterflies when I'm supposed to be here for my dead sister. I look at my lap, my face pounding with wave after wave of guilt.

"Hailey?" Duke taps my foot with the side of his shoe.

I look up. "Hmm?"

"Lina just went. She said, 'Never have I ever been on the subway.'"

"Wait, seriously?"

I blink at Lina, who cocks her head to the side. "Um, *yeah*, seriously. Is there something wrong with that?"

"Uh, no. Sorry." How is that even possible, living in New York? I don't know, but I put a finger down, and Sylvie hands me the bottle. I tip it back, but nothing comes out.

"Oh *no*," Sylvie whines. "Are we out already?"

"I guess so."

Sylvie juts out her bottom lip and turns to Jocelyn. "Joc," she says in a baby voice, "will you go and get us a few more bottles?"

"Me?" Jocelyn asks.

"You're closest to the door," Sylvie points out. It's technically true, but only by a matter of a foot or so.

Divya lifts her head off Jocelyn's lap. "Wait, can you also get us some rosé? I don't *love* champagne, TBH."

"This sounds like a lot for me to carry," Jocelyn says dubiously.

"Maybe Hailey can go with you." Sylvie looks at me expectantly. Just like with Duke and the window, I know I can't refuse.

"Yeah, sure." I clamber off the bed. "C'mon, Joc. I'll help."

Sylvie turns back to Jocelyn. "See? You'll have fun. Now go. We can't keep playing without drinks!"

"I know—sorry!" Jocelyn leaps off the bed. "I was just comfortable the way I was lying. We'll be back ASAP."

Jocelyn glares at me as we walk down the hallway. "Thanks for making me look like a total bitch back there."

"Because I said I was down to help you?"

She rolls her eyes. "I would have totally gotten up in a second. Now I just look like an ungrateful piece of shit."

"What are you trying to act grateful for?"

"Um, hello?" As we turn onto the mezzanine, she gestures over the half-wall to the great room below. "They invited me *here*."

"Your parents aren't down there?" I assumed Jocelyn was like the rest of the crew in Sylvie's bedroom: a longtime family friend of the Avalons.

"Um, no. My parents are home on our farm in Wisconsin."

"How'd you meet Sylvie and Duke, then?"

She side-eyes me suspiciously. "What, you want to know if it was as *epic* as your tic-tac-toe maneuver?"

I shrug. "I was just asking."

"I went to Columbia for a year before culinary school. Sylvie and I were randomly paired as first-year roommates, and we became, like, instant best friends. We'd go out to eat at all these amazing restaurants her family owns, and that's how I realized

I wanted to be a chef. Obviously, her family has a ton of connections in the hospitality world, so they've been helping me out with informational interviews and externship opportunities. I'm super indebted to the Avalons—and before you judge me, I know *you're* not from this world either."

My heart shoots into my throat, but I try not to let it show on my face. Does Jocelyn recognize me? I fight to keep my voice steady. "What do you mean?"

She huffs a laugh. "I saw your face when you found out Lina had never been on the subway. I know what you're doing, Hailey. You're trying to get ahead, just like me—only, I've known the Avalons a lot longer than you have."

"Does it have to be some kind of competition?"

She doesn't answer as she leads me down the stairs, around the edge of the great room, and over to the bar.

"Something to drink?" asks the bartender.

"We're grabbing some things for Sylvie and Duke," Jocelyn says with her nose turned up. The twins' names have an immediate and visible effect on the bartender, who waves us around the bar with a sweep of his arm and lets us snag whatever we want from the wine fridge. Each of us holding two bottles, we make our way back toward the stairs.

"Hailey?" I turn at the sound of my name. Over by the gleaming grand piano, Gracie Avalon waves to me. Standing next to her is a white woman in her sixties with high cheekbones and a sleek silver bob. "Come over so I can introduce you to Emmeline," Gracie says.

Grimacing, I hold up the champagne. "I told Sylvie I would bring these up to her. Do you mind if I come right back?"

"Why doesn't Jocelyn carry them up for you?" Gracie asks.

Whatever light was behind Jocelyn's eyes disappears. She looks like she'd rather swing one of the bottles into my skull. But with Gracie watching her, Jocelyn plasters on a smile. "I'm happy to take them for you."

"You sure?" I ask.

"Totally."

She tucks one of her bottles under her arm and grabs both of mine with her newly free hand. Before I let go, she jerks me in close, and even though she's still smiling, there's venom in her stare.

"Careful, Hailey," Jocelyn whispers. "I was here first."

CHAPTER 10

Jocelyn stalks off toward the staircase, leaving me stunned. Is this how she reacted when Leah started spending time with the Avalons, too? The look in her eyes just now was scary, like she wanted to hit me, or wrap her hands around my neck...

... or slip me a lethal dose of painkillers. What if it wasn't Tommy, but Jocelyn who killed my sister? I know from their DMs that Sylvie started inviting Leah to all sorts of outings. If Jocelyn felt like Leah was stealing the spotlight, threatening her chances of getting ahead, how far would she have gone to steal the spotlight back?

A chill goes down my spine, and it only gets pricklier as I walk over to meet Emmeline Gilbane, Leah's boss from last summer. This is the editor who forced my sister to cover the Sunday Service grand opening, even though Leah was scared for her safety. *It is too late to find a replacement,* she wrote in that cruel text. *In any case, maintaining professional boundaries with sources is a crucial part of this job, and you must learn that.* What kind of woman *says* that after a fellow woman confesses that she was violated?

I'm pretty sure I know the answer: a monster.

"Hello, there." Emmeline extends a bony hand. She has short stiletto nails, painted black at the pointy tips.

Gracie smiles warmly. "Hailey, this is my friend Emmeline Gilbane. She's the editor-in-chief of the *Gotham Sentinel*. Emmeline, this is the twins' new friend Hailey. She's a writing major at Pratt, and she's just beginning her journalism career. I figured you two *had* to meet."

How are these two women friends? One lifts people up; the other forces them to come face to face with assholes who hurt them. Whatever. I might learn something useful about Leah from Emmeline.

"It's nice to meet you, Ms. Gilbane. I'm a big fan of the *Sentinel*."

If she notices any resemblance between me and Leah, it isn't apparent on her face. "Is that so?" She raises a slender eyebrow. "What do you like about it?"

Gracie raises her eyebrows expectantly. She wants me to pass this test. Luckily, after two whole days posted up at the bar at Sweet Bean, I came prepared. "I was obsessed with that feature you did earlier this year on the secret power players behind New York Fashion Week."

Emmeline looks surprised. "Really? Did you know that's one of my favorite *Sentinel* projects of all time?"

Gracie beams at me. As a matter of fact, I did know that. As I researched Emmeline in anticipation of meeting her tonight, I found a social media post where she shared a link to the feature and said how much she loved it.

"Trinity Hoxton is such a great writer," I go on. "I love everything she's been doing recently: the profile of the jeweler working with black diamonds; the story on virtual reality shopping..."

"I'm impressed with how familiar you are with the newspaper. Some people try to bullshit me, but you're clearly a reader."

Nope. Just trying to figure out what the hell happened to my sister.

Gracie turns to Emmeline. "Don't you think Hailey would be a wonderful fit for a summer internship? She's so well-versed in the kind of work you do, *and* she's already building out a strong network of sources!" She gestures around at the gala.

Emmeline twists a sapphire ring around her finger. "Potentially, yes."

"How should Hailey go about applying?" Gracie asks.

The editor's lips flatten into one thin line. "I thought I told you: we paused our internship program this summer."

Gracie sighs. "*I* thought maybe you'd reconsidered."

"No," Emmeline says firmly.

"Why'd you pause the program?" I interject. "Um—if you don't mind me asking."

Emmeline's gaze flits to her left. There's a theory that people's eyes go in that direction when they're lying about something. "Our intern last summer, she ... she had a mental health crisis. It was incredibly unfortunate, and it compelled us to reexamine the kind of work we're having our interns do."

"Oh, Emmeline." Gracie pats her friend's arm, looking concerned. "You know you can't blame yourself for what happened to that poor girl."

"Yes, I know," Emmeline snaps. She twists the ring around and around her finger.

Gracie turns to me with a sorry expression. "She took her own life," she explains.

I clap my hand over my heart, which is secretly pounding like a jackhammer. "Oh my God. That's awful."

"Yes." With a curt nod, Emmeline clears her throat. "Anyway, I'm going to get another drink. Hailey, it was lovely meeting you. While I can't offer you an internship at this time, I'd be happy to show you around the newsroom any time you wish. Just let me know."

"Oh, okay. Thank you so much, Ms. Gilbane. It was great meeting you, too."

Emmeline pries herself away from the conversation and makes her way toward the bar.

"Hailey, why don't you go upstairs and find the twins," Gracie suggests. "I'm going to join Emmeline for a drink." With a frown, she watches the editor weave around other party guests. Then she turns back to me. "The loss was really hard on Emmeline, and I think she could use some friend time. You did great, though."

"Thanks."

She rubs my arm before hurrying off in Emmeline's wake. I follow Emmeline's silver bob all the way across the room, my pulse pounding behind my eyes.

Gracie may be convinced that Emmeline's still grieving Leah's death, but if you ask me, the editor-in-chief of the *Gotham Sentinel* didn't seem sad. She seemed nervous.

—

When I get back to Sylvie's bedroom, the group is in the process of peeling themselves off the bed and putting their shoes back on. Jocelyn avoids making eye contact with me, instead hovering next to Sylvie and loudly recounting the story of when they picked out Sylvie's hot-pink Louboutin pumps together, and "wasn't that *sooo* much fun?"

"Where are we going?" I ask Duke.

He holds up his phone. "My mom just texted that we should come down and hear the mayor's speech."

I raise my eyebrows. "The *mayor* is here?"

Duke shrugs. "My mom's friends with everyone."

Down in the great room, the eight of us stand shoulder-to-shoulder near the window. The mayor takes center stage at the top of the steps to the foyer, where a microphone stand has been set up. As she launches into her speech in support of the Avalon Hospitality Group's philanthropic work, Gracie herself watches from the foot of the stairs, dabbing tears from the corners of her eyes with a tissue.

Over to my left, sporting a much stonier expression, is Emmeline Gilbane. Her eyes are glazed over and focused somewhere in the middle distance—certainly not on the speech taking place. Between her shifty eyes and her fidgety hands, I *know* she was nervous when Leah came up in conversation. Emmeline obviously wasn't the person who crossed a line at the Haven, but what if she's been protecting whoever did?

I think through everyone else who might know more about Leah's death than they're letting on. There's Jocelyn, who's over there linking arms with Sylvie as the mayor speaks. She doesn't come from money the way nearly everyone else in this room does. For Jocelyn, the Avalons and all their connections are a one-way ticket out of rural Wisconsin, and she's terrified to lose that. But is she terrified enough to kill?

Then there's Tommy Sunday, who isn't here tonight—thank God. I didn't want to have to hug him again, let alone look at him, with his slicked-back hair and his face that reminds me of a lion. Tommy's a proven creep; Leah would have known she'd see him at the Sunday Service grand opening, and it was plausible that he could have gotten back from Bridgehampton in time to see her at the Haven on Wednesday night.

And I can't forget about my parents, who almost certainly saw Leah's texts with Emmeline. Not only did they never bring them up, but they made it seem very "case closed" that Leah ended her life because of work stress. Did they consciously lie? And if so, why? Leah was their favorite daughter. Their golden child. If someone killed her, my parents would sooner kill *them* than offer them protection.

The mayor's going on and on about the astronomical amount of money the Avalon Hospitality Group has raised this year alone. It makes me wonder... what if someone paid my parents off so they wouldn't share what they knew? I wouldn't say my parents are *struggling* when it comes to money, but for the past few years, their financial situation has been a little strained. Mom's single-handedly paying for my grandparents' assisted-living home, and on top of that, I know she's freaked out that her company's had multiple rounds of layoffs in the past few years. Any day, she could end up on the chopping block.

The great room erupts in applause, pulling me out of my thoughts and back to my present surroundings. Duke puts a hand on the small of my back. "Wanna go raid the kitchen for extra dessert?"

Sylvie and the twins' friends are migrating back toward the stairs, but dessert with Duke sounds good too—and no, *not* because I like the feeling of his palm on my bare skin. "I'm down. Let's do it."

He grabs my hand and guides me across the room. "They always order a shit ton of catering for these things, and like half of it ends up going to waste."

"We're doing a public service, is what you're saying."

Duke smirks at me. "I like the way you think."

He leads me around the corner, past a dining room table that could probably seat two dozen people, and then through an archway that leads to the gleaming kitchen. The uniformed catering staff bustles around, carrying trays in and out of the other archway, which leads out to the great room. In the center of the kitchen is a marble-topped island—and it's covered with silver trays of beautiful, untouched desserts.

"What do you like?" Duke asks.

"I-it all looks so good," I stammer, like I'm scared to offend any one of the delicacies. I've never seen such exquisite treats: glistening berry tarts, dark-chocolate truffles with milk-chocolate swirls, macarons dusted in gold.

"I'll get us a little of everything," Duke assures me. The caterers see him, but pay him no mind as he throws open a cabinet, grabs himself a plate, and starts loading it up with desserts. When there's no room left on the plate, he carries it with him and nods for me to follow him out of the room.

He steers me to a quieter wing of the home, and into a library with dark-blue paneled walls and bookshelves that go all the way up to the ceiling. There's a writing desk with a winged armchair and a leather couch the color of caramel.

"It was my dad's office," Duke says. He sets the plate down on the coffee table and eases himself onto the couch, where he looks at me and pats the cushion beside him. The two of us, alone on a couch in a cozy room? The butterflies come back, and I'm not sure I'll be able to stop them. What if I don't even *want* to stop them?

You are here for Leah.

Right. I join Duke on the couch and pluck a gold-dusted macaron off the plate. I cover my mouth as I swallow. "Whoa, this is really good."

"Yeah, I love those things. Macaroons? Macarons? I forget. But my mom always gets them for her parties." He laughs. "She served these same ones, but silver, at a birthday party she threw for her friend's Chihuahua the other week."

I snort. "She threw a birthday party for a Chihuahua?"

Duke smiles. "That's my mom. She loves pumping people up."

"And dogs." I smile back at him. "She's really cool."

"Yeah. She is." He pauses. A shadow crosses over his face. "By the way, I'm so sorry about what happened with my grandpa when you first got here. I hate when he gets like that. It sucks for my mom, and it's so awkward for anyone standing around them."

Duke seems like he wants to open up to me, and I'll gladly let him. "How often does your grandpa get like that?"

"Uh, pretty much all the time?" Duke laughs darkly. "I mean, I get it. He's running a massive company and he doesn't have his right-hand man anymore."

"That was your dad?"

"Yeah. My dad was my grandpa's only son, and they were

best friends. Ten years ago, the plan was for my grandpa to retire and my dad to take over. But then my dad got sick—prostate cancer." He looks at his knees.

"Oh, Duke."

"He died six months later," he says. "Prostate cancer is super survivable, if you catch it early. But my dad hated going to the doctor, and by the time my dad was diagnosed, it was too late."

"I'm so sorry."

"Thanks." Duke sighs and shakes his head. "So, yeah. You asked about my grandpa. In his eyes, none of us will ever be as smart, talented, good at business, *whatever*, as my dad was. So he's super hard on us—my mom especially, since she's the 'outsider' who married into the family. And that only makes my mom want to please him more. She works a *ton*. She figures if she can keep getting good press for the company, he'll go easier on her."

"Has it worked?"

Duke winces. "You saw the two of them out there. You tell me."

"Ugh. Your poor mom."

"He won't let her catch a break."

"But your grandpa has to retire someday," I point out. "Someone's going to have to take over." That's when I remember how Rex referred to Duke: *a future leader of the family business*. My eyes go wide. "Wait, Duke, are *you* going to be CEO?"

"That's the plan."

"Are you excited?"

He shrugs. "Yeah! I mean, I think so? I've always known it would happen at some point, so I guess it just seems normal to me. Like, I dunno . . . do you think the British royals get excited about being royalty?"

"That's fair." My heart beats faster. The Avalons *are* royalty, in a way: they have an empire, a line of succession, a penthouse palace, seemingly endless financial resources...

...and I can't deny there's a sense of magic in just being near them.

"My grandpa will probably work for another ten years, and then I'll be up," Duke says. "He's started giving me all these training sessions so I can learn the ropes."

"What about Sylvie? Is she going to work for the company too?"

"Oh yeah, for sure. She's already helping my mom with marketing and publicity stuff." I remember Sylvie's first DMs to Leah, when she reached out after the speakeasy-themed open house to invite Leah out to dinner. Her message had seemed so friendly, but of course, she was also pushing the family business. "My mom and my sister are super close," Duke adds.

"That's so nice."

"Yeah. Speaking of close... uh, do you mind if I..." He scoots closer to me. My breath catches in my throat. But he's only trying to reach for one of the berry tarts.

Why am I disappointed he wasn't trying to reach for me?

Disgusted with myself, I get up off the couch and cross the carpeted floor to the wheeled ladder that helps you reach books on the top shelves. "You know what? I have *always* wanted to use one of these." I'm not sure where I'm going with this, but it was the only way I could think to put some distance between us. I grab one of the rungs and look over my shoulder. "Can I try climbing it?"

Duke grins. "You're weird—you know that?"

"I'm somewhat aware."

"I like it, for the record."

I face the ladder and start to climb, but it isn't that tall, and it only takes me a few seconds to reach the top. Maybe this wasn't my smartest plan of all time. Letting go with one hand, I swing myself around to say "ta-da"—but the word turns into a shriek when the ladder starts to roll. I'm careening out of control. Duke leaps to his feet. Sidestepping the coffee table, he races across the room and grabs hold of the ladder just before I smash into the wall, where an oil painting hangs in a gilded frame.

"Gotcha," he says, grinning.

"Oh my God."

"That was epic." Duke laughs. Between this and leaning on the windows in the great room, this guy likes a rush. Maybe that's what happens when you grow up in a palace, the way rich people with boring corporate jobs go heli-skiing and white-water rafting on the weekends. "You're okay, right?" he asks.

My pulse is still pounding, but I nod. "Thanks for the save."

"My pleasure. Here, I'll spot you on the way down."

Great. In trying to kill the sexual tension, I managed to make it way more charged. Hating myself more with every move, I climb back down the ladder—directly into the cocoon of Duke's body. My back is against his chest when my feet touch the floor.

His hands are still on the ladder, and his arms surround me. The next thing I know, his lips are at my ear. "Turn around."

I know what's about to happen, and fuck, what am I supposed to do right now? If I say I just want to be friends, he might never invite me to hang with his family again. Some guys take rejection so personally. But how much of me wants to kiss him to find out what happened to Leah, and how much of me wants to kiss him... just to kiss him? To enjoy this bit of magic I earned all on my own?

I turn around. My nose is against his chest.

"Hey, you," Duke whispers. "Question."

"Hmm?"

"Can I kiss you?"

"Of course you can."

He slides his hand to the back of my head, grabs a fistful of hair at the roots, and gently tugs. Before I know what's happening, my face is tilted up with nowhere else to go. He rakes his teeth over his bottom lip, leaving it plump and extra red before he leans down and presses his mouth to mine. I can't help it when I moan in response.

"You like that?" he asks.

"Mmm-hmm." I nod.

He kisses me again; then, he moves his lips to my ear. "Keep quiet so nobody hears us."

Fuck. The ache between my legs is out of control. I hate myself for giving in to this. My sister is dead—murdered, most likely. And I'm making out with Duke Avalon in his dad's study.

I let my guilt become a glass prison. Duke's tongue may be pressing its way through my teeth, and his free hand may be charting a course down my body, but in my head, there's a wall between us. A wall that makes me numb to my surroundings—to everything except my own self-loathing.

My body is stiff, wooden, but I force it through the motions, reminding myself that this is what I need to do. It works for at least a few minutes, until Duke thrusts his knee between my legs and grinds himself against me. The ache between my legs is gone. Now I just feel trapped—pinned against the ladder—and at the same time, like I'm tumbling toward a cliff's edge without anything to stop my momentum.

"Wait." I pull back from the kiss, as far back as the ladder will let me go.

Duke looks worried. "Everything okay?"

"I just like to move slow, if that's all right. I'm sorry."

"Whoa, whoa, Hailey, don't be sorry. We can move at whatever pace feels right for you." Duke cradles my cheeks and kisses my forehead.

Leah was obsessed with guys doing that. She'd come home after a date with one of her high school boyfriends, screaming, "He just kissed me on the forehead!" To her, it was the ultimate romantic gesture: a sign of protectiveness and tenderness all rolled into one.

I wasn't on the giving or receiving end of *any* forehead kissing, so I'd just roll my eyes and say something sarcastic, like, "Wow, when's the wedding?"

But this time, it's different. This time, I want Duke to like me—to like Hailey, I mean. Looking up into his eyes, I giggle. "Do you know how much I love it when people kiss my forehead?"

He looks taken aback. "Really?"

"Is that so weird?"

"No—sorry. It just surprised me. I knew a girl last summer who said the same thing."

INTERNSHIP LOG

LEAH FALK

June 28

Today, I feel . . . I don't know. Confused. (To future Leah who's trying to use this internship log to write her essay: sorry I low-key turned it into a journal.) There's this guy I've hung out with at a few parties now. I don't mind talking to him, but he's definitely into me, and I don't like him that way. He has a sleazy vibe that gives me the ick. Here's the problem, though: everyone he's close to is like, BFFs with my boss. His whole circle is in the Sentinel all the time. If he makes a move, I don't want to reject him and piss him off. That would be so awkward. But then what am I supposed to do???

CHAPTER 11

Duke and Leah were together. If there's anyone with intel on what happened to my sister, it *has* to be him. I know I should be thrilled by this step forward in my investigation, but as I stand in the spray of the shower on Saturday morning, processing everything that happened at the Avalons' last night, my mind keeps coming back to the same angry thought.

Leah claimed Duke first.

Why, even in death, does my sister have to steal the things I want just for myself?

Sometimes I don't even know if you miss her.

My guilt rears its head, the pressure starting in my chest and building up until tears spring from my eyes, mixing with the hot water as they rain down my cheeks. I turn the faucet to the left. Hotter. The water stings when it hits my skin. I turn it even farther, wincing as the water scalds me. The pain is nearly unbearable now, my skin as red as a tomato, and I turn the faucet farther. My body deserves to burn. The bathroom is filled with steam when suddenly, the water turns to ice, and I gasp like I'm gulping down air after a near-drowning experience. I must have used up all the hot water—but the jets of ice feel twistedly satisfying too. The longer I stand in the frigid stream, shivering, the less I feel. Only when I'm finally numb do I turn the water off.

When I get out of the shower and tap my phone, I see four new messages from Duke.

> **DUKE**
> Had so much fun with you last night! Thanks for coming
> Except when you almost died on the rolling ladder
> Thank god I was there to save you
> Lmk when we can hang again ;)

I'm not sure how to reply. I need to keep Duke close so I can learn more about Leah, but after what we did last night, being alone with him feels too complicated. I put on my clothes, trudge out to the kitchen, and chuck my phone onto the island, where I slump onto a stool and dig my fingertips into my temples.

Ivy wanders into the kitchen wearing a cute pair of linen overalls and a backpack slung over one shoulder. Her hair is in a messy topknot, with a few strands falling down and framing her face. "Uh-oh," she says when she sees me. "What happened last night?"

While she fills up her stainless-steel tumbler with cold brew, I take her through my troubling conversations with Jocelyn and Emmeline. I add that Duke and Leah had some kind of romance last summer, but I don't tell her how I found out; it's too shameful to talk about what happened in the study.

"Jocelyn and Emmeline both sound super suspicious," Ivy says.

"And then there's Janie," I add, "my sister's roommate from last summer. I don't know if this means anything, but she told me how envious she was of Leah."

"Enough to kill her?"

I groan, placing my forehead on the counter. "I don't know."

I look up and catch Ivy wrinkling her nose. "It seems like sort of a stretch, to be honest. Even if she was super envious of Leah, what would killing her do? It's not like she got to trade places with her. But who knows? People do weird things. What do you think you're going to do now?"

Putting my head back down and closing my eyes for the rest of the day sounds nice. I glance at my phone, where another new text just came in—this one from Sylvie. "I don't know," I tell Ivy. "I'm gonna use today to figure out a plan for the next week."

"Well, speaking of next week"—she twirls a loose strand of hair around her finger—"you know that show at my gallery I told you about? I know you have way bigger things going on, so feel free to ignore me, but opening night is on Tuesday, if you want to come check it out. Zayn and Killian are going to stop by too. But no pressure! Obviously. And you can think about it. Okay, I'm gonna stop rambling now and leave for work—how's that?" Her cheeks flush pink. She grabs her tumbler and heads for the door.

That's when it hits me that Ivy just invited me to her art show. My brain's so fried, I could barely keep up. She must think I'm not interested. "Wait—Ivy?"

She spins around. "Yeah?"

"I'd love to come to your show." It's the least I can do to say thank you for letting me sleep on an air mattress right outside her room for an undefined amount of time.

Her face brightens. "Oh! Awesome!" She bites her bottom lip, but her smile still forces its way through. "Well, I'll see you later, Noa."

"See ya."

She rounds the corner into the front hallway, and I listen to the zip of her backpack, the jingle of her keys, and the opening and closing of the door. My stomach sinks at the click of the lock—the final confirmation that Ivy's gone for the day. I liked sharing ideas with her. She's refreshingly logical. That's not the only reason I wish she were still here. Ivy's a warm light that I could bask in for hours, a crackling campfire on a cold, dark night. When I think about going to her art show on Tuesday, I know it's more than a way to say thank you for letting me crash on her floor; it's something I genuinely *want* to do—something that makes my chest flutter.

I need to stop with all the feelings already. Grabbing my phone, I open the text from Sylvie.

> **SYLVIE**
> Hey!! So good to see you last night! My mom said things were a bit weird with Emmeline—toootally not your fault, in case you were worried!! She's been going through some tough stuff
>
> Why don't you come to the City Crop fundraiser on Wednesday? There should be other helpful contacts for you to meet ☺

Just like that, I know exactly what to do about Duke—at least in the short-term. First, I reply to Sylvie, telling her I'd love to come to the City Crop fundraiser. Though I obviously don't mention it, I'm hopeful the event will give me a chance to question Tommy, since City Crop is his nonprofit. Then I reply to Duke:

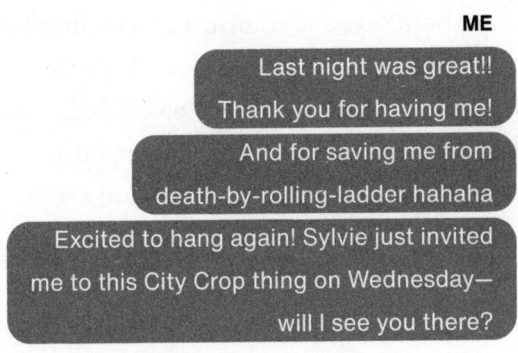

A group hang at a party? That sounds innocent enough. Then panic shoots through me. It sounds innocent enough—as long as the party isn't anywhere near my town. If anyone recognizes me there, I'm screwed. I ask Duke where the party is. He names a mega-wealthy town in North Jersey that's forty-five minutes away from where I grew up. I should be all right . . . but who knows? I tell Duke I'm in, before turning my phone over and resting my forehead on the island again. This is all getting very real.

—

On Tuesday evening, I set off on foot to the art gallery with Zayn and Killian, who pass a cheap bottle of grapefruit-flavored prosecco back and forth between them. They offer to share it with me, but I decline. I'm still feeling stuck in my prison of guilt.

We wander down zigzagging streets lined with unmarked industrial buildings and colorful spray-painted walls. Up ahead, string lights twinkle over the sidewalk outside one of the warehouses, and as we get closer, I hear laughter and upbeat music. We walk through an open garage door into a cavernous space with art lining the walls, and a crowd of artsy-looking twentysomethings milling around in the middle.

Ivy stands out immediately in a neon-green dress and silver platform sandals. When she sees us, she excuses herself from a group conversation and rushes over.

Killian wraps her in a hug. "You okay?"

Ivy lets out a squeak of a laugh. "Oh, just the most anxious I've ever been in my life."

"Why?"

Ivy lowers her voice. "You know how I've always dreamed of having strangers see my work?"

"Yeah..."

"Well, now strangers are seeing my work. I have a heart attack every time someone wanders over to my little section."

Zayn grabs her shoulders. "Ivy. You've survived group critiques with fine-arts majors. You can survive anything."

"But these are real art people!"

"Well, can *we* check out your photos?" Killian asks. "We are, after all, your best friends, and therefore contractually obligated to like everything you create."

That makes her smile. "Fine. But, for the record, I'm still nervous for you to see them." Ivy seems to direct the last comment to me, or maybe that's just where her eyes happened to land.

She leads us over to the rear left corner of the room, to a spot on the wall with four framed photos hanging in a grid. Each is a self-portrait of Ivy sitting and staring into the camera. Her pose is identical in all of them—confident, with her legs slightly spread and her back straight—but the settings and stylings differ in each one.

Ivy starts by pointing to the one on the top left. "I took that one on the L train at three a.m. after a Pride dance party." She looks at me, smirking. "That glitter was stuck in my hair for weeks."

Then she points to the one next to it. Seated on a park bench, she wears a pretty pink dress that matches the cherry blossoms behind her. "I took that one when I was visiting my grandparents in Tokyo over spring break."

She takes us through the remaining two: one in her childhood bedroom in Connecticut; the other in her bedroom in the loft, where all she wears is a sports bra and underwear. When I realize I've been staring at the final photo for a few seconds longer than the other three, my cheeks go hot, and I make a point to look everywhere *but* at Ivy with her clothes off.

While Zayn and Killian inspect the photos up close, I hang back, surveying them with my arms crossed.

Ivy winces. "Do you hate them?"

"Oh my God, no—I think they're awesome." I'm only sulking because I'm still overwhelmed by everything that happened at the gala, especially between me and Duke—but that's not something I want to talk about.

"Really?"

"Yeah. I was standing back so I could take them all in

together and figure out what they mean." I tilt my head to the side, in the hope of it freeing something smart for me to say. "Do you feel like one of these is the *real* you?"

"Actually, it's the opposite," Ivy says. "The point is that I'm not just one of these identities; I'm all of them at the same time." I can hear her finding her confidence the more she speaks about her work. "I can be soft and hard; traditional and rebellious; calm and chaotic . . . and it's okay if I feel a bunch of totally opposite things at the same time. Because I'm a human, and being a human is fucking complicated." She giggles.

"That's really cool, Ivy."

"Thanks, Noa." She squeezes my arm before she goes over to talk to Zayn and Killian. I don't follow her right away. For a few minutes longer, I stare at her piece from back here, replaying her words in my head. *Being a human is fucking complicated.* I want to believe it. I really do. Instead, I make a beeline for the refreshments table to pour myself a very full plastic cup of wine.

We stick around until closing. Then the four of us walk back to the loft. Zayn and Ivy skip ahead, singing along to pop music playing tinnily out of Zayn's phone. Killian is next in line, texting the hot barista. I trail in the back, drinking the wine I poured for the road and playing a silent game with myself: list the proof I miss my sister.

One: I came to New York to piece together her death. *But maybe you only did that to prove you're not heartless.*

Two: I teared up the other day when someone came into my subway car wearing strawberries-and-cream perfume. *Performative.*

Three: I was fucking sad when she died! *Then why did you feel so alive when you threw your first party without her around?*

This game isn't working. Guilt squeezes my insides. Sure, Ivy may be okay feeling a bunch of totally opposite things at the same time, but as far as I can tell, she's also a fundamentally good person. She can be soft and hard, traditional and rebellious, and all the other cute contradictions she mentioned. But I don't see how someone who allegedly misses their dead sister can feel what I've been feeling: stinging, childlike devastation at the thought of Leah kissing Duke first. Good sister or bad sister: at the end of the day, I can only be one.

Someone loops their arm around my elbow—Ivy. "Save me," she says. "They switched to show tunes." I've been so lost in thought that I didn't even notice when Zayn and Killian broke out into a rendition of "Defying Gravity" from *Wicked*.

Ivy pulls me closer into her side, and then I do start to notice things: how our bare arms fuse together—our skin tacky in the summer heat—and the smell of her intoxicating spicy perfume that always wafts from her area of the loft.

"Noa, do you know how grateful I am that you came tonight?" I'm not sure if she's tipsy from gallery wine, or high off her first exhibition—or both—but her words tumble out of her mouth. "They *had* to come"—she nods at Zayn and Killian—"but you didn't. And I appreciate that so much."

"I'm so happy I came. It was really cool."

"I think *you're* really cool."

"I'm so not."

"Yes, you are." I open my mouth to protest again, but she presses her index finger to my lips. "Uh-uh. It's my night and I make the rules." Her eyes twinkle in the glow of a streetlamp.

"Fine," I say against the pad of her finger. She takes it away, but I could swear it lingers for longer than it needs to on my bottom lip.

"Say 'Thank you for the lovely compliment, Ivy.'"

"Thank you for the lovely compliment, Ivy."

"You are so welcome!" She giggles and rests her head on my shoulder. "Ugh, this is the best night ever. I don't want it to be over."

Back at the loft, she rummages through the fridge for another bottle of grapefruit prosecco. "Nightcap, anyone?"

"I'm working the early shift tomorrow," Zayn says, groaning.

"Killian? Noa?"

"I'm in," Killian says, already on his way to the cabinet for cups.

My guilt squeezes me harder than it has all night, because I'm still not over her touching my lips during the walk home, and I want to stay up and spend more time with her, but I've already given in to enough distractions since I got to the city, and I can't stray even further from the actual reason I'm here. I fake a yawn. "I should probably get some sleep too."

Ivy's face falls. Ugh. She deserves to celebrate her big night, and I *also* feel guilty letting my own shit get in the way of that.

"Actually, you know what? I'll hang out for a little longer."

"You sure?" Ivy asks.

"Yeah."

Her face lights up. She pops the cork and pours three cups of the fizzing rosy drink, which we carry into the living area. Killian takes the armchair, while Ivy and I sprawl out on opposite sofas. I do my best to keep up with the conversation, but my head is a cyclone of shameful thoughts. I chug my prosecco and go back to the fridge for a refill. On my way back from the kitchen, the loft teeters slightly. I'm normally not a fan of being drunk, but right now, I *do* like the thought of being numb.

Killian slams down his drink and leaps to his feet.

"Whoa," Ivy says.

Killian holds up his phone. "Hot Barista just got home—*and he says I should come over.*"

"Go, go, go!" Ivy cheers.

Killian rushes for the door, hugging each of us on his way out, and then it's just me and Ivy—and a big, square coffee table between us.

"You feel so far away," she says, and before I know it, she's plopping down on the end of my sofa. She puts her back against the armrest and her feet up on the middle cushion—same as me—so that our bodies form one squiggly line. She presses the sole of her foot against mine, and everything feels fizzy and sweet, like prosecco. "Oh my God," Ivy says, laughing. "How are my feet so much bigger than yours?"

"You're like six inches taller than me."

"I *am*?"

"I'm five two!"

"*No.*"

"Yes."

"You have tall energy," she says.

"What's that supposed to mean?"

She snorts again. "I have no idea." We both start to giggle. These drinks have gone to our heads. "It's definitely a compliment, though."

Mimicking our interaction from earlier, I tilt my head, bat my eyelashes, and say, "Thank you for the lovely compliment, Ivy."

"Yes!" She pushes herself off the armrest and holds out her

hand for a high five. I lunge for it and miss. We laugh harder. "Let's try again," she says. This time, we nail it. Now we're holding hands. Without breaking eye contact, Ivy finishes the rest of her drink. Her lips glisten with prosecco. I wonder how they would taste, if I just leaned forward...

NO. My guilty conscience yanks me out of my bubbly grapefruit haze. What happened with Duke was bad enough; I'm not about to add Ivy to the mix. I let go of her hand, cutting off our electric current, and grab her empty cup instead. "Lemme get you a refill." I climb off the couch and hurry to the kitchen.

Ivy looks over her shoulder. "You didn't have to do that."

"It's no problem." I pick up the bottle and eye what's left. "Oh no. We're all out." What would have happened if we'd both had more?

Ivy gets up and stretches her arms above her head. "I should probably get to sleep, anyway. I have to be back at the gallery in the morning."

"I should go to sleep too." Tomorrow's the City Crop fundraiser, and I need to be on my A game. I look at Ivy and nod to the door by the stove. "You can take the bathroom first, if you want."

"Thanks. I'll be quick." She walks along the same side of the island where I'm standing, even though there's way more room on the other side. On the way, she squeezes my shoulder. "Thanks again for tonight. It was awesome."

"Anytime."

As Ivy shuts the door behind her, a part of me is relieved to be stopping this night in its tracks. But another part of me wishes we were still on the couch, holding hands.

CHAPTER 12

Standing in front of Zayn's full-length mirror, I make an announcement. "I'm not drinking tonight."

"Uh, okay?"

"I'm just stating it out loud so I can hold myself accountable."

"Did you get sick from the grapefruit prosecco or something?" they ask.

"No, I just . . . feel like I should take the night off." *So that I don't do something selfish like kissing someone cute when I'm supposed to be focusing on Leah.* That moment on the couch with Ivy was way too close of a call.

I tug at the hem of the pale blue dress I'm planning to wear to the City Crop fundraiser. "Is this too short? Maybe I can adjust the straps to make it longer. . . ."

Zayn, sitting cross-legged on their bed, scrutinizes me over their laptop screen. They've been sending emails to potential future podcast guests. "What are you talking about?" they ask. "You could wear that dress to my abuela's church and be *fine*."

I loosen the straps, but then it shows more of my cleavage. "Ugh. Maybe I should just change."

Zayn sets their laptop aside and shuffles to the edge of their bed. "Noa, look at me. No more messing around with the dress. What's going on?"

With a sigh, I let go of the straps and turn to my friend, arms crossed. "My sister might have been murdered, Zayn." The words sound hollow, even to me. Probably because they only tell half the story.

"I know, but you've seemed extra stressed-out these past few days. I feel like it started after the gala. Is it Emmeline? Jocelyn?" They look at me with such sincere concern that I feel obligated to share a little more of the truth.

With a sigh, I plop down next to them on the mattress. "Something happened with Duke," I say quietly. I don't mention Ivy because nothing *did* happen between us. It just . . . almost did. Thankfully, I reined myself in before I did something I regretted.

"What happened with Duke?" Zayn asks.

"We kissed."

Zayn stares at me, wide-eyed.

"I know, it's fucked up." I hunch over with my face in my hands.

"Wait, no." Zayn puts a hand on my shoulder. I look up. "I was only surprised because I don't think it's that big of a deal! So what if you kissed?"

"Doesn't it seem a little . . . I don't know . . . heartless?"

They look doubtful. "To have one little moment of joy amid

all the shit you're dealing with? I don't think so, Noa. I think, actually, you deserve it. And Duke's *hot.*"

With a sigh, I stare at my knees. "I guess," I mumble, knowing full well that my guilt isn't just coming from kissing Duke.

"What else is bothering you?" Zayn prods. I used to love listening to them do interviews over the phone for the school paper. Their questions were always concise and open-ended: the exact kind of phrasing that prompted a vivid response. Maybe I could try to tell Zayn about the guilt eating away at me.

"You know how I told you that Duke and Leah also had a thing last summer?"

"Yeah..."

I twist my fingers into a Gordian knot. "Well, when I found that out, I felt kind of... pissed off."

"At...?"

"At Leah."

Zayn takes their hand off my shoulder.

"See? I told you. I'm heartless." This time, Zayn doesn't jump in to correct me, and when I force myself to look into their warm, brown eyes, I see confusion staring back at me. Or maybe it's repulsion.

Too late, they rearrange their features into a more neutral expression. "Noa," they say tentatively, "I *really* feel like you should talk to a therapist."

Great; they think I'm messed-up enough to need professional intervention. Ignoring their comment, I check the time on my phone. "I should go. It's a long train ride from here."

"Noa, wait..."

"No, seriously. I have to take the L to the four, and then switch to the six."

"I feel like you're mad at me."

"Trust me, I'm not." I grab my purse off Zayn's desk and hike it over my shoulder. "I'm just mad at myself."

In the lobby of the Avalon Central Park East hotel, the ceiling drips with crystal chandeliers, the floor is an icy white marble, and the air-conditioning gives me goose bumps. Sylvie stands near the elevator bank, her thumbs tapping away at her phone. Her chestnut hair is in a slicked-back ponytail, and her face is largely obscured by a giant pair of designer sunglasses, which she pushes up on top of her head as soon as she sees me striding toward her.

"Hi, doll!"

"Hey!" I do my best to summon Hailey's up-for-anything attitude. "Thanks so much for inviting me to this."

She kisses the air next to each of my cheeks. "Oh my God, you are so welcome. It's really the least we can do, after the awkwardness with Emmeline. That is *not* the kind of networking opportunity we promised you, and I don't want you thinking we're a bunch of liars!" Sylvie links an arm through mine and steers me toward the elevators, bypassing the young woman with the City Crop clipboard. "She's with me," Sylvie mentions over her shoulder. She jams her finger onto the button.

"Oh, Miss Avalon! You'll need these." The clipboard woman darts over. She reaches into the burlap sack slung over her shoulder and pulls out two smaller burlap sacks, one for each of us.

"The others are on the rooftop already," Sylvie explains as

we wait for the elevator. "Jocelyn just got a big externship offer, and she was dying to go up and start celebrating."

"An externship offer? From Tommy Sunday?"

"Actually, no." Sylvie raises her eyebrows. "She applied to work at Josephine Desjardins's restaurant in Union Square, and she ended up getting it all on her own. Sometimes I forget that Joc is like a legitimately amazing chef."

"Whoa." I don't know much about the New York restaurant scene, but even I've heard of Josephine Desjardins. She's a judge on a Netflix cooking competition show, and every mom in the New Jersey suburbs is obsessed with her line of high-quality cast-iron cookware. I force a smile. "Good for Jocelyn!"

"Yeah, totally. She didn't need us after all!" Sylvie's smile is pinched. She changes the subject as we board the elevator. "So. You and Duke, eh?" She smirks and waggles her eyebrows.

Me and Duke. My chest feels like one giant knot. "What about us?"

"A little birdie told me you might have kissed."

"Uh..." My heart thumps under the growing pressure.

"Oh my God, babe, don't be embarrassed. We're twins! We know everything about each other." She steps closer and rests a hand above my elbow. "I brought it up because I wanted you to know how happy he was after you left on Friday night. He was all smiley—it was *so* cute."

"Aww." I can barely make a sound without my throat catching.

"Right? I'm not just saying this because he's my twin: Duke is *such* a good guy, and he deserves someone awesome."

A light bulb flicks on in my head. This is it—a chance to put my new friendship with Sylvie to good use. But just then, the elevator *dings*, and the doors open onto a lively rooftop terrace with an unobstructed view of the Central Park Reservoir.

"Welcome to the City Crop fundraiser!" chirps another clipboard-wielding employee. "You have your bags?"

Sylvie and I hold up our burlap sacks.

"Fabulous! So, here's the way it works. As you move down the row of planters just behind me, you'll pick whatever 'crops' you want to eat—all of them grown right here in New York City, at the amazing farms powered by City Crop. Then you'll give your crops to Tommy and his team, and they'll cook you up something delicious."

Peering out over the crowd, I see steam rising from a makeshift kitchen set up under a pergola. Tommy is in the middle of the fray, barking orders at his sous chefs and mopping sweat off his forehead.

We thank her for the tutorial and wander over to the first planter, which isn't so much a planter as it is a wicker basket full of produce, like you'd see at the grocery store. I guess it was too much of a stretch to have the wealthiest people in Manhattan *actually* pick their own food.

"Want one of these?" Sylvie holds up a peach.

"Sure, thanks." I open my sack so she can drop it in. I don't want to lose the thread of the conversation we were having in the elevator. "Um, really quickly, back to what you were saying before . . ."

"Hmm?"

"Duke mentioned a girl he was seeing last summer. Is she still in the picture at all? He didn't say when or how that ended, so I just wanted to make sure. . . ."

"He told you about Leah?" Sylvie raises her eyebrows.

My heart's jackhammering now. "Maybe? All he said was that she loved forehead kisses."

Sylvie's face relaxes into a sad smile. "Aww, yeah. That was definitely Leah." She sighs. "Sorry to bring down the mood, but she's the same girl Emmeline was upset about—the *Sentinel* intern who died last summer."

"How did she die again?"

"Suicide," Sylvie says. "She OD'd on oxy. I felt so, so bad for Duke. And her family, obviously. But Duke was so good to her."

Duke couldn't have been at Leah's funeral, because if he had been, he would have recognized me. That's the only reason I know he wasn't there. On the day of, it would have been easy to miss him. Hundreds of people showed up to the synagogue that morning; pretty soon, it was standing room only. And besides, I was way too shell-shocked to register anything that was happening around me. It was all a blur, from the crowded synagogue to the more intimate gathering at the cemetery, where the rabbi pulled the lever that lowered her coffin into the earth—so heart-wrenchingly final, that part—and then our family took turns shoveling dirt into the grave.

"Were you close with her, too?" I ask Sylvie.

"Not as close as Duke, but yeah, we hung out. I would have hung out with her more," she adds, "but I was sidelined with this awful injury last summer." She dumps some tomatoes into both of our bags.

"What happened?"

"I fucked up my knee playing squash with Duke. I lunged for a drop shot, and I don't know what happened, but I landed all wrong and tore my ACL. It hurt *sooo* bad. I had to get surgery, and I was on crutches, like, all summer. Overall, not cute."

We reach the end of the produce baskets and hand over our burlap sacks to a harried-looking sous chef.

"Order up!" Tommy screams, slamming some kind of quesadilla onto the table in front of him. The leafy green garnish quivers on impact.

The chef catches sight of us as he whirls back around. "Well, well, well! Looking good tonight, ladies." He winks, then turns to yell at the guy on the fry top.

"He's such a flirt," I say quietly to Sylvie as we wait for our food to be ready.

She waves her hand. "Nah, he's just a friendly guy. I've only ever had super-professional interactions with him."

I can't say I'm surprised, given her family is the reason Tommy has his own restaurant. I'm sure he wouldn't dare lay a hand on Sylvie, but I can't necessarily say the same for my sister.

"ORDER UP!"

A server hands me a pretty salad with tomatoes, grilled peaches, and fresh mozzarella. Once Sylvie also collects her plate, she leads me around the rooftop pool to the other side of the terrace, where the same group from Friday night is clustered around a high-top. Duke, the first to spot us, puts down his drink and jogs toward us. The memories rush back of him tugging my hair, and whispering in my ear, and kissing the side of my neck.... The next thing I know, my stomach is doing flips without my permission.

"Damn, Hails. You look amazing." Duke's eyes rove over my spaghetti-strap dress. This is why I wish it were a little less revealing.

"Thanks. So do you."

He gives me a one-armed hug, careful not to bump my plate.

God, he smells good—like spiced tobacco and the buttery-soft leather couch in his dad's study.

When Jocelyn spots us, she shrieks and waves us over. *"Sylvie! Hailey! Come celebrate with me!"*

Either Jocelyn's already drunk off the mostly empty glass of rosé in her hand, or she's decided she doesn't hate me anymore. I'm betting on already drunk. Maybe she pregamed the fundraiser.

I set my plate down on the high-top, squeezing in between Owen and Jocelyn. Duke grabs me a glass of rosé from a roving caterer's tray, elbows Owen to the side, squeezes in next to me, and passes me the glass.

"Cheers," Duke says. "To a good night."

"To a good night." I pretend to take a sip.

He bites his bottom lip, the same way he did before he kissed me on Friday. I turn to my left. "Uh, I think we should also be cheers-ing to Jocelyn, right?"

At the sound of her name, Jocelyn bounces on the balls of her feet.

"Joc, I heard about Josephine Desjardins. That's amazing—congratulations." I get the rest of the table's attention. "To Jocelyn!"

"To Jocelyn!" Everyone repeats, clinking their glasses.

"That's really sweet of you, Hailey." Jocelyn squeezes my shoulder, and when I turn to her, she seems surprisingly lucid. Maybe she's not as drunk as I thought. "Um, do you mind if we talk for a second, over there?" She nods to a private corner of the terrace. For a second, I wonder if she's going to try to push me over the edge—eliminate the competition, once and for all. But then I see the redness creeping up the fair skin of her neck, and the vulnerable expression in her eyes. Something tells me Jocelyn has other plans.

I follow her over to the corner, stealthily ditching my wine along the way. Her blond hair has been pin-straight the other times I've seen her, but tonight she wears it wavy and tossed to one side of her head. It's wilder, and it looks good.

Jocelyn exhales and relaxes her shoulders, which she'd been holding up by her ears. "Hailey, I wanted to apologize for being an absolute jerk on Friday."

I raise my eyebrows. *This,* I wasn't expecting.

"I was so, so stressed waiting to hear back about all these externship applications, and I realize I was taking it out on people who totally didn't deserve it, like you. You've been nothing but perfectly nice to me, and I want you to know I appreciate that. And I hope we can be friends." She gives me a tentative, small smile.

"Of course we can." She was at the Sunday Service grand opening; therefore, we *have* to be friends.

"Thank God." We hug, and she lets out a relieved-sounding laugh. "Um, actually, are you around this coming Tuesday and Wednesday?"

"I think so. Why?"

"Lina's parents have this *amazing* house in Montauk, and they're not there during the week, so they said we can use it to do a little girls' trip for my birthday. Do you want to come?"

I don't even pause. "I'd love to."

"Oh my gosh, yay! It's going to be so much fun. You have no idea how badly I need to blow off steam. I've been a wreck—as you know."

"Jeez, I'm sorry you were so stressed out about job stuff."

Jocelyn sighs. "It was a nightmare, honestly." She peers over my shoulder, back toward the high-top, and lowers her voice. "Between us, I really didn't want that Sunday Service externship. But I felt like I had to go for it just in case my other options didn't pan out."

"Really? Why didn't you want it?"

"Please don't repeat this, but Tommy Sunday gives me the *ick*. I saw what he did when he hugged you the other night at the bar."

"You saw that? It happened so fast, for a second, I thought I'd—"

"—imagined it? Yeah, that's Tommy for you. I'm sorry that happened to you, Hailey. I should have said something, but . . ." She crosses her arms, looks down, and shakes her head. "It was all so complicated."

"Hey, don't worry about it. It's easy to *know* when you should say something, but it can be harder to actually *do* it."

"Especially when you might be depending on the guy for a job."

We both shudder.

"It's all so messed up," Jocelyn murmurs.

That's when I realize this could be my chance to find out if Tommy was at the Haven the Wednesday before Leah's death. I know for a fact that Jocelyn was there. When I stalked her Instagram in one of my Sweet Bean study sessions, I found a photo she'd posted from that night, of her and Sylvie clinking cups of some electric-green frozen drink. "You know, I'm so happy we're talking about this, because Tommy's the one reason I've been worried about getting closer to the Avalons. Does he ever try to, like, hang out with you guys? At parties, or bars, or . . . ?"

"Luckily, no." Jocelyn scratches her chin. "I feel like the only places I've ever seen him are here and Sunday Service."

"That's it?"

She nods. "That's it."

INTERNSHIP LOG

LEAH FALK

August 7

I've been trying to hold him off for as long as possible, but tonight, I failed. I was covering this event at a shitty bar. I felt like I had to say yes because I was invited by another friend of the Sentinel. I knew he'd be there. If he made another move, I figured I'd tell him (again) that I want to go slow. Well, he was pretty drunk, and he made another move. I told him I wanted to go slow, but he didn't want to hear it this time. He called me a tease. I told him I needed some space, so I left and went to the bathroom, but I didn't realize he followed me. It was a one-person bathroom and he shoved me through the door, locking it behind us. He said he wanted me. I said no. He said, "Other girls don't say no." I'll remember that disgusting line for as long as I live, because the very next second, he pushed me into the counter and kissed me and shoved his hand up my skirt. I couldn't push him off me. The only thing I could think to do was headbutt him. It worked. He stumbled back and I ran out and I left the club and now I'm home in bed, shaking. This internship used to be a dream, but now it feels like a nightmare.

CHAPTER 13

Tommy Sunday might be the scum of the Earth, but he isn't the source who "behaved extremely inappropriately" at the Haven. Not unless Jocelyn is lying to me—but after everything she just revealed, I don't see her going above and beyond to protect the chef's reputation.

Someone touches me lightly on the arm—Sylvie. "What are you two *doing* over here?" she asks with a giggle. There's a hollowness to her laugh, as though she's suspicious of what we could possibly have to talk about on our own.

"I was apologizing for being a jerk on Friday," Jocelyn says. She doesn't mention anything about Tommy.

"Oh, cute." Sylvie seems completely uninterested in knowing more about the apology. She looks at me. "Do you want to come say hi to my mom? We can introduce you to a few journalism people."

A jolt of adrenaline courses through my veins. "Oh wow! That would be great."

I talk to a bubbly nightlife blogger named Lily, who says she can put me in touch with a bunch of editors with freelance budgets. "I'm happy to connect you," she says. "Influencing pays *so* much better than writing, and these days, I'm getting enough spon-con deals that I don't have to write as much as I used to. What's your email?"

What somehow hasn't occurred to me up until now is that any connections I make through the Avalons are worthless. I can't give this woman my *actual* email. It has my real name in it, and I'm supposed to be Hailey Star. On the spot, I can only think of one alternative: my first email address from when I was little—the throwaway one I still use when I don't want my actual inbox getting clogged with spam. My face is hotter than the surface of the sun as I spell it out letter by letter.

Lily squints at the address she just typed into her phone. Then she looks at me like I must be joking. "It's . . . 'tswizzleforever'?"

"Yep." *I'm a Swiftie. Sue me.*

"That's . . . cool." Her tone says otherwise. She's not going to connect me to anyone, and I can't blame her.

The next three networking conversations are similarly doomed. "Actually, my email was recently hacked, and I still have to make a new one," I explain to the next person. "Want to give me yours, and I'll follow up as soon as I can?" Of course, I can't follow up with *any* of these people, unless I plan to keep up my Hailey Star alias for the rest of my life.

At some point, I'll have to cut things off with the Avalons too. Either that, or come clean about who I really am. Maybe I'll do that once I figure out what happened to Leah, once and for all. They'll understand, won't they? Sylvie and Duke seem as close as two siblings can be. I'm sure they'd do the same for each other if they were in my position.

The sun begins to set, and tiki torches are lit along the perimeter of the terrace. While I've been pointlessly networking on behalf of Hailey Star, Jocelyn's been getting drunk—for real, this time—and insisting everyone else keep up with her. When I rejoin the group, now lounging in a cabana, Lina and Mateo are making out, Divya is asleep, and Jocelyn is talking loudly in Sylvie's ear. Sylvie looks exhausted as she turns to Duke. "I hate to break it to you, but there is no way in hell I'm going to Rutherford's party tonight."

"What? No!" Duke balks at his sister as he wiggles over to make room for me on the cushion.

"Sorry. I'm wiped." Sylvie leans in and lowers her voice. "And I wouldn't bring Joc, if I were you. She'll probably puke in the back seat."

Duke frowns. "Mateo? Lina? You guys are still coming, right?"

The couple comes up for air, looks at Duke, and then at each other. Lina winces. "Sorry, Duke. I think we're gonna head back to my place." Mateo looks pleased with himself.

"You all suck," Duke chides. He doesn't even bother asking Divya, who's out cold. "Owen, what about you?"

I wait for his answer with bated breath. If Owen says no, the party won't be an innocent group hang anymore; it'll be a date for me and Duke.

"Dude, I'm in. His sister liked one of my Stories last week, and I think she's gonna be there tonight." *Phew*. Owen fist-bumps Duke. He's short and skinny, with a patchy brown mustache and beard. He's constantly flexing his mosquito-bite biceps and poking them to see how hard they are, and on Friday, he was bragging to Duke and Mateo about some questionably legal supplements he read about online and ordered from some sketchy website.

"Yeahhh, buddy." Duke playfully punches Owen in the shoulder. "And, Hails, you're coming, right?"

I smile at him. "Of course."

"You wanna head out soon?" Duke asks.

"Sure. Let me just use the bathroom first." I climb off the daybed and make my way inside, past the cook station, where Tommy Sunday is still barking orders at his sous chefs. At the elevators, I turn left, following the signs for the bathroom.

From around the corner up ahead, I hear voices—arguing. They sound familiar, so I stop in my tracks to listen in on what they're saying.

"... upset you showed up so late. The photographers have all left. It's going to look like you weren't even here." That's Gracie Avalon's voice: gentle and sweet, even as she tries to convey a problem.

"You want to know why I wasn't here earlier?" Rex Avalon growls in response. "I was stuck at the office, trying to un-fuck a situation *you* should be dealing with."

"What do you mean?"

"I have reporters banging down my goddamn door about the Dumbo property."

"Oh no. Still?"

"*Still,* Grace. That's what happens when you're too nice to these people. I swear to God, I'm going to wring the neck of the next reporter who asks me to comment on why we're building over a park."

"Well, people are concerned that—"

"Tell them there are plenty of other places to do their hippy-dippy farmers' market crap. And make sure they get the message. Do your goddamn job."

"I *am* doing my—"

"I don't wanna hear it. I'm going to get something to eat." With that, Rex barrels around the corner and storms out to the terrace without even looking my way. I wait a beat before rounding the corner so Gracie doesn't realize I heard her getting reamed out by her father-in-law—but she isn't here.

I go into the bathroom. Gracie stands at the sinks, gazing into the mirror and using a tissue to dab at her eyes, which are shiny and bloodshot. She sniffs loudly when she sees my reflection. "Oh, Hailey! I'm sorry you have to see me like this. I'm a mess."

"Uh, is everything okay?"

"Oh, the joys of working for your father-in-law!" She lets out a weak laugh. "Whenever he has journalists breathing down his neck about something, he becomes *impossible* to deal with."

"That sounds . . . stressful."

"It certainly can be." She stuffs the tissue in her purse and turns around. "But how are *you*? Are you having a good time? I saw you mingling with some of the journalists who are here." She waggles her fingers like a puppet master operating a marionette.

"Yeah!" The word *journalist* feels like a stretch for the woman who also does spon-con deals, but it's not like I'll be following up with her anyway. "It was great chatting with them."

"Oh, that's wonderful to hear. I love when I can help facilitate those kinds of connections. Are you sticking around longer, or are you and the kids heading out?"

"We're heading out," I reply. "I'm going to a party with Duke and Owen."

"Ah!" She claps a hand over her heart. "I love it." She leans in with a conspiratorial smirk. "To be honest, I wish I could get the heck out of here, too."

"Well, hopefully the rest of your night goes okay," I say as I start to make my way toward the stalls.

Gracie takes one last look in the mirror before heading for the door. "If I can keep that man from killing any journalists, I'll consider it a success!"

Once she's gone, I rush into the nearest stall and slam the door behind me, as Rex's and Gracie's words replay themselves in my mind.

I'm going to wring the neck of the next reporter who asks me to comment . . .

If I can keep that man from killing any journalists . . .

I think about the story my sister wanted to pitch to the *New York Times*'s social justice editor, Noelle Rice. I hadn't considered it until just now, but what if that *pitch* had something to do with her death? Maybe she'd uncovered something damning about Rex's business practices, and he found out she was trying to make it public, and then he . . . then he . . .

My legs shake as I use the bathroom and walk to the sinks. I just heard Rex Avalon threaten to murder a reporter with his own bare hands. Gracie might have been joking about keeping him from killing any journalists tonight, but if you ask me, Rex doesn't seem like the joking type. I hold the insides of my wrists under the ice-cold water. Leah used to do this when she was nervous about an exam, a dance recital, or a big soccer game. I'd tell her it was weird, and a waste of water, but now I can't pretend it doesn't help steady me.

My phone lights up with a text from Duke.

DUKE
At the elevators. You ready to go?

I'm ready to run back to La Forêt, change into my pajamas, and make a miso mushroom rice bowl. Ivy's face flashes through my mind. Ignoring the tug in my heart, I turn off the tap, dry my hands, and text Duke that I'm on my way.

CHAPTER 14

Duke, Owen, and I Uber back to the Avalons' building, where we get in the elevator and rocket up to the penthouse. The boys have been talking about the party this whole time, but I've barely been paying attention; my head's still spinning from what I overheard between Rex and Gracie at the City Crop fundraiser.

Duke squeezes my shoulder as the elevator doors slide open. "That's cool with you, right, Hails?"

"What did you say? Sorry, I was thinking about something else." We step out into the foyer.

"I said it's cool if we stay over at Rutherford's, right?"

"Oh." A sleepover with Duke? I'm supposed to be *limiting* our alone time. "Uh . . . is that okay with Rutherford?" I ask, realizing I don't even know whether "Rutherford" is this person's first or last name.

"For sure," he says. "Sounds like a bunch of people are gonna crash there."

At least we won't have a room to ourselves. Or will we? Judging by the town, this "Rutherford" guy probably lives in a mansion. "All right, I guess that's fine," I reply. If we have to spend the night together, maybe I can pull some details out of Duke about his grandfather's shady business practices—get a sense of what story Leah might have wanted to pitch to the *New York Times* before she died.

"Awesome," he says. "I'll run upstairs and grab us some comfy clothes for later. Owen, you go grab some shit from the bar, okay?"

"What do you wanna drink?" Owen asks.

"I dunno, it's all good. Whatever you want."

"I can't drink tonight, dude. I'm still on antibiotics from strep."

Duke snorts. "Sucks to suck, bro." Owen's cheeks turn pink. Duke looks at me. "Hails, any requests?"

I shake my head. I'm not going to pretend to have taste in drinks that cost hundreds of dollars. After the gala, I looked up the champagne Jocelyn had swiped from the fridge behind the bar. It was $460 a bottle. The boys take off, and I stand in the foyer next to the water feature, waiting for them to return.

Duke jogs back up the steps first, a tote bag slung over his shoulder and a set of car keys dangling from his finger.

"Are we driving?" I assumed we'd be taking another Uber.

Duke grins. "The X5."

"You haven't had too much to drink?"

"I only had two glasses of wine at that thing. I'm under the legal limit."

"Maybe Owen could drive," I point out. "He's totally sober."

"No fucking way," Duke says. "Nobody drives the X5 but

me." He glances over his shoulder. The faint clanking of glass bottles means Owen's still stocking up on drinks. He turns back to me, the grin still on his face. "We probably have a minute or two." He saunters toward me, holding out his free hand. I give him mine. He pulls me toward him, like we're ballroom dancers, and stoops to kiss the spot above my collarbone. He trails kisses up the side of my neck and along my jaw toward my mouth.

But before he can get there, Owen bounds up the steps, each hand clasping two glass bottles. "You pervs ready to go?"

"You *wish* you were getting any," Duke fires back.

"Shut up, bro," Owen replies. "I'm definitely hooking up with Addison tonight."

Duke laughs. "Good luck, man. I hear Rutherford's sister loves strep."

We take the elevator down to the parking garage, where Duke leads us toward a gleaming black BMW X5. He unlocks the doors.

"I call shotgun!" Owen cries, racing to the car. He opens the passenger-side door, dumps the bottles on the floor of the car, and hops into the front seat triumphantly.

Duke rolls his eyes. "You okay in the back, or do you want me to make him move?"

"I think I'll survive in the back."

"You sure?"

"Positive."

The car rumbles when Duke turns on the ignition. He swivels around to look at me before he backs out of the parking space. "You won't believe how fast this thing goes. Wait till we get out of the city."

Owen jabs at the volume buttons on the center console. A thudding bass drum rattles my insides. We battle our way through Manhattan traffic to the George Washington Bridge, where the inky-black Hudson River sprawls beneath us, separating New York from New Jersey.

"Finally," Duke says. We're on a dark, narrow road with trees on either side, and not another car in sight. "I'm gunning this shit. Owen, try not to piss yourself."

Owen swears at Duke, but his voice is drowned out by the revving of the engine as Duke presses down on the accelerator. My stomach leaps to my throat, and I grab onto the door handle as we seem to double our speed. Leah would drive fast on those nighttime drives we used to take, but never like this. The boys whoop.

Duke smacks Owen in the arm. "Since I'm driving your ass to the party, you have to be the drink bitch."

"Fuck you, man."

"Owen, do it. I'm letting you bring Dom Pérignon to your dumbass friend's party. Open one of the bottles."

Owen reaches down to grab a bottle of champagne. He twists off the metal wiring.

My stomach lurches. "Wait, Duke, you're not going to drink that, are you?" Duke doesn't answer, because Owen deftly pops the cork and shoves the bottle into Duke's mouth so he can swallow what would have sprayed out the top. Duke having a couple of glasses of wine earlier in the evening was one thing, but I'm not okay with him drinking *while* driving.

"Wait," I plead again, but Duke grabs the bottle out of Owen's hand. "Duke, please, don't! Wait until we get there."

It's like Duke can't even hear me. I watch in horror as he

chugs what has to be two or three glasses' worth of champagne. He passes the bottle back to Owen. Catching my eye in the rearview mirror, he grins at me. His lips are wet and shiny. "It's fine, Hails. We do this all the time."

As if that's supposed to make me feel better. Fear coursing through me, I look out the window, wondering if Duke could just let me out of the car. But it's pitch-black, and who knows where we are? There's nothing but trees out there. "How much longer until we're there?"

"Chill," Owen says. "It's like ten minutes."

I stare at the clock on the dashboard, willing the minutes to evaporate. One goes by. Then another.

BANG.

I scream as my body bounces off the seat. *Breathe, Noa. We're fine. It was just a pothole.* But Duke is swearing: a shower of champagne just rained down all over the front of the car. My panic spikes as he takes a hand off the wheel, reaches over Owen's lap, and opens the glove compartment. "Where the fuck are my napkins? Are you gonna help me, or just sit there like—"

There's a flash of brown and white in the headlights. And as the boys keep messing around in the front seat, I'm the only one who sees it.

"Duke!" I scream at the top of my lungs. "Deer!"

It all happens too quickly to process. Duke looks up and turns the wheel sharply to the right, and with a screech of tires, we careen off the side of the road. I hear screams, including the one erupting from my own lungs. I feel the car shuddering as it tries to stop, but it can't. There's a crunching thud as we collide with a tree. The headlights disappear. The horn blares. My body snaps forward but my seat belt holds me in place.

The car isn't moving anymore. I blink. Pat my chest and the tops of my thighs. Flex my fingers and toes.

Oh my God.

I'm alive, and I'm okay.

"Duke?"

Duke sits in the front seat with a dazed expression on his face, the airbag deflated on his lap. He stares straight ahead at the spiderwebbed windshield. "Fuck my fucking life," he moans. "I'm fucked. *I'm fucked.*"

At least he's alive. "Owen?" I shuffle over and peer into the passenger seat.

When I see Owen's body, I scream.

He's slumped over the dashboard. There's blood on the cracked windshield. Blood on the airbag. Blood seeping down the side of his face.

"Duke, Owen's hurt!" Why isn't he doing anything to help? I climb between the two front seats. "Owen?" I touch his shoulder.

Miraculously, his body stirs. Slowly, slowly, he places his palms on the dashboard and starts to push himself up. I help him until he's resting against the seatback. Blood oozes from a gash above his left eyebrow, and there are cuts and scrapes on his forearms.

Duke is still sitting there cursing.

"Oh my God, you're alive." I want to hug him, even though I don't particularly like him. "Are you okay?"

Owen touches his forehead, winces, then pulls his hand away to inspect the blood. "Shit. Is it bad?"

"I don't know. It *looks* awful. Your face is covered in blood. Owen, I think we should call an ambulance."

"Nahhhh, dude." Owen moans.

At the same time, Duke says more firmly: "No."

"But—"

"Hailey"—Duke presses his fingers into his temples—"can you get out of here and give us a sec to talk?"

Dumbfounded, I turn back to Owen. His face is more blood than skin. "Are you *sure* you're okay?"

"I'm gooood, I'm gooood." He sounds a little out of it.

"He said he's good, Hailey," Duke snaps. The iciness of his voice chills me to the bone.

I grab my bag and try the door, which isn't crumpled like the front of the car. Thank God, it opens. I get out and slam it behind me. I stumble to the back of the BMW and lean against the trunk. If not an ambulance, I should call the cops right now. Duke was literally drinking and driving, and he got us into an accident that could have killed all three of us.

And yet, I don't reach for my phone. No sooner has the thought of dialing 911 crossed my mind than I cast the prospect aside. If I get Duke in trouble with the law, there's no way he'll ever speak to me again. He's known me for, what, a week? The rest of the family would probably write me off, too. As generous as they've been, there's no way they'd side with me over Duke. And then how would I find out anything more about Leah? I'd be nowhere—just a selfish girl who came to the city on the pretense of solving a murder but ended up partying with the rich and famous for a week before crashing back down to Earth.

Besides, Owen's awake and claiming to be fine. It's not like his life hinges on me calling for help.

The silence of the woods makes it easy to hear the boys' muffled conversation from inside the car.

"Dude, I got you, bro," Duke says to Owen. "I'm gonna get us out of here."

"Thanks, man."

"Hello?" Now it sounds like Duke is on the phone. "Hey, I got in an accident. I need you to come over here. I'm on the Palisades. I'm almost at Nine W." There's a pause. "Okay. Thanks."

Duke gets out of the car and walks over to me. "Hails? You okay?" This isn't the thrill-seeking Duke who made me lean against the ninetieth-floor window with him. He can call me "Hails" all he wants, but I can hear the anxious edge to his voice.

"Yeah." I try not to flinch when he takes my hand.

"Good." He looks down and caresses my skin with his thumb. "I'm sorry I snapped back there. It's all taken care of now. Everything's gonna be fine."

"Did you call for help?"

"Yeah, they're on their way. Listen, you should get out of here. Call an Uber."

"Okay." Can I *afford* an Uber from here? Let's see. I pull out my phone and plug in my address in Jersey. It's a lot closer than Brooklyn, but still, yikes. This is going to be expensive—but I have to get out of here. Inwardly cringing, I accept the pricey fare.

"Is he close?" Duke asks.

"He's twenty-two minutes away."

"Shit. Seriously?" He cranes his neck toward the road, as though he might be able to will the guy to drive faster.

"We're in the middle of nowhere."

"I know. It just, uh . . . it just sucks that you have to wait." Duke turns back to me and squeezes my hand. "Hey, Hails?"

"Hmm?" I look up at him. He cups my jaw and kisses me

softly on the lips. The moment our mouths touch, my blood turns to acid. It singes my insides like a shot of cheap liquor. I'm the first one to pull back. "Maybe you should go check on Owen."

"Yeah, good call," he says. Duke kisses my forehead before striding around to the passenger side of the car. When he's gone, I wipe off his saliva with the back of my hand.

A little while later, Duke and I are leaning against the back of the car when a pair of headlights approaches from the way we came. "I wonder if that's my driver," I murmur, praying I can finally leave. I check my phone, and my heart sinks. The car's still seven minutes away.

Duke stares at the approaching car, which rolls to a stop nearby.

"Took them long enough," he says.

Both front doors open at the same time. Two middle-aged men get out, each of them dressed in jeans and a polo shirt. Who did Duke call for help?

"Duke," one of them calls out.

"I'll text you," Duke mutters. Then, like a dog summoned by its owner, he leaves the BMW and jogs across the road to the men. The one who called his name opens the back door for Duke to slide in, then slams the door behind him. The second man makes a beeline for the wrecked BMW. When he gets here, he goes straight to the passenger-side door without saying a word to me.

"Hey, you're Owen?" he asks.

"Yep," Owen replies weakly.

"Hi, Owen. My name's Leo. I'll be right back and we'll talk."

"Cool, man."

The man—Leo—carries the bottles of alcohol back to his own car and stuffs them in the trunk. Then he returns to Owen's side of the car and starts whispering.

Who *are* these men, and what's going on here?

I crouch to the ground, my hands and knees in the dirt. As quietly as I can, I creep to the edge of the car so I can hear what they're saying around the corner.

"If the story goes that Duke was driving this car, we're in big trouble," Leo says. "Duke was drinking, so if he's driving the car, it's an embarrassment; it costs the Avalon family their reputation, and your best friend goes to jail."

"But you're sober," Leo goes on. "If *you're* driving the car, it's just an accident and nobody cares. You can't be arrested. You saw a deer in the road and swerved to avoid it. It happens."

Holy shit. They're asking Owen to take the blame for the accident *Duke* caused.

"It's not your car. It's not your insurance. You're not responsible for anything," Leo says. "We all work together and the Avalons will compensate you for your support."

"Compensate?" Owen murmurs. "What do you mean?"

Leo leans in closer. "As in, you'll be paid."

When my Uber arrives on the scene, I hurry across the road and get in the back without looking over my shoulder.

"Whoa," the driver says as he surveys the scene in his headlights. "You guys were in an accident? Are you okay?"

I nod.

"What happened?"

"There was a deer."

"Oh, damn," he says as we pull away. "Buddy of mine almost hit one the other day. They're outta control around here."

I nod again, my thoughts racing. Duke just drove drunk, crashed his car, and paid off Owen to take the blame for it. One phone call, and he made his problems go away like magic. I feel sick that I was ever attracted to Duke. Really and truly nauseated. I fell for Duke's charm—for Sylvie insisting he was *such a good guy.* As shame curdles in my stomach, I wrap my arms around my waist and slump against the window, wondering if Leah ever felt this way too. And the longer I think about Leah, and Duke, and the two of them together, the harder it is to avoid another terrifying new question: What other crimes has Duke swept under the rug?

CHAPTER 15

DUKE

Text me when you get home so I know you're okay

My car's fucked because of Owen. Why did I let him drive??? FML

Next time we hang out, let's just stay in and chill 😞

Duke obviously knows that I know he was the one driving. He must assume that I'll accept whatever version of reality he dictates to me. He's pretty slick, not saying anything incriminating in his texts—sending me the lie as if it's always been the truth.

I stare at the texts as the Uber turns onto my street, my stomach in knots at the thought of hanging out with him again. But I have to do it; I have to know if Duke killed Leah, then made it look like she'd done it to herself.

After everything I've seen tonight, there's no question he was capable of it.

Just so he stops bothering me, I thumbs-up Duke's last message and let him know I'm home, and that I'm exhausted and getting into bed ASAP. He has the gall to write back: *Sweet dreams.*

It takes me a few tries to get the key in the lock in the front door. My hands shake like the lid of a pot full of boiling water.

When I finally get inside and close the door behind me, the upstairs hall light flicks on. Dad appears at the top of the stairs wearing boxers and an old white T-shirt, his thinning hair rumpled from sleep. "Noa?" He rubs his eyes and blinks at me.

"Sorry to wake you. You can go back to bed." I lock the door behind me. When I turn around, Dad's still standing in the same spot, bearing down on me.

He surveys my party outfit and scoffs. "What the hell are you doing coming home in the middle of the night? We're getting up for work in a few hours."

My whole body starts to shake as I try to find words for what happened to me tonight. The champagne. The deer. The screams. The crash. The blood streaming down Owen's face. Those terrifying moments when I thought he was dead, and Duke didn't seem to care. *Duke.* I've kissed the guy who might have killed my sister.

When I don't respond right away, Dad throws his hand in the air. "For the love of God, do you ever think of anyone but yourself?"

My back against the door, I slide to the ground in a fit of sobs. The tears come hard and fast, like a flash flood, barreling through my flimsy defenses. I pull my knees up to my chest and bury my face in my crossed arms.

Then I hear Mom. "What's going on?" she asks, a frantic edge to her voice.

Now that I've cracked myself open, there's no reining these feelings back in. I lift my head, my face streaked with tears. They're both standing there on the stairs, looking dumbfounded. "Why didn't you tell me the truth about Leah? I found her phone in your bedroom safe. I saw her texts with Emmeline Gilbane, and I know she didn't kill herself because she was stressed about her workload. Fuck, I don't even think she killed herself!"

At the bottom of the stairs, my parents freeze in their tracks. Now they're the ones who can't find the words to reply.

"Guess what? I haven't just been visiting Zayn this past week. I've been looking into what actually happened to Leah, and I know the truth is more complicated than the story you told everyone. So either you can tell me what *really* happened, or I'll figure it out for myself. Your choice."

Mom looks at Dad. Dad pinches the bridge of his nose. "Let's sit down," he mutters.

I use the bathroom and clean myself up before joining my parents in the living room. They each perch on the edge of an armchair. I sit alone in the center of the couch, facing them. I raise my eyebrows. "Well?"

Dad holds his palm up. "Enough with the attitude, Noa."

"She's upset, Rob," Mom says gently. She turns to me. "But we *are* all in this together, Noa."

"How so?" I snap. If we're all in this together, then why

did they stash Leah's phone in a safe and hide the whole truth from me?

My parents look at each other, then back at me. "Because we also don't know the full story of what happened to Leah," Mom says quietly.

"Wait... what?" I ask.

"We saw those texts with Emmeline," Mom says. "They were obviously alarming, but at the time, we were just s-so d-devastated...." She's too choked up to keep talking.

"We couldn't *begin* to go down that other road," Dad says sharply.

"Not then, at least," Mom says. "You know what a toll it took on us. We decided we'd give ourselves a year to grieve before we even started to think about this other stuff."

We were all crushed by Leah's death, but while I had senior year and college applications to help distract me, my parents became ghosts of their former selves. Dad took the semester off teaching, and Mom's company let her go on leave for a while. They stayed at home, growing more gaunt as the weeks went on. Eventually, Mom's sister stepped in and dragged them both to a support group.

"A whole *year*?" I ask in disbelief. "Why so long?"

Mom flinches. "Everyone grieves at different paces, Noa."

"What's that, a line from one of your books?" I remember the stack I found in her bedside drawer.

"Noa," Dad warns me, but I keep going.

"Sorry, but I'm frustrated that you didn't tell me any of this. Just because you didn't want to look into it, that doesn't mean I wouldn't have wanted to."

"Oh, really?" Dad snaps, his aggression rearing its head again. "That's what you would have wanted?"

"You don't believe me? *You're* the ones who sat on this evidence for a year. At least I *did* something as soon as I found her messages."

Dad's nostrils flare. He leans forward, elbows resting on his knees, and when he speaks, his voice is deadly calm. "Noa, do you know what else we saw when we went through Leah's messages? Something you might be familiar with."

"Rob . . . ," Mom says weakly.

My pulse thuds behind my eyes.

"We saw that she texted you the day before she died," Dad says. "She said she was scared, and you didn't fucking answer her—or even mention it to us." He leans closer, fire blazing in his bloodshot eyes. "You know what *else* I've never said to you, Noa? That if you hadn't ignored that text, your sister might still be alive."

"*Rob.*"

Dad glares at me, a sick triumph in his eyes, as his bullet rips through my heart. I slump against the back of the couch. Dad pushes himself to standing and motions for Mom to follow him. "Let's go back to bed, Dawn."

Mom bites her lip, looking as though there's something she wants to say.

"Come on," Dad pushes.

Mom sighs. "Let's talk in the morning," she says quickly. Then she scurries up the stairs in Dad's wake.

When the shock wears off, I start to sob. Hard. I stumble out to the backyard, and with shaky thumbs, I text Zayn.

ME
Can we FaceTime?

ZAYN
Are you okay???

ME
I really need someone to talk to

ZAYN
One sec. Let me go up to the roof

I'm huddled on a patio chair, my knees drawn up to my chest, when the name Zayn Torres pops up on my phone. I'm still sobbing when I answer the call.

"Holy shit, Noa," Zayn says. "Are you okay? Where are you?"

"My house."

"I thought you were on the Upper East Side."

"I was. But then..." Another flood of tears cuts me off as the night catches up with me again.

"What happened?" In the fluorescent glow of the roof light, Zayn looks scared. "Noa, talk to me."

I start with what somehow feels like the easy stuff: the fundraiser, the car crash, the cover-up. But when I get to the part about coming home and confronting my parents, I start to sputter. Suddenly, I'm hyperventilating.

"Noa, breathe. *Breeeathe.*"

"I'm sorry," I say, gasping. "There's some stuff I've never told you before. Stuff I've never told anyone." All year, I've tried to push down the guilt, but it always comes bobbing back to the surface. Maybe it's time that I admit what I did.

So, for the first time, I tell Zayn the whole story, from the blowout fight with Leah, to the text she sent to me the day before she died, to my parents discovering my most shameful secret of all: that I'm the one to blame for Leah's death. As soon as I'm done repeating the words Dad hurled at me in the living room, I dissolve into yet another fit of tears. God, I need to pull myself together. I don't deserve to weep like this. I'm not the victim here.

"Okay, hold up," Zayn says, flashing their palm. When my tears keep coming, they sharpen their tone. "Noa, *seriously*."

I bite the back of my hand to stop my sobs.

"Will you listen to me? I don't care what your dad said: Leah's death isn't your fault."

"Yes, it is, Zayn!"

"No, it's not!"

"I'm a shitty sister. There's something wrong with me. You said it yourself yesterday: I need to see a therapist."

Zayn balks. "I didn't say that because I think something's wrong with you. I said it because I was worried about you, Noa. It sounded like you were dealing with some difficult shit."

"Oh." I don't know what else to say.

Zayn rolls their eyes. "As I was *saying*," they continue pointedly, "Leah's . . . death . . . is not . . . your . . . fault. Okay? It's the fault of whoever killed her. That's it. Period."

"But I could have stopped it," I protest.

Zayn takes a deep breath and lets it all out. "No offense, because I promise you're one of the most determined people I've ever met, but do you really think you could have stopped it? Like, really?"

"What's that supposed to mean?" I mutter.

"Think about Duke bribing his friend to take the blame tonight," Zayn says emphatically. "The people Leah hung out with last summer are more privileged than we can possibly imagine. Whoever killed your sister, they would have found a way to silence her, whether you were at that restaurant or not."

If I hadn't been through the car crash and its aftermath, I might have objected to Zayn's argument. But now, as their words wash over me, I realize they have a point. The Avalons and their social circle are powerful enough to literally reshape reality. What chance would I have stood?

"Okay, fine," I reluctantly concede. "But, Zayn, I'm still a monster. I still, like, *enjoyed* this pool party I threw the other week because Leah wasn't there to steal the spotlight for once. How can I possibly miss her and feel that at the same time?"

"Oh, Noa. You're not a monster. You're a human."

Ivy's voice pops into my head—what she said to me at her art show. I refused to embrace it, but here's Zayn insisting it's true, even after hearing my confessions. "And being a human is fucking complicated," I say.

"Exactly," Zayn replies.

Warmth spreads through my chest, and I manage a weak smile. "Do you know how much I love you?"

"Do you know how much I love *you*?"

"Is it a lot?"

"It's bigger than a lot."

"Same here."

We chat for a little longer, until we've passed the same yawn back and forth three times.

"I think we should get some sleep," Zayn says. "You coming back here tomorrow?"

"Is that okay?"

"Of course it's okay. Ivy came back from dinner tonight and asked why you weren't home."

"She did?"

"Mmm-hmm." Zayn gives me a knowing smirk.

"What?"

"Oh, nothing."

"Zayn Skye Torres."

"She just said she had a great time hanging out with you after her art show." They shrug, but a smile still lingers on their face. "Anyway, I'll see you tomorrow."

My cheeks are warm. I'm definitely blushing. "See you tomorrow."

When I hang up, I feel a lot lighter than I did before—lighter than I've felt since last summer. I spend a few minutes appreciating the summer night: the chirp of crickets, and the green glow of fireflies. Then I go upstairs to my room, change into my pajamas, and fall into the deepest sleep I've had all year.

When my eyes flit open, daylight streams through the window, and the sky is a bright blue. I check the time. Jeez—it's almost one in the afternoon. I can't remember the last time I slept this late, but apparently, I needed the rest. Sitting up, my body feels lighter, my head clearer.

The door to the backyard slides open and shut. Dad teaches

in person every day, but Mom works from home a couple of days a week. She must be taking her lunch break outside. I make my bed and plod downstairs in my pajamas. Dust motes dance in a sunbeam streaking across the foyer, and something about this whole scene reminds me of weekend mornings when Leah and I were little, and we'd watch our cartoons in the family room while Mom and Dad slept in. We'd lie on our stomachs on the area rug, which was so much more fun than the couch, for some reason. It was one of those times when the two of us could just *be*.

Remembering that Mom wanted to talk to me in the morning, I cross through the kitchen and go out to the backyard, where Mom is on all fours in the grass, with her head in the plants. She's wearing a white linen shirt and comfy cotton shorts—her classic work-from-home uniform—and a pair of yellow gardening gloves the same color as the marigolds blooming all around her. Mom got really into gardening this year on the recommendation of someone in her support group.

"Mom?"

She looks up and sits back on her heels. "You're up."

"Yeah." After last night's showdown in the living room, there's obviously some tension between us, but I want to know what was on the tip of her tongue at the end of the conversation. What was the thing she wanted to say, before Dad convinced her to follow him upstairs? I wander across the warm patio stones and into the grass, where Alistair and I played cornhole with Millie and Reza at the pool party. "What are you up to?"

"Just doing some weeding." She nods at a tangle of uprooted plant matter in the grass. "It's what I do on all my lunch breaks now."

"You do this on every lunch break?"

"It's better to do it often so they don't get out of control." Mom shrugs. "I don't mind. Gives me something to do."

"You... want some help?"

Mom looks surprised. "Sure," she says. "Uh, there's an extra pair of gardening gloves over by the barbecue."

When I return to the garden, gloves on, Mom shows me how to pull up the weeds from the roots, instead of just tearing off the leaves and stems, like I do at first.

"Aren't there tools you can use to make this easier?" I take in the size of the garden, which stretches around the edge of the whole backyard.

"There are," she says, "but, I don't know. I like the manual work. It's been helping me stay present in the moment. Otherwise, I just—" Her voice catches in her throat. "I just get the most terrible thoughts."

We're both silent for a few seconds, and I wonder if she's thinking about last night's argument too. "Hey, Mom?"

"Yeah?"

"I'm sorry for what I said last night... about your books, and your grieving process, and stuff."

"I appreciate that." She yanks a weed out by the root and tosses it into the pile. "I'm sorry Dad was so hard on you. He's been... a *lot*."

"Yeah."

"I've been begging him to see a therapist, especially after the incident in his class."

"He won't do it?"

"Refuses."

"But he goes to the support group. How is it that different?"

Mom sighs and sits back on her heels. She wipes the sweat from her forehead with the back of her glove. "I think there are things your dad is scared to talk about."

"Like what?"

She gets to her feet. "I should probably just show you."

"Is this what you were going to bring up last night?"

"Wait here," she says.

Mom disappears into the house and comes back a few minutes later with a spiral-bound notebook tucked under her arm. As she steps into the backyard, she glances left and right, like she's double-checking we're alone. Whatever she's about to show me, I have a feeling Dad wouldn't want me to see it. Mom crosses the backyard and kneels beside me.

"What's that?" I ask, staring at the notebook.

She takes a deep breath. "It's true that Dad and I were devastated, and we wanted to give ourselves a year before we dove back into what happened."

"Okay..."

"But, between us, I also suspect your dad was ashamed of some of the things we found in here." She pulls the notebook from under her arm. "We found this in Leah's apartment. We've been keeping it in the safe, too."

Now that I see it, I think I remember it being stuffed at the bottom of the safe when I was looking for Leah's phone, but at the time, I didn't think twice about it.

"What is it?" I ask, easing it from her hands.

Mom opens the cover for me. In the center of the first page, I instantly recognize my sister's perfect handwriting. "It's her internship log."

INTERNSHIP LOG

LEAH FALK

August 8

I didn't sleep all night. I'm embarrassed to tell anyone what happened in the bathroom because I feel like it was my fault. I knew he was into me. I was too afraid to turn him down sooner. I should have known this would happen.

There I go again. I know you're not supposed to blame yourself when something like this happens, but it's so hard. I'm scared of what Emmeline will say if I tell her what happened. She might take my side, being a woman and all, or she might get mad at me, given her close ties to him.

I think I'm just being anxious, as usual. What woman with any moral compass whatsoever wouldn't take my side here? OK. I'm writing it here to hold myself accountable: I'm going to text Emmeline and tell her I can't cover the Sunday Service grand opening on Friday.

INTERNSHIP LOG

LEAH FALK

August 8

As if my life couldn't get any worse, I was just accidentally included on an email from Emmeline I wasn't supposed to see—because it was about me. And it was the most horrifying thing I've ever read.

I've worked my ass off this summer, and I've done a damn good job. I've gladly taken every assignment they've given me. I've stayed up late working on drafts and turned in the cleanest copy imaginable. I've taken my edits well. Now I know that none of it mattered. Do I even matter? Or am I just some fucking object?

I'm crying so hard right now. I feel hopeless, knowing how this is the way the world works. There, that's what I learned in this fucking internship: that nobody does anything out of the goodness of their heart. There's a saying that has to do with this. What is it, again? Oh yeah.

There's no such thing as a free lunch.

INTERNSHIP LOG

LEAH FALK

August 8

I've never felt this level of rage before, and I need to channel it into something productive. So, here's an internship update for you: I'm going to take this story to the New York Times. I reached out to the social justice editor there, saying I have a pitch. If she's interested, I'll show her the emails Emmeline accidentally looped me into. I hope it'll be enough proof to move forward, but in case it isn't, I've decided I'm going to go to the Sunday Service opening tomorrow. I'm going to make Emmeline think I'm bending to her will—that I'm trying to get back in her good books. But I'll actually be trying to pull more information out of people—stuff that could help my story for the Times.

I'm in way over my head, seeing as all I've ever done is society reporting. This is the kind of journalism that Noa's always wanted to do: big stuff, with big consequences. She'll know how to handle this. I reached out to her to see if she can come to Sunday Service with me. We could report it together—we could have a joint byline. Maybe then, she'd finally forgive me. Maybe then, I could finally forgive myself for what I did to her.

I still feel so guilty. I knew she'd be furious about the

Sentinel internship, but what was I supposed to do, not have a job this summer? Dad would have disowned me!! Noa has no idea how lucky she is. She's always been off the hook.

There I go again, trying to make this guilt go away. I'm such a shitty sister. I just want things to be good between me and Noa. I hope she gets back to me and we can do this together.

I'm scared of what might happen when I expose them, but if I don't do anything—if I stay silent—nothing will ever change.

CHAPTER 16

Before she gets back to work, Mom drives me to the train station. Instead of braking to let me out, she puts the car in park. She takes a deep breath and wipes her palms on her shorts. "You know, I had half a mind not to show you that notebook."

"Because Dad would be upset?"

Mom wrings her hands. "Because I'm worried about you," she says, and turns to me with fear in her eyes. "I appreciate everything you're doing, but it's dangerous, Noa."

"I'll be fine." Last night's car crash would indicate otherwise, but she doesn't need to know that. "And anyway, I'm eighteen now, so . . ."

Mom sighs. "I know I technically can't stop you. But you're still my daughter."

"The best thing you can do right now is help me." I reach across the center console and take her hand, feeling closer to Mom than I have in a very long time. "I know you're not ready to fully investigate this, but I have questions you might know the answers to."

"Like what?"

I glance at the time. I still have a few minutes before the train comes. "Actually . . . I was wondering if I could ask you about Janie."

"Leah's roommate?"

"Yeah. I went to see her the other day."

Mom looks startled. "You went to the—to the apartment?"

"Yeah."

"Oh. Wow." She closes her eyes and breathes out a jet of air.

"Is it all right if I ask you . . . How did Janie seem that day?"

After a beat, Mom opens her eyes again. "Shocked? Shaking? Crying? Why?"

"Well, when I went to see her, she said she was envious of all the cool stuff Leah got to do for the *Sentinel*. I know it seems super far-fetched, but you don't think she might have . . . ?"

Mom's eyes go wide. "No, there's no way," she says emphatically. "The best actor in the *world* couldn't have faked the reaction she was having. She was as much of a wreck as we were."

"You're sure?"

"Positive. And once you read that"—she nods at the notebook clutched in my hand—"you won't think Janie had anything to do with it. Trust me."

"Okay."

She unbuckles her seat belt and leans over to hug me. Half an hour later, I'm crying on the train to Manhattan. Leah's internship log is spread open across my lap. With the pads of my fingers, I wipe the tears from under my eyes before they rain down and smudge words that I never thought I'd read.

First of all, I can see why this internship log wrecked Dad—not that I feel sorry for him. Once Leah started using the notebook as more of a journal, she'd go on for pages about the pressure he put on her to succeed. When she got to college, she was finally free—at least, freer than she'd ever been before—and she let loose. She partied. And she missed nearly every deadline for summer internship applications. She was freaking out. When she saw that the *Sentinel* was still hiring, she went for it.

Apparently, I'm not the only one who thought she was the world's shittiest sister. Leah felt guilty, too. She knew I'd be upset when she accepted that internship, but she went ahead and did it anyway, petrified of what Dad might say if she came home from college without a job.

Maybe Leah was right during our fight: I *was* oblivious—at least about certain things. Like just how much pressure Dad put on her to be perfect. All eyes were on the oldest daughter, the one who did everything first. By the time I got to ballet class or soccer practice, it didn't really matter how I performed, because my sister had already paved the way. There's a freedom in being the one nobody's watching.

Leah tasted that freedom when she finally got to college, and Dad couldn't breathe down her neck the way he used to. It's no wonder she missed the boat on summer internship applications. When she took the job at the *Sentinel,* she wasn't trying to steal my dream; she was trying not to let down Dad. I've never had to worry about that kind of thing. If there's anything I stressed about growing up, it was that Dad didn't care whether I let him down or not.

I remember dinners when Leah would proudly announce she got ninety-eight percent on some test, and Dad would be like, "What about the other two?" Then there was the time when Leah sprained her ankle playing soccer, and she was devastated to miss a big game; instead of comforting her, Dad kept harping on how the injury was her fault, and if she'd only been quicker on her feet, she could have prevented it. Whenever that stuff happened, Leah would get so upset, and I'd be like, "Why are you complaining? At least Mom and Dad pay attention to you." Now I see we were both just products of the same messed-up situation. And last summer, we *both* made choices we shouldn't have—choices we both would regret for the rest of our lives. But that didn't make us bad people.

I'll never get a chance to apologize to Leah face to face, but I hope I can still make peace with her. With a sniff, I flip back through the notebook. When Leah texted me the day before the Sunday Service grand opening, asking me to join her, it wasn't *only* because she was scared to run into her attacker. She also wanted to expose a secret—something so damning, she thought it worthy of the *New York Times*.

And she wanted to do it together.

My mind goes back to Rex at the City Crop fundraiser. Jeez, was that only yesterday? So much has happened since then. *I swear to God, I'm going to wring the neck of the next reporter who asks me to comment on why we're building over a park,* he growled at Gracie. And that was over a story that was already public knowledge; what would Rex have done if he realized what Leah had uncovered?

Speaking of which, what *did* she uncover when Emmeline Gilbane accidentally looped her in on those emails? It had something to do with Leah, and it sounds like it was related to my sister speaking up about what happened at the Haven.

The attack at the Haven . . . the accidental emails . . . the pitch to the *New York Times* . . . all these things are somehow connected to Leah's death. I can feel it. I just need to fill in the blanks, like who attacked her, and what those emails said.

I put on the noise-canceling headphones I grabbed from my room, and for the rest of the train ride, I listen to Leah's interviews again. And by the time I get back to Brooklyn, there's something I'm dying to do.

I jab my finger into the button next to Loft 4A. The door unlocks, and I let myself into the lobby, where I breathe in the warm smell of herbs, spices, and incense and let it all out with a sigh of relief. I'm home.

Ivy opens the door of the loft and immediately wraps me in a hug. "Oh my God, Noa. Zayn told us about the crash and the shit your dad said. I can't believe what happened." Breathing in her familiar fragrance, I sink into her arms, and she holds me like that for what might be a full minute. Then she pulls back and peers into my eyes. "Are you okay?"

Where do I even begin?

"Sorry, loaded question."

"Don't be sorry. You helped me a lot, actually."

She tilts her head. "I did?"

Over her shoulder, Zayn appears at the end of the corridor, smiling at me. I wave, then look at Ivy. "It's kind of a long story, but I've been feeling really guilty since Leah died, and last night, with my parents, it was like the worst *ever*. But then I remembered what you told me at the gallery. That being a human is fucking complicated."

She grins. So do I. Then she hugs me again. "I'm so happy you're back," she whispers. My heart flutters like it did that night on the couch, after her art show, only this time, I don't feel ashamed.

I hug Zayn, and then Killian, who also came over to say hi. "We were about to start making dinner," he says. "You hungry?"

I put a hand on my stomach. I had a granola bar before Mom drove me to the train station, but the last actual meal I ate was that salad at the City Crop fundraiser. "I'm starving, actually."

As we all pitch in to make a giant pot of pasta with homemade kale pesto, I tell the group about the internship log, reading passages aloud so they can get the full picture. After we eat, and we're done doing the dishes, I turn to Zayn to pitch them my idea.

Last night, toward the end of our FaceTime, they were telling me about some new upgrades they'd made to their makeshift recording studio upstairs. "I just got this epic new audio equipment and editing software," they said. "It's gonna make the sound quality a thousand times better."

"Hey, Zayn, you know that new equipment and software you were telling me about last night?" I ask. "Do you think you could use it to adjust the volume on a Voice Note from Leah's phone?"

"I think so," they say. "Why?"

"Remember that interview I played for you? With Sylvie Avalon, at the Sunday Service grand opening?"

"Yeah..."

"And remember how there was that weird part at the end, where they'd stopped talking, and it sounded like Sylvie stormed off and Leah forgot to stop recording?"

"Yeah," they say, more eagerly.

"Well, I was listening to it again on the train this afternoon—this time, with my super-intense noise-canceling headphones. I could be wrong, but I think I heard voices at the end. Like maybe Sylvie didn't storm off; maybe she stayed, and they just started talking super quietly. I cranked up the volume as much as I could, but I still couldn't make it out."

Zayn's already halfway to the stairs.

A few minutes later, I hover over their shoulder as they pull up the editing software on their computer. Ivy and Killian sit behind us on Zayn's bed, watching intently.

"You got the audio file?" I ask Zayn, looking up from Leah's phone.

There's a *whoosh* sound as it lands in Zayn's email inbox. "Yup. Lemme just download it, and then we can open it in the program." Zayn clicks around on the screen for a minute. "Okay, you ready?" Their cursor hovers over a Play button.

"Ready."

The next thing I know, the room is filled with the din of a packed restaurant. Zayn's speakers are incredible; it sounds like we're *there* at Sunday Service, the voices and music and clinking of glasses echoing under the vaulted ceiling. When I hear Leah's voice, it's like she's standing right beside me.

Ivy and Killian haven't listened to the interview before, so Zayn lets it play from the beginning.

LEAH: Hey, can I ask you a few quick questions for the Sentinel?

SYLVIE: Of course. Come, sit down.

LEAH: Did we wander into some kind of satanic ritual, or is it just me?

SYLVIE: [Laughs.] Isn't it so sexy, though? I'm obsessed with it. Can you believe all these candles are real?

LEAH: I heard some members of the former congregation were actually pretty upset with what they did to the space.

SYLVIE: Well, I don't know anything about that. Why are you asking me?

LEAH: I'm a journalist. I'm trying to learn about all sides of the story.

SYLVIE: [Laughs.] Okay, Miss Journalist, but you haven't even asked me about this amazing food and this incredible drink! My mind is blown. This is the beef tartare; this is a goat cheese tart; and see these little latkes with smoked salmon and caviar? They're going to change your life. And I'm drinking an extra-dirty vodka martini. The olives are smoked, and I'm telling you, it takes the classic cocktail to a whole new level.

LEAH: Wow. That's some high praise. But your family owns the restaurant, right?

```
SYLVIE: Leah, come on.

LEAH: What?

SYLVIE: Why are you being like this?

LEAH: Like what?

SYLVIE: If you're going to be like that, this
interview is over.
```

"This is the part where you can't hear them anymore," I explain. Even with Zayn's powerful speakers, the background din becomes louder than the girls' voices. On the bed, Ivy and Killian lean forward in apparent attempts to make anything out.

"I can't tell what they're saying," Ivy says, "but they're definitely saying something."

"Do you think there's anything you can do?" I ask Zayn.

Their forehead wrinkled with concentration, they click around on the screen, pulling up all kinds of toolbars and sliders. "I'm still getting the hang of this, so bear with me," they say. "I'm trying to see if I can dial down the background noise and amp up their voices."

My heart pounds as I watch Zayn work.

"Let's try this." Zayn presses Play, and we listen with bated breath. The girls' voices are definitely clearer from the start, the surrounding chatter more muffled than before. But after Sylvie threatens to end the interview, my stomach sinks. It's still too hard to hear what they're saying.

"Jeez," Killian says, "how did they even hear *each other*?"

"They must have been talking really quietly," Ivy murmurs.

"I'm gonna try one more thing," Zayn says. They must sense my desperation in the way I'm clinging to the back of their chair. As they fiddle around with the sliders again, I say a silent prayer to whatever celestial beings may be listening. *Please let this work. Please let this work. Please let this work.*

"All right," Zayn announces. "Let's try... this."

They press Play again.

This time, it's different; the background noise is even quieter than before. I hold my breath as Leah asks her question.

And then, remarkably, I can make out what comes next.

"Holy shit!" Killian exclaims.

"Shhh!" Ivy smacks him.

SYLVIE: You know what I mean. You're supposed to ask nice stuff.

LEAH: "Supposed to"? What does that mean, Sylvie?

SYLVIE: [Sighs.] Leah, are you upset about what happened at the Haven?

LEAH: Of course I am. I was there to do my job and he wouldn't listen when I said no. Do you know what he told me?

SYLVIE: What?

LEAH: "Other girls don't say no."

SYLVIE: [Sighs.] Well, I'm disgusted to hear that a member of my family behaved so appallingly. I want you to know that I don't support what he did, and that isn't what our family stands for. I'll make sure my mom talks to him.

LEAH: Oh really? That isn't what your family stands for?

SYLVIE: Really.

LEAH: Okay.

SYLVIE: Oh shit, you're still recording, aren't you? I have to go, Leah. Pass me my crutches.

LEAH: Bye.

My roommates and I exchange wide-eyed looks, and I know we're all thinking the same thing. The person who attacked Leah at the Haven was a man in the Avalon family.
"Duke." Zayn spits out his name.
"But what about Rex?" Ivy asks.
I check Google Maps. The Haven opens at four p.m. tomorrow.

I get to the Haven at four-fifteen p.m. Hopefully, since I'm here on the earlier side, the staff will be freer to talk to me, and not bogged down making the $5 happy hour blue raspberry mojitos and bubble gum martinis advertised on the chalkboard sign outside. I hop onto a stool and rest my forearms on the bar. When I feel how sticky the bar top is, I immediately regret my decision.

"Hey," I say to the man wiping glasses behind the bar.

He looks up. He's thirtysomething, with the long, tired face of someone who pours shots for wasted high school and college kids until four in the morning. "Hey. What can I get you?"

"A ginger ale, please."

"You got it." He fires the soda gun, shuffles over, and sets the glass down in front of me. "Anything else?"

"Yes, actually." I stir the straw around my glass. "I was actually hoping to talk to anyone who was working at the Haven last summer."

The bartender scratches the back of his neck. "I started in the fall, but my manager's been here forever. He's just checking something in the back room, but he should be out in a sec."

"Thanks so much."

I take a sip of ginger ale, which mostly tastes like water. Then I pull out my phone.

DUKE

Hey, you. What are your plans this weekend? You wanna do something?

ME

Hey!! I'm actually back home visiting my parents for a bit. Then I have Jocelyn's birthday trip to Montauk!

DUKE

Oh noooooo

I miss you lol

When are you back from Jocelyn's?

ME

I think Wednesday night

DUKE

Kk. That Friday I have to go to this giant party for the Sentinel's 50th anniversary. Wanna come??

ME

Yeah, sounds great!

The idea of seeing Duke at all makes me cringe, but at least this *Sentinel* thing is another big party, which will limit our one-on-one time. I glance up at the sound of a door swinging shut. A short, middle-aged white guy with a bushy orange beard makes his way across the empty dance floor, toward the bar.

"Hey, A.J." The bartender nods in my direction. "She's asking to talk to someone who worked here last summer."

I wave at A.J., trying to appear friendly, and not like an undercover detective trying to bust them for serving underage kids. The fact that I'm only eighteen probably works in my favor. Still, A.J. peers at me skeptically as he joins the other guy behind the bar. He crosses his arms and puffs out his chest as far as it'll go. "How can I help you?"

I'd better cut right to the chase. Plus, a rowdy group of teenage girls just barged through the door and swarmed one of the high-tops. They're already talking about doing a pitcher of the blue raspberry mojitos.

I look A.J. in the eye and tell him the truth. "My sister was murdered last summer, and we still don't know who did it. I'm trying to figure out what happened in the days leading up to her death, and I know she came here two nights before." I tell him the date, and show him a photo of Leah. "Is there any chance you remember her?"

He lets out a small burst of laughter and replies in a patronizing tone. "Honey, I'm sorry to hear about your sister, but do you know many people I serve on any given night?"

"This girl was here too." I pull up a photo of Sylvie.

A.J. shakes his head, right as another big group stumbles through the door of the bar. "Listen, I have people to serve, so—"

"What about him?" I shove a photo of Duke in his face.

A.J. is midway through an eye roll when he stops and squints at the phone. "Wait. I *do* know that guy." The expression on his ruddy face turns angry. "The little fucker was here last summer." A.J. smacks the bar. "I remember it now—your sister too."

I lean forward. "What do you remember?"

He points from the back of the bar to the front door. "Your sister comes running outta the bathroom crying, and busts outta here. *That* piece of shit," he points at my phone, "follows her out of the bathroom, hands covering his face like this." He cups his hands around his nose and mouth.

"The bathroom is where she was assaulted!" I exclaim, remembering Leah's internship log.

"Is *that* what happened in there?" A.J. asks.

"I thought you knew."

"How would I know?"

"You called him a piece of shit."

"Yeah, because the guy had a gushing nosebleed, and he didn't have the sense to clean it up on his own in the bathroom," A.J. complains. "Instead, he comes running over here, blubbering like a baby, asking if I have any ice. Whatever happened, your sister must have fought him off real good in there. He got blood all over my fuckin' floor."

CHAPTER 17

Back at the loft on Friday evening, I reread Leah's internship log with my disturbing new insight.

There's this guy I've hung out with at a few parties now. I don't mind talking to him, but he's definitely into me, and I don't like him that way. He has a sleazy vibe that gives me the ick.

The whole time, she was talking about Duke Avalon.

Between Duke mentioning the forehead kisses and Sylvie remembering how "good" he was to my sister, I sort of wrote Duke off as an assault suspect. But I was wrong. I wonder if Leah asked him for forehead kisses to steer him away from other parts of her body.

If he made another move, I figured I'd tell him (again) that I want to go slow. Well, he was pretty drunk, and he made another move. I told him I wanted to go slow, but he didn't want to hear it this time. He called me a tease. I told him I needed some space, so I left and went to the bathroom, but I didn't realize he followed me. It was a one-person bathroom and he shoved me through the door, locking it behind us. He said he wanted me. I said no. He said, "Other girls don't say no." I'll remember that disgusting line for as long as I live, because the very next second, he pushed me into the counter and kissed me and shoved his hand up my skirt.

"I want to kill Duke Avalon," I mutter under my breath, hunched over the kitchen island while Zayn sits next to me on their laptop. I was sick the first time I read these entries in Leah's internship log, but reading them again and knowing it was Duke is a whole new level of nauseating.

"What are you gonna do the next time you see him?" Zayn asks. "I feel like he'll want to kiss you."

"That's at the very least," I say, groaning as fear blooms in my belly. "But what do I do? Call him out? Get shunned by his family when I'm *this* close to finding out what really happened to Leah? Oh God. I sound just like my sister." Another wave of nausea hits me as I flip back to the first entry where Leah wrote about Duke.

If he makes a move, I don't want to reject him and piss him off. That would be so awkward. But then what am I supposed to do???

I want to reach through paper and celestial planes and hug

my sister tight. *We're in this together,* I say in my head, in case she's listening... somewhere.

"There must be something you can look into without having to see Duke," Zayn reasons.

"I do need to learn more about this email Leah was accidentally looped in on." I flip to the second-to-last entry in the log and read it aloud: "'As if my life couldn't get any worse, I was just accidentally included on an email from Emmeline I wasn't supposed to see—because it was about me. And it was the most horrifying thing I've ever read.' This happened after she told Emmeline about the assault," I add.

"Oh God. Emmeline did that horrifying thing where you're shit-talking somebody, but then you accidentally include the person you're shit-talking." It happened one time to Zayn when we were in high school. They meant to send me a text about their plans to break up with their partner, Kit, but since Kit was on their mind, Zayn accidentally sent *them* the message. Zayn was mortified—although, at least it got the job done.

"It sounds *exactly* like that kind of email." I drum my nails on the surface of the island. "The question is, how the hell do I find it?"

Subject: Informational interview?

From: Hailey Star
To: Emmeline Gilbane

Hi Ms. Gilbane,

It was great to meet you at Gracie Avalon's gala.

Thank you so much for offering to meet with me for an informational interview! If you're available sometime in the next week, I'd love to hear more about your pathway in journalism, as well as what you're looking for in a *Gotham Sentinel* reporter. It's my dream to write for you someday!

Thank you so much for your time.

Sincerely,
Hailey

Subject: Informational interview?

From: Emmeline Gilbane
To: Hailey Star

Hi Hailey,

It was lovely to meet you and see your passion for good journalism! Next week is quite busy as we prepare for the *Sentinel*'s 50th anniversary party, but I should have time for a conversation on Thursday at 10 a.m., if you're available. Let me know.
 —Emmeline

I spend the weekend lying low, since I told Duke I was in Jersey with my parents. On Saturday, there's a summer solstice potluck on the roof of Zayn's building. Zayn, Ivy, Killian, and I stuff tote bags with fresh tomatoes and berries from the farmers' market, the unsold pastries from Sweet Bean that day, and a few bottles of grapefruit prosecco.

Up on the roof, blankets are spread out over the cement, with people sitting around playing instruments, making crafts, drinking, eating, and, in the case of a few bold residents, doing yoga in their underwear. While Zayn and Killian get swept up in a lively game of charades, Ivy takes out her sketchbook, and I find myself content with lying there on my side, my eyes following the gentle strokes of her pencil. I don't mean to, but eventually I doze off in the balmy breeze. When I jolt awake, Ivy giggles and flips her sketchbook around. "I couldn't resist," she says. It's a contour drawing of my sleeping body.

"Wow."

"'Wow' as in, 'It's weird that I watched you sleep'?"

"No! 'Wow' as in I'm obsessed with this." I take the sketchbook from her hands so I can look at the drawing more closely. I smile as my eyes trace the lines, and my next words spill out before I realize what's happening. "I'm kind of obsessed with *you*."

Ivy takes back her sketchbook and tears out the page with the drawing. "I'm kind of obsessed with you too. Clearly." She places the drawing in my lap—but first, she scrawls something in the bottom corner of the page. It's her signature, with a tiny heart next to her name.

Then it's Tuesday, and I'm walking with my backpack toward the sleek, black building under the FDR Drive. Delicate silver lettering on the door of the black building says:

BREEZE

Next to the door is a buzzer, which I press. There's a click, and a blast of cold air hits me as I push open the door. I'm standing in a small, windowless reception room, where a guy in a suit greets me from behind a desk.

"Welcome to Breeze," he says. "Your name?"

"Hailey Star." *Please don't ask for ID. Please don't ask for ID.*

"And whose party are you with?"

"Lina Lawrence-Kalu?"

He clicks a few things on his computer. "Thank you, Miss Star. You're all checked in. You can leave your bag here and head on through to the lounge." With a sweep of his arm, he directs me to the sliding door behind him.

The "lounge" looks like a cross between an airport gate and a study where rich old men drink whisky and smoke cigars. There's brown leather furniture, a bar stocked with top-shelf liquor and dispensers of fancy nuts, and, on the walls, a bunch of giant framed photos of Manhattan from above. Turning my attention to the floor-to-ceiling windows lining the opposite wall, I spot our ride to the Hamptons.

A helicopter.

Fear shoots through my chest like lightning, and I try to ignore the mental image of our chopper losing power and crash-landing in the East River. I'm a risk-taker, but I like *calculated* risks. And flying in a helicopter doesn't meet that threshold. But I can't let my nervousness show on my face, because there's Jocelyn, popping out of an armchair and hurrying to me with outstretched arms.

"Hailey!" she squeals, wrapping me in a hug.

"Happy almost-birthday!"

"Aww, thank you, but how *are* you? I heard about the crash. Thank God you were all okay."

"I'm totally fine." *Physically.*

"Fucking Owen does *not* know how to drive." Sylvie glides over from another armchair with a flute of champagne dangling between her fingers. She gives me a one-armed hug, then steps back and runs her hand through her blow-dried brown hair. She looks so chill—but is she . . . too chill? I wonder if she was sold the lie that Owen was driving the BMW, or if she knows the truth, and she's helping cover for Duke.

It wouldn't be the first time, I realize, as Sylvie's piercing green eyes flit to the left. When we were in line for food at the City Crop fundraiser, Sylvie said Duke had been "so good" to my sister last summer. But she was fully aware that he'd assaulted Leah at the Haven; this I know, because she and Leah discussed it in the interview I was finally able to listen to the other day. My blood runs cold. Suddenly, the helicopter is the least of my concerns.

While we wait for Lina and Divya, Jocelyn gives me a rundown of our Montauk itinerary. "As soon we get there, we can Uber to the grocery store to stock up on supplies. Then I'm thinking we do the beach, and then later, everyone can come up and chill by the pool while I start getting dinner ready."

"It's your birthday trip," I cut in. "You don't have to cook for everyone!"

"No, Hailey, I want to," Jocelyn insists. Her eyes sparkle as she bounces on the balls of her feet. "Cooking for people is my favorite thing in the world. I have a whole four-course meal planned. I can't wait."

When Lina and Divya arrive, the man from reception leads the five of us out back to the tarmac. We meet our pilot, who gives us a brief safety demonstration, before we climb into the helicopter and strap ourselves into our seats. The blades start to spin, and my stomach lurches as we lift off the ground with ease.

Only Jocelyn stares out the window as the city grows smaller beneath us. Sylvie, Lina, and Divya are on their phones. I venture a quick glance at the view, but it gives me a head rush and makes my palms sweat. Instead, I spend most of the ride watching Sylvie, wondering just how far she's gone to protect her dear twin brother.

CHAPTER 18

Forty minutes later, we touch down in East Hampton, where the air tastes fresher, with a hint of brine. As our pilot unloads our luggage, Lina summons an Uber to drive us the rest of the way to her family's house.

I've never been to the Hamptons or Montauk before. We drive down a quiet two-lane highway with the ocean to our right. Low bushes line the road, but every so often, I catch a glimpse of the turquoise waves sparkling in the late June sun.

Our SUV stops at a white gate set into the bushes. Lina taps something on her phone, and the gate swings open, beckoning us in. We follow the gravel driveway around a bend, and then I see it out the front window: an ultramodern mansion made of grayed wood and glass. I searched the address online, and saw the property was featured in *Architectural Digest* last year, and that it's valued at $25 million. Lina's mom is a famous fashion designer from Nigeria, and her dad owns a commercial real estate development company with offices in New York and

London. The family has homes in Manhattan, Montauk, London, and Lagos, and apparently they own a whole *island* somewhere in the Caribbean.

After the car drives off, we carry our luggage up to the door. "Lina," I say, "this place is *gorgeous*."

"Yeah, it's supercute," she replies lazily. "The pool's out back, the tennis courts are over there, and the beach is right down those steps." She taps her phone again to unlock the front door.

"Wait till you see the inside," Jocelyn says. "It's *so* nice."

Inside, the white and beige decor looks as perfect as it did in the *Architectural Digest* photos. It's bright, airy, and open-concept; from the foyer, I can see straight through to the gleaming marble kitchen and out the back windows, where there's an infinity pool and a bunch of daybeds overlooking the ocean.

"So who wants to come to the store?" Jocelyn asks brightly, except Sylvie, Lina, and Divya have already dropped their bags and started making their way to the backyard. I think I'm the only one who even heard her. Wincing, she turns to me and scratches the back of her neck. "You up for a grocery run?"

Just like when Sylvie sent me and Jocelyn to grab more drinks at the gala, it's the two of us outsiders who get in another car to buy groceries. I feel icky walking into the grocery store—like we're the other girls' servants or something. Jocelyn grabs a cart, whips out a handwritten shopping list, and steers us toward the produce section.

At least it turns out to be fun shopping with a soon-to-be-professional chef. Jocelyn shows me how to test an avocado's ripeness without bruising it, and how to smell the skin of tomatoes to find the most delicious ones. At the fish and meat counters, she knows exactly what to ask for and how much, and she beams as she accepts her packages, wrapped in paper and tied with twine.

The house is quiet when we get back. While we were out, the other girls claimed their bedrooms, changed into their swimsuits, and made their way down to the Lawrence-Kalus' private slice of beach. Jocelyn sighs as she heaves her grocery bags onto the kitchen island to unpack them.

"Are you all right?" I ask.

"Yeah, I'm great!" she says brightly, but her words have a hollowness to them. The moment glints with opportunity.

"Are you sure? Just between us . . . I don't know the other girls quite as well, but I feel like Sylvie sometimes . . ." I pause like I'm searching for the right words, but really, I'm studying Jocelyn. She's frozen with a block of cheese halfway out of the bag, listening intently.

"Sometimes isn't as nice as she seems?" Jocelyn finishes for me.

My heart skips a beat. "Yeah."

But no sooner have the words left her mouth than Jocelyn blinks and shakes her head like she's coming out of a trance. "Sylvie's a good person and a good friend!" she says in that same hollow voice as before. "I think she was just tired and needed to relax so she could be fully present tonight, you know?"

"Gotcha," I murmur as I go back to slotting cans of tangerine seltzer—Sylvie's favorite flavor, according to Jocelyn—on the top shelf of the fridge.

We eventually make our way down to the beach, where Sylvie is evidently done resting up—that is, if she ever was to begin with. She and Divya are on all fours, posing for photos at the edge of the water. They shriek with laughter whenever the waves splash them from behind. "I want to join!" Jocelyn cries, bounding so fast down the rest of the stairs, I'm terrified she's going to trip in her platform sandals.

When their photo shoot is over, and the girls have all decided which shots they're going to post, Sylvie declares she's bored of the beach and ready for wine by the pool. Jocelyn puts her sandals back on, leaps to her feet, and shakes the sand out of her towel, ready to go. She and I haven't even been down here for an hour.

The rest of the day is more of the same, with Sylvie calling the shots, even though it's Lina's house and Jocelyn's birthday. There's a power structure in place that no one talks about but everyone seems to embrace.

Well, almost.

Jocelyn's four-course dinner is incredible—legitimately one of the best home-cooked meals I've had in my life. She makes shrimp and corn fritters as an hors d'oeuvre, mango gazpacho as an appetizer, steak for the main, and blueberry cobbler for dessert. By the time we're finished eating and doing the dishes, it's nearly eleven o'clock. Out the window, it's hard to see where ocean ends and night sky begins; the only clue is the twinkling of stars.

The group starts meandering over to the couches to relax, but Jocelyn clears her throat. "Um, I kind of had an idea for something we could do tonight."

Sylvie raises her eyebrows. "Oh yeah?"

Redness creeps up the fair skin of Jocelyn's neck. "I was thinking we could do a little campfire on the beach. We could stay out there until midnight, when it's officially my birthday."

A beach bonfire actually sounds like fun to me. While we were down there earlier, I noticed a firepit set up with plenty of wood ready to go. But Sylvie pouts. "Really? We all showered before dinner. I don't know if I wanna get sandy again."

"Same," Divya says, flopping onto a couch and already reaching for the remote.

The wounded look on Jocelyn's face makes me genuinely ache for her. "I'll come down to the beach with you," I offer.

Sylvie eyes the two of us with an arched eyebrow, like a boss who suddenly realizes their workers have the power to unionize. But then she shrugs and joins Divya on the couch. "If you guys wanna do that, go for it. We'll be up here."

"No problem," Jocelyn says. "C'mon, Hailey." She grabs a fresh bottle of rosé from the fridge, a lighter from the drawer, and our paper shopping bags from earlier to use as kindling, and then strides out of the room. I hurry after her, wondering if now she might be more forthcoming with her feelings on Sylvie.

In the light of our phone flashlights, we walk carefully down the stairs to the beach. Jocelyn is quiet.

"I can take care of the fire," I say, grabbing the lighter and the shopping bags. "You just hang out."

"You sure?"

"Joc, you just cooked me one of the best meals of my life. I'm sure."

"Thanks."

"Thank *you*."

She chuckles and takes a swig of wine. She's been drinking steadily since she started cooking this afternoon, so she's a little less guarded than she was before. "None of them even said thank you for the meal," Jocelyn muses. "I know we're all splitting the cost of food and drinks while we're here, but like I cooked everything. *And* did the dishes."

"You don't have to rationalize it, Joc. They should have thanked you."

Jocelyn sighs. "Yeah."

While Jocelyn works at the rosé, I light the paper bags and add kindling, followed by larger logs from the pile on the beach. We both sit down in the sand, the flames casting a warm orange glow on our faces. The waves lap gently against the shore.

"Can I ask you something?" Jocelyn blurts.

"Sure." Panic shoots through my chest.

"Was Owen really driving the car the other night, when you crashed?"

Oh, thank God. For a second, I thought she was on to my real identity, somehow. But now, I have to decide how I want to answer her question. I could lie and stay loyal to the Avalons, or I could tell the truth and see what else it compels Jocelyn to divulge.

I lower my voice. "This is just between us, right?"

"Obviously." She nudges the side of my foot with hers. "We're on the same team."

"Okay." I take a deep breath. "It was Duke." I thought I'd be anxious admitting the truth, but actually, it's a relief to not be complicit anymore.

Jocelyn smacks the sand. "I knew it!"

"How'd you know?"

"He would never let someone else drive his car, and definitely not *Owen*. God, the fucking Avalons. They're something else." She shakes her head and takes another swig of wine. "What actually happened that night?"

As the fire crackles between us, I tell Jocelyn how Duke crashed the car, then called his lawyers instead of emergency services. I repeat the exchange I overheard between Owen and the lawyer, Leo, who explained that the Avalons would pay him off if he took the blame for the accident.

"Wow," she murmurs. "Wow, wow, wow."

"In the Breeze lounge, Sylvie said something about Owen being a terrible driver. Do you think she was lying? Or does she really believe it was him?"

"Hailey. Come on." She gives me a look.

"What?"

"She was *obviously* lying."

"You're sure?" It would add up, since I know Sylvie lied about Duke being "so good" to Leah.

"Positive." Jocelyn's voice is grim. "Lemme tell you, there's nothing that family won't do to protect each other."

A chill goes down my spine. "What else have they done?"

Jocelyn goes quiet for a few seconds.

My heart thumps. "Joc?"

"Oh my God."

"What?" I ask urgently.

Jocelyn holds up her phone, grinning. "It's officially my birthday."

When the fire dies down, we get up and brush the sand off our bodies. Jocelyn, who consumed the better part of the wine, is more than a little unsteady as we make our way to the stairs. She giggles. "Why is walking in sand so *hard*?"

In the light of my phone's flashlight, I watch as her ankle rolls sideways. She drops the wine bottle, which hits a rock and shatters. I lunge, trying to catch Jocelyn as she falls, but she's at least five inches taller than me, so when I grab her arm, her weight ends up pulling me down too. I stick my arm out to cushion the blow as we both crash to the ground in a heap. *Ow.* There's a searing pain in my palm, and when I touch it with my other hand, I gasp. There's a shard of glass sticking straight out of my flesh, and blood trickling down my wrist. "Careful—there's a ton of glass from the wine bottle," I warn Jocelyn. "Some just went into my hand."

"Shit." She finds her phone in the sand and aims the flashlight at my palm. "Oh God, Hailey!"

Wincing, I ease the glass out, but the bleeding is bad. I grab my phone off the beach. Holding my bloody hand away from my clothes, I lead the way back to the house. I slide open the back door and go inside. Sylvie, Lina, and Divya are splayed out on the couches in the next room, chatting and drinking while some late-night show plays on the TV.

Lina's eyes go wide when she sees the blood trailing down my arm. "Oh my God. Do not come anywhere near these white couches."

"Do you have any Band-Aids?" I ask.

Sylvie, at least, is more helpful. She points down the hall just outside the kitchen. "I think I saw a box of them under the sink in my en suite bathroom. Want me to check for you?"

"No, it's okay, I'm closer." I hurry to the first guest suite, and then into the bathroom. Sure enough, there's a box of Band-Aids under the sink. I turn on the faucet and rinse the blood off my skin to survey the actual damage. Phew: the cut itself doesn't seem to be that bad. I don't think I need stitches or anything. It briefly occurred to me that if I'd had to go to the emergency room, the hospital staff would have asked for my name and ID. I would have been screwed.

As I lay the Band-Aid over my cut, my eyes catch on something peeking out of Sylvie's toiletry bag next to the sink. A label on a clear orange bottle, and a word that makes sirens go off in my brain.

My hand shaking, and not from the blood loss, I nudge the toiletry bag open wider, so I can read the label clearly.

OXYCODONE

The same drug that killed Leah.

"What are you doing?"

Gasping, I retract my hand and look up into the mirror. Standing in the bathroom doorway, her green eyes glaring at me, is Sylvie.

CHAPTER 19

"Why were you going through my toiletry bag?" Sylvie snaps.

Think fast. Why was I going through her toiletry bag? "Um, I realized I should probably put something on my cut, so it doesn't get infected. I cut myself on glass from a bottle that was sitting in the sand for an hour, so who knows what could have gotten in there, you know? You don't have any Neosporin, do you?" I fight to keep my voice from wavering.

Sylvie's face relaxes. "Uh, I might, actually. Let me check." She walks over, grabs her bag, and roots around inside. To get a better view, she takes out a tube of sunscreen, a pot of lotion, and the bottle of oxycodone.

"Oh, damn," I say as casually as I can. "What's the oxy for?"

"It's left over from my knee surgery last summer," Sylvie replies breezily.

"Ah."

"They gave me a ridiculous amount. I like *get* the opioid crisis now. Here." She pulls out a tube of Neosporin and unscrews the cap. I peel back the Band-Aid, and Sylvie squeezes a dollop onto the cut. "Yikes, it went pretty deep, huh? You sure this doesn't need stitches?"

"I think it's fine." I press the Band-Aid back down. "Thanks so much. And sorry for going through your stuff. I started panicking that some weird beach bacteria had gotten into my bloodstream, and it would make its way to my brain, and you guys would wake up tomorrow to find me dead! I guess I can be a bit of a hypochondriac."

Sylvie waves her hand. "No worries. Sorry I freaked. I'm a little jumpy. Divya brought gummies. You want one?"

"I'm good, but thank you." The last thing I need is to be even jumpier right now.

We all hang out in the living room a little while longer, but I'm totally lost in my head. I drift in and out of sleep all night in the king-size bed in one of the mansions' many guest rooms. In the morning, I help Jocelyn make pancakes for her birthday, and then we head to the marina to spend the day on Lina's family's yacht. But as we lie on the front of the boat in our bikinis, living what should be the literal *dream*, all I can think about is how last summer, Sylvie Avalon was prescribed a self-proclaimed "ridiculous" amount of the same pills that killed my sister.

After a lavish dinner at the Avalons' restaurant in Southampton, where we never so much as lay eyes on a bill, we take a sunset helicopter ride back to the city. I have to admit it's jarring to descend the grimy steps to the subway, my foot accidentally landing on a squashed cockroach carcass. But as I tap my phone and walk through the turnstile, there's also something strangely relieving about being back in charge of my own destiny: to pay a fare and know exactly what I'm getting in return, instead of wondering what I unofficially owe when I accept things for free.

I think of what Leah wrote in her internship log. *There's no such thing as a free lunch.* It's true, isn't it? I didn't pay *money* for the food I just ate, but that dinner at the Avalons' restaurant still cost me something. My *loyalty* was the price—because how could I ever divulge the truth about the car crash when I've also accepted so much free shit from them? I'd rather just pay for my own damn dinner instead of getting tangled up in this spider's web.

Leah got tangled up, too. She tried to break free by telling Emmeline about Duke's attack, but the spider ended up getting to her before she could escape. But who was the spider, and what, exactly, happened? I need to see those emails Leah was accidentally included on, and I can't get to them from her phone because her Sentinel account was deactivated.

The next morning, I put on the skirt and blouse I wore for my college admissions interviews and take the subway to East 50th Street, transferring from the L to an uptown E. The *Gotham Sentinel* building is a castle of concrete, six stories tall, with the name of the newspaper carved into the stone above the doorway. There's a sandwich shop next door, where I pause to check my reflection in the front window. I'm just an innocent college student, eager to learn more about a career in journalism.

I walk through the double doors and up to the security desk. "Hi there," I say to the guy on duty. "I'm going to the fourth floor?"

"You got ID?" he asks in a bored-sounding voice.

Two seconds in, and I'm already in major trouble. I have two pieces of ID on me, but one is mine, and the other is Leah's. Neither says Hailey Star. I reach into my bag for my wallet. Maybe he'll just glance at the photo to make sure it's me . . . or maybe he'll call up to Emmeline and tell her someone with the last name Falk is here to see her. Stalling for time while I think of what to do, I pretend to be having a hard time getting my own ID out of its see-through pocket. "S-sorry," I stammer. "One sec. It's really jammed in there."

The guy leans forward and peers through the see-through pocket. "No worries; you're good." He presses a button and nods to my left, where a green light flashes next to the turnstile. "You can head on up."

With trembling fingers, I close my wallet and toss it back in my bag. That was way too close of a call for my liking.

I've regained my composure by the time I reach the fourth floor. Rolling back my shoulders, I step out into the hallway, where I'm face to face with glass double doors emblazoned with the newspaper's name in frosted lettering. When the receptionist on the other side looks up, the glass doors make a clicking noise, and he motions for me to come through.

"I'm Hailey Star, here to meet with Emmeline Gilbane?"

"Right this way, Ms. Star." The receptionist—Miles, according to his name tag—gets up from his chair. He looks to be in his early twenties, with light-brown skin and a bleach-blond buzz cut. He motions for me to follow him.

He leads me into a corridor where the walls are lined with framed copies of the *Sentinel* and gestures to the first one on our left. "That was the front page of the inaugural issue," he says.

"Fifty years ago, right?" I ask.

The receptionist looks impressed. "How'd you know that?"

"I'm going to the anniversary party tomorrow."

"Oh my God, no way. I wasn't sure if I'd get an invite, but Emmeline just told me I could come." He does a little dance move with his arms.

"I guess I'll see you there," I say.

"I'm *pumped*. I've never been to Sunday Service before. Have you?"

My heart skips a beat. I've been putting off texting Duke to ask for the time and location of the party. Now I know I'll be returning to the place where Leah spent her last hours alive. "Once," I reply. "It was . . . nice."

"Welcome to the bullpen," Miles says, leading me into a large, open room where workers sit in rows at long desks. I see designers working on layouts, editors poring over galleys, writers slamming away at their keyboards.

"Wow," I murmur as my eyes try to soak it all in. I want to be part of the fray—maybe not here at the *Sentinel*, but in *some* newsroom, somewhere. I've always been good at writing, but that's not the main reason I was first drawn to journalism. Movies, TV shows, and even some politicians make journalists out to be sleazy and dishonest. I guess it can be true, like those British tabloid reporters who made Meghan Markle's life hell. But journalists also have the power to affect positive real-world change by shedding light on untold stories—like the *Boston Globe* reporters who uncovered widespread sexual abuse in the Catholic Church, and the *New York Times* reporters who exposed Harvey Weinstein as a serial sexual predator. Back in high school, Zayn and I reported on how our school's decision to only stock the girls' bathrooms with free menstrual products affected trans and nonbinary students. A trans eleventh grader told us the school once shot him down when he raised the issue on his own. But shortly after our piece went public, free pads and tampons started appearing in all the bathrooms.

The *Sentinel*'s bullpen is built panopticon-style, with stairs leading up to a mezzanine that rings the room. At the top of the steps, Miles stops in front of a frosted glass door:

    EMMELINE GILBANE

    EDITOR-IN-CHIEF

He knocks.

A familiar voice comes from inside. "Yes?"

"Hailey Star is here to see you."

"Lovely! She can come right in."

Emmeline sits at a brushed-steel desk the same color as her sleek silver bob. There's a keyboard and mouse in front of her, and a laptop and giant monitor off to one side. "Hailey! It's so nice to see you again." Her tone is pleasant, if not a little stiff.

The wall behind her is covered in framed photos of the editor-in-chief posing arm in arm with various important people; Gracie's and Rex's faces smile at me from a few of them. Emmeline gestures to the chair in front of her. "Come sit down."

"It's nice to see you again too, Ms. Gilbane. Thanks so much for meeting with me today, when I know you're busy getting ready for the anniversary party."

"It's my pleasure."

The first thing I do as I move toward the desk is scan the surface for Emmeline's phone. There it is, lying face-up near her elbow. I take a mental snapshot of the oxblood case.

"So, tell me," Emmeline says after we make a bit of small talk about my commute from Brooklyn, "how can I be most useful to you? What would you like to know?"

"I guess, um, everything! How did you first get into journalism?" As she starts to answer, I pull out my phone. Emmeline slows her speech and cocks an eyebrow. "I hope you don't mind if I take some notes as you talk," I say quickly. "I want to make sure I remember everything."

"Oh." Emmeline waves her hand. "Yes, of course."

She continues her story, but instead of opening my Notes app, I start a new text to Killian, who agreed to help me out today. I send him one word.

ME
GO.

KILLIAN
Coming right up.

Within seconds, Emmeline's phone vibrates and lights up with an email notification. She clicks the side button and keeps talking. Shoot.

ME
She looked, but didn't swipe.

KILLIAN
I'll try again.

The second time he sends her an email, she wrinkles her eyebrows at her phone, but she still doesn't take the bait. It isn't until the third email that Emmeline looks at the screen more closely, and her eyes go wide. I know what she sees there: a series of emails from a fake account Killian and I created this morning, with the subject line: "URGENT: Huge, timely scoop for the *Sentinel*." I'm fully aware there's nothing in the bodies of those emails, but Emmeline isn't.

"Excuse me," she says, and swipes the notification. Her passcode screen pops up. I watch her index finger like a hawk as she taps at the numbers. I immediately text the code to Killian so I don't forget it.

ME
040243
SUCCESS. TYSM.

KILLIAN
pleasure doing business with you

"Hmph." Emmeline frowns at her screen. "So weird," she mutters. "Sorry about that."

"Don't be sorry," I tell her in earnest, because I just got Emmeline's passcode. Now all I have to do is get her phone.

CHAPTER 20

Back at the loft, I hear sniffling.

It's after dinner, and I'm upstairs, deciding what to wear to the party tomorrow. The sounds aren't coming from Zayn, who's sitting at their desk with noise-canceling headphones on, editing their podcast and oblivious to the world around them, and they aren't coming from Killian, who, last I checked, was downstairs in the living room playing *The Sims* instead of working on his play.

Ivy was quiet during dinner, and barely touched her pad see ew from the Thai takeout place she usually loves. I press my ear to the velvet curtain that separates our two sleeping areas. My heart sinks. Ivy isn't just sniffling anymore; she's full-on crying.

"Ivy?"

The crying stops. She sniffs.

"What's wrong?"

Her voice is weak and strained. "I just had a bad day."

"Can I come in?"

"Okay."

Gently, I sweep the curtain to the side. Ivy sits curled up on her beanbag chair, her cheeks splotchy and wet. "Oh, Ivy." She covers her face with her hands. I rush to the beanbag chair and wrap my arms around her. "What's going on?"

"Y-you know my piece? At the gallery?"

"Yeah," I say, instantly defensive without even knowing the full story.

"Some people came in and said the meanest stuff about it."

"No."

She nods. "I should have known. I could tell right away they were classic, like, *art* people."

"How could you tell they were art people?"

"Because one of the guys had a mustache like this." Still sobbing, Ivy traces the shape of a handlebar mustache with curls at the end. It's so tragic and ridiculous and absolutely freaking adorable, it's impossible not to giggle. Ivy does the same.

"Sorry," I say.

"No, it's okay. I needed a laugh."

"Tell me what Mr. Mustache did."

Ivy sniffs. "So, he and his friend start checking out the exhibit. And you've been to the gallery: you know it's not that big of a space. When it's mostly empty—which it was—you can hear what people are saying as long as they're not whispering. So, they get to my photos, and Mr. Mustache is like"—she deepens her voice and tucks in her chin—"'If you're going to be this derivative, at least make the composition *slightly* compelling.'" Ivy presses her face into her palms as a fresh wave of sobs overtakes her.

"Oh no, Ivy, stop. Fuck Mr. Mustache."

"I tried not to let it bother me. I tried to just focus on my work the rest of the day. But, Noa, I've been spiraling. What if it is derivative? What if I'm incapable of having original ideas? What if my career is over before it's even begun, and—"

"Whoa, whoa, whoa." I hold her against my chest, whispering into her ear as her tears soak my shirt. "Your career is nowhere near over, Ivy."

"It is," she whines. "If my first-ever piece in a gallery is *that* uninspiring, the next ones are only going to be worse."

"Ivy, your piece was super inspiring."

She gives me a look. "You didn't even *get it* at first."

I sigh, thinking back to that night at the gallery. It was only two weeks ago, but it feels like eons have gone by. "I was in a very different headspace that night. And actually, it was your piece that helped me get out of it."

She sniffs. "What do you mean?"

Just then, Killian lets out a cry of victory. *"My Sims are finally doing it!"* he calls up from the kitchen.

We both roll our eyes. "Do you want to go up to the roof?" I ask Ivy.

She nods.

We leave the loft and climb the zigzagging stairs to the very top, to the metal door marked *ROOF*. I push it open and lead the way outside, where the sun is sinking toward Manhattan's jagged skyline in the distance. The sunset is stunning tonight, the sky a rippling watercolor of blue, pink, and purple. "Nature's so bisexual tonight," I joke as I gesture to the colors, which match the flag pin I wear on my backpack.

Ivy lets out a weak laugh as we wander over to the low cement wall at the edge of the roof. We lean on our forearms, side by side, and gaze out at the sunset. The glittering lights of Manhattan are so far away from here, like a fantasy world encased in a snow globe. It's one thing to stare at it from a distance, but it's another to be trapped inside the snow globe. When it gets turned upside down and shaken, you end up losing your bearings—your whole sense of self.

"So, what were you saying downstairs, about being in a different headspace when you first saw the piece?"

"Oh yeah." I take a deep breath, only to find that I'm already calm. "Things between me and my sister were always kind of messy, including when she died. And for a while, I hated myself for it."

Ivy lays a hand over mine, the softest hand I've ever felt in my life. Like the petal of a lily. Her touch—so safe, familiar, and pure—is everything my time with the Avalons is *not*. With a small smile, I keep going. I tell her everything I told Zayn over FaceTime from my backyard in New Jersey, only now, it's with a newfound confidence that branches down to the tips of my fingers and toes. "We both felt guilty about the way we treated each other, and that's fair. But we're not, like, terrible people. It's like the message of your piece: being a human is complicated, and that's okay. So . . ." I turn to her. "Thank you for helping me realize that."

She's teary again, but in a happy way. I'm amazed at just how beautiful her eyes look up close—how the light of the setting sun makes her chestnut-brown pupils seem flecked with gold. Or maybe she just sparkles on her own. "You're welcome," she says, her voice breathy. It catches in her throat. "And, Noa?"

"Hmm?"

"For the record, you couldn't be a terrible person if you

tried." She squeezes my hand, and sparks fly up my arm and down my body like wildfire. As we share a smirk, I step closer. Our faces are almost touching, my eyes in line with her silver septum ring.

Her free hand finds my waist, and I shiver as the pad of her thumb traces a graceful arc around my hip bone. She's wearing a muscle tank that shows off the sides of her torso, and I put my hand on the warm skin there, my palm resting on the delicate black fir tree tattooed on her rib cage. When I lift my chin, her lips are there waiting for mine.

Kissing Ivy feels like I'm floating off the roof and into the sky. I follow her lead as she opens her mouth, the heat of her tongue matching the fire blazing inside me. I pull her even closer, deepening the kiss. A kiss that isn't some secret form of currency—just the magic between two girls in the glow of a bisexual sunset. Whatever happens between me and Ivy from here, I promise myself to bottle this moment forever: the feeling of being with someone who likes me for me, and not for what I can do for them. This feeling, and those kinds of people, *exist*. I wish I could have reminded Leah before she died, but tomorrow night, I'm going to do my best to show her.

CHAPTER 21

When I turn onto Park Avenue, my eyes find the red carpet cascading down the steps of Sunday Service. It's Friday evening, and in front of the old church, valets open car doors for guests in tuxes and gowns. Photographers dart around on the sidewalk, the flashbulbs of their cameras going off. Curious pedestrians who failed to score an invite to the *Gotham Sentinel*'s fiftieth anniversary party slow down to survey the scene.

I make my way toward the restaurant in the black strapless tulle gown I wore to my cousin's wedding. It isn't until I get to the red carpet that I force myself to look at Duke, waiting for me at the base of the steps, his legs slightly spread and his hands in the pockets of his deep-blue tuxedo pants. He flashes me the same boyish gap-toothed grin that wooed me when I first met him. I return the smile as hatred burns in my chest. I can't look at Duke without seeing him forcing himself on my sister—without hearing him say those awful words to her. *Other girls don't say no.*

"Hey, you," I bring myself to say.

"Hey, *you*." He takes my hand, and the next thing I know, he's twirling me around, whistling to show his approval. I know he's trying to put the night of the car crash behind us, and it sickens me that I have to act like it's working.

A flurry of flashbulbs goes off as I spin. Duke jerks his head toward the restaurant. "Look at us, back where it all began."

"Should I challenge you to tic-tac-toe again?"

"Hmm." He steps closer. "I can think of some other ways to have fun."

When he reaches out and cups my jaw, I know what's coming. "Not in front of all the cameras." I turn my head so his lips collide with my cheek instead. Even *that* makes me feel contaminated, but it's better than having his mouth on mine.

We walk up the front steps, Duke's hand on the small of my back until he yanks open the heavy wooden door for me. Again, I have the sensation of tumbling into some kind of underworld, the place as dark and full of candles as the first time I was here. The only difference is that just beyond the check-in desk, there's a ten-foot-tall cardboard replica of a *Gotham Sentinel* front page, where the main headline proclaims: *MANHATTAN'S MOST POWERFUL PAPER FOR 50 YEARS AND COUNTING*. I wander over to look at the sign while Duke gives our names to the hostess, but it isn't long before his hands are on my shoulders, holding on firmly.

He talks straight into my ear, so I can hear him over the pounding music. "Fifty years and counting thanks to us."

"Thanks to us?" I call back.

"*Us*. Like, my family."

"What do you mean?"

"My grandpa was explaining it to me the other night. We were having one of our training sessions where he teaches me how the whole business works, since eventually, I'm gonna be running it, you know? Anyway, I always thought newspapers made money just from people, you know, buying the newspapers. Which they do. But a way bigger portion of their money comes from—"

"Ads, right?"

"Oh. You knew that already."

I lift my chin. "I want to go into journalism, remember?" When Leah announced she'd be interning at the *Sentinel*, I thought I'd have to give up on my dream of becoming an investigative reporter. Now I'm proud that my plan is to follow in her footsteps. She wanted us to do this together.

"Oh yeah. Well, we can definitely hook you up with a job at the *Sentinel*, if that's what you want." Duke squeezes my shoulders. "Because you know who the paper's biggest advertising client is?"

"Who?" I ask, even though I can already guess what he's going to say.

"The Avalon Hospitality Group. We're basically keeping this paper afloat." He lowers his voice. "Don't tell anyone, but it's great for us, 'cause it means they're always gonna print good things about the company. No one from the *Sentinel* is gonna blast us for building a new hotel on some stupid park. Genius, right?"

"Hmm."

"And it gets even better." Duke can barely contain his gleeful laugh. "When Sunday Service first opened, there were these religious freaks who kept protesting us turning a church into a restaurant. *Sooo* dumb, but they kinda started going viral. So my mom calls Emmeline Gilbane, and Emmeline gets a reporter to dig up some dirt on the guy who was leading the protests. They wrote this whole story on how the guy had been cheating on his wife for decades. Some Christian, right?" Duke snorts.

My skin is crawling, and not because some protester cheated on his wife. From the sounds of it, the Avalons aren't just buying space in the *Sentinel* to advertise their hotels and restaurants; they're also buying good press, and the power to downplay their scandals. It's all so twisted. A journalist's job is supposed to be reporting the truth—not writing flattering stories or strategic hit pieces that entice rich people like the Avalons to keep forking over money.

I think about Leah's *Sentinel* clips from last summer. Is that all she was hired to do? I remember one of the more heartbreaking entries in her internship log, where she wondered how much her hard work actually mattered. She'd fallen in love with society reporting, only to learn she was nothing more than a cog in a corrupt machine. *It is too late to find a replacement,* her own boss had written back to her when she'd asked to be excused from the grand opening of an Avalon-owned restaurant. *In any case, maintaining professional boundaries with sources is a crucial part of this job, and you must learn that.* Rich of Emmeline to cite "professionalism" as a reason that Leah had to work that night.

As Duke slides his hands down the sides of my torso, I think about what happened between Leah and Duke—and how the sick, symbiotic relationship between the Avalons and the *Sentinel* played into it. Leah was never into Duke; she saw through him from the start, which is more than I can say for myself. She'd been with enough guys in high school and college to pick up on his sleazy vibes, no problem. But the deeper she sank into the role she was hired to play, the harder it became for my sister to say no to him.

Duke smacks my ass, and I gasp. It takes everything in me not to knee him between the legs.

"Someone's on edge," he says. "Champagne?"

"No thanks."

He sidles up beside me. "How about we find somewhere private, then?"

"Duke, we just got here."

"So?"

"Don't you two look dashing!"

I spin around, grateful to see Sylvie gliding toward us, with Jocelyn following along in her wake. Sylvie's in a bright orange statement gown with a slit that goes up to her waist, and her hair is twisted into an elaborate braided chignon. Jocelyn wears a comparatively subdued pale pink number, her long blond hair in a sleek ponytail. Abandoning Duke's side, I hurry over to greet the girls.

Jocelyn lights up when she sees me, and steps out from behind Sylvie to hug me first. "I missed you!" she says sincerely.

Sylvie scoffs. "Um, you guys saw each other two days ago."

Jocelyn carries on as though she didn't hear the comment; she's too busy extricating my wrist from around her shoulder. "How's your hand? Is it all right?"

"I haven't looked under the Band-Aid, but I think so."

She pouts. "I still feel *so* bad for dropping the bottle and then pulling you down into the sand with me."

"Sounds hot." Duke appears at my side again, waggling his eyebrows. I want to rip them clean off his face.

"Actually, I cut myself on glass," I say flatly, holding up the bandaged palm he hasn't even asked me about yet.

"Oh shit. You okay?"

"I'm fine."

"Sorry we're a bit late," Sylvie purrs as she hugs her brother. "Joc and I went to get our hair done, and this whole situation took forever." She gestures to the side of her head.

"No prob," Duke replies. "We just got here."

Jocelyn smiles placidly at Duke, and I wonder what's going through her head, now that she knows he lied about the car crash. Not that she was surprised to hear he'd pinned it on Owen, or that Sylvie was complicit in the same lie. From the sounds of it, that kind of behavior was normal for the Avalons. I remember what Jocelyn told me on the beach in Montauk, her face glowing ominously in the firelight: *There's nothing that family won't do to protect each other.*

What *else* does Jocelyn know?

"Drinks, anyone?" Sylvie asks.

Duke elbows me playfully. "I think this one could loosen up a bit." He's clearly annoyed that I've snubbed him twice already since we've gotten here. Leave it to a guy to blame his rejection on something being wrong with the woman who turned him down.

We press deeper into the already-crowded restaurant. I recognize the mayor and her husband; at least two cast members from *The Real Housewives of New York City*, which Leah used to watch religiously; and a few famous actors and models who'd probably have me feeling starstruck if I weren't distracted by much more important things. To ensure I'm not left alone with Duke, I make constant conversation with Sylvie and Jocelyn as we make our way around the crowded space. I ask them a million questions about their outfits, their jewelry, the trip they're taking to Paris at the end of the summer to shop for their fall wardrobes.

"You should totally come," Sylvie says. "We'll make it a girls' trip: me, you, Joc, Divya, Lina. We already have a suite booked, so it's no big deal to add another person."

"That would be amazing," I say as I scan the room for Emmeline Gilbane's silver bob. But the next familiar face who comes our way isn't the editor-in-chief of the *Sentinel*.

"My darlings!" Gracie parts the crowd and strides toward us with outstretched arms. She hugs us each in turn, embracing me just as tightly as she did her own children. She holds me at arm's length and squeezes my shoulders. "Hailey, honey, Emmeline was just telling me what a lovely meeting you two had the other day. She said you have a very promising future ahead of you."

"I was just telling Hailey that we should get her a job at the *Sentinel*," Duke tells Gracie.

She smiles at me, the corners of her eyes crinkling. "I'm certain I'll be able to work something out when you're done with college. If I can help a smart, young woman get ahead in her career, I always will."

Her words trigger an eerie sense of déjà vu. She said something similar to Leah at the nineteen twenties–themed open house last summer. At the time, Leah believed that Gracie genuinely wanted to help her. She didn't see the offer for what it really was: a chance for the Avalons to control her, and in doing so, to maximize their positive press. Now they want to do the same thing with me.

Rex Avalon excuses himself from a conversation and wanders over to us. He's dressed in a white tuxedo that matches his hair and goatee. After we've all greeted each other, Gracie turns to her father-in-law and puts a hand on his arm. "Rex, we were just discussing how Hailey would love to work for the *Sentinel* when she finishes college. She had a wonderful meeting with Emmeline the other day."

"Oh yeah?" Rex surveys me up and down. "Good. The world needs more journalists with their heads screwed on straight."

"Hailey definitely has a good head on her shoulders," Sylvie chimes in. She turns to me. "When you work for the *Sentinel*, we'll brainstorm so many great story ideas. I'll obviously bring you to all the best events. *Ooh!* Maybe we'll do a trip to one of our resorts to celebrate."

Gracie beams at us. "Girls, I'm already loving this collab."

I've listened to Leah's Voice Notes and read every page of her internship log. This is the same game they played with her. I don't blame my sister for falling into their trap. Now I'm going to get us both out. "Speaking of the *Sentinel*, has anyone seen Emmeline?" I ask. "I was hoping to find her and thank her again for speaking with me."

"She's very popular tonight, as you can imagine." Gracie looks back over her shoulder. "Last I saw, she was somewhere back there in the middle of the fray."

I turn to Duke. "I'm gonna see if I can find her, okay? I'll be back as soon as I can." Before he has a chance to reply, I peel away from the group and start to make my way through the dense crowd.

When I finally spot Emmeline, she's deep in conversation with a woman I've seen in a movie before. My eyes travel up and down the editor-in-chief's fitted silver gown. Her dress doesn't have any pockets, and she isn't carrying a bag. Seemingly ready to wrap up the conversation, the actress gives Emmeline a one-armed hug and an air kiss on each cheek, but before she goes, the editor-in-chief motions for her to wait just one second. She cranes her neck, snaps her fingers, and calls someone's name.

Miles, the receptionist I met at the *Sentinel* headquarters, jumps to attention. He darts away from whomever he was talking to and races over to his boss. Emmeline gestures for Miles to take a picture of her and the actress. *This* must be the reason she invited him to the party at the last minute: she needed a personal photographer, just in case the professionals weren't nearby to snap her with every A-lister in attendance. Nodding enthusiastically, Miles pulls out a phone from the inside pocket of his lavender dinner jacket.

My heart leaps as I recognize Emmeline's oxblood case.

As soon as the actress drifts away, I seize my chance to slither up to the editor-in-chief. "Hi, Ms. Gilbane!"

"Oh, hi, Hailey." She smiles at me, but with a hint of impatience. Out of the corner of my eye, I can already see more party guests queuing up to greet their host.

"I just wanted to come over and say thank you again for meeting with me the other day. I learned so much."

"It was my pleasure. Anything you need as you move forward in your career, let me know."

Because you think I'm dating Duke, and you need to stay in the Avalons' good graces. "Hey, Miles." I wave to him.

He raises his eyebrows as though he's surprised I remembered his name, but he nods at me all the same. "Hey!"

"Would you mind taking a picture of us, too?"

Miles shrugs. "Okay."

I flash Emmeline a bashful smile. "You don't mind, do you?"

"Of course not. Are you sure you don't want it on your phone?"

I'm very sure. "It's in Duke's pocket! Not enough room in here." I pat my clutch, feeling the hard shell of my phone case beneath the fabric. "I'll find Miles after and have him send it to me."

"All right," Emmeline says, evidently ready to move on to the next interaction. We smile for the camera, the flash goes off, and Miles gives us a thumbs-up.

"Thanks so much, Ms. Gilbane!" I shake her hand. "Hopefully, I'll see you again soon!"

The editor-in-chief is already striding over to embrace another guest, and she waves for Miles to come with her. I'll have to catch up with him later; hopefully, when he's had a few drinks and he's less likely to realize when anything's amiss.

I'm making my way through the crowd to find Jocelyn or Sylvie—really, anyone who isn't Duke—when a hand lands heavily on my bare shoulder. "Why, hello there."

When I turn around, my stomach turns to stone. I should have amended my goal just now: anyone who wasn't Duke or Tommy Sunday. The chef leers at me in his white jacket, lifting his matching hat to rake his nails through his sweaty hair.

"Hailey, right? You're friends with the Avalons? We met here the other night." He glances brazenly at my chest, and I uncross my arms to make my cleavage less pronounced. Gross, but at least Tommy Sunday makes it obvious that he's a sleazy piece of shit. That's one dark-as-hell silver lining.

"Yeah, hi." I give him a pinched smile and jerk my thumb

over my shoulder. "Um, I was actually just on my way to find them, so—"

His hand closes around my wrist. "What happened to your palm?" he asks. A fleck of spit hits me in the eye.

"I cut myself on some glass." I try to pull my hand away, but Tommy holds on tight.

"That sounds serious," he says in a patronizing voice. Then he cocks an eyebrow. His lips curl into a smirk. "What kind of trouble did you get yourself into?"

"*Hailey!* There you are!" Out of nowhere, Jocelyn practically body-checks three people out of the way so she can hightail it over to me. She grabs my arm and yanks me sideways, hard enough to free me from Tommy's clutches. Relief rushes through me. Jocelyn gives Tommy a quick wave. "I've been looking for this one everywhere! Gotta steal her for something important—sorry!" She tugs me through the crowd, toward the other side of the restaurant.

"Where are we going?" I ask Jocelyn.

"Away from *him*." She looks behind us. "Okay, phew. He's talking to Rex now." She stops hustling and lets go of my arm. "You okay? I looked over and I saw him come up to you, and then I saw him grab your wrist, and I was like, *Oh God. She needs saving.*"

I don't have any words; I just throw my arms around Jocelyn and hug her as tight as I can.

"Your heart—it's racing," she says.

"I was scared when he wouldn't let go of me." It isn't until I speak the words that I realize just how true they are. My pulse pounds behind my eyes, and my hands are numb and shaky. My lips tremble when I try to say more. First Duke, then Tommy...

The weight of their sleazy advances is adding up, and the pressure is starting to suffocate me.

Jocelyn looks like she's going to cry, too. "Oh, Hailey."

She squeezes me even tighter, and that's when I decide to tell her what's been weighing on me. "Hey, Joc?"

"Yeah?"

"Remember when we were on the beach the other night, and you said the Avalons would do anything to protect each other?"

Her body goes rigid as a board. She lets go of me and steps back. Her shoulders are up by her ears. "You didn't tell them I said that, did you?"

"No—oh my God, no." She starts to drop her shoulders—but then I ask her my next question. "Did Leah Falk really die by suicide last summer?"

CHAPTER 22

Even in the candlelight, I can tell Jocelyn's face is white as a sheet. "Why are you asking about Leah Falk?" she asks.

I can't tell Jocelyn who I really am. Not yet, at least. If word gets back to the Avalons before I've stolen Emmeline's phone, I'll be banished from this whole world before I ever figure out what happened to my sister. "Because she and Duke had a thing last summer, right?" I swallow hard. "I just... wanted to know more."

Jocelyn nods tentatively. "Th-they dated."

My stomach churns. "I was just curious what really happened. At the City Crop thing, Sylvie said Leah overdosed on oxy, but I know the Avalons lie sometimes, so, I was just wondering..."

"W-wondering what?"

Blood pounds in my ears, blocking out the chatter, the music, the clinking of glasses—everything but the six inches of space between my face and Jocelyn's. I try as hard as I can to keep my voice even. "Just . . . wondering if that's what really happened."

Jocelyn blinks at me, and as she picks at her bottom lip, I imagine gears turning in her head. "Sylvie said she overdosed?"

"Yeah."

Jocelyn nods. "That's what happened."

"Are you sure?"

She gives me a pleading look as she digs her nail into her lip. "What is it, Joc?"

She squeezes her eyes shut. "Just ask the Avalons, okay?"

My pulse thumps. "But the Avalons lie. You were the one who told me that. Why should I ask them?"

"Because I just don't want anything to do with it, okay?" When she opens her eyes, a tear leaks down her face. She wipes it away instantly. "Sorry," she adds weakly.

"It's okay," I reply, even though it's not. I wish I could pull the secrets out of her, but this conversation has clearly freaked her out, and I don't want to ruin the alliance we've built. Besides, a flash of lavender just caught my eye. Miles is carefully charting a course across the restaurant, a very full martini glass in his hand. He must be off picture duty now that the bulk of the guests have arrived and the professionals who were snapping photos outside have made their way in. Hopefully, he still has Emmeline's phone in his pocket. "Hey, there's someone over there I need to go talk to," I tell Jocelyn. "Can I come find you in a bit?"

She nods eagerly. "Of course."

I squeeze her hand. "And thank you again for saving me back there."

"Anytime."

After making sure Duke isn't anywhere near me, I take off

in Miles's direction. On the way, I pass Owen, who has a bandage over his eyebrow and another on his cheek. He nods at me knowingly. Two members of the same complicit club. Shuddering, I keep weaving through the crowd until I find Miles seated at a table with a sharply dressed man I remember seeing in the bullpen yesterday. Somehow, in the minute or so since I first saw him with the martini, his glass is now half empty.

"Hey, Miles!"

"Hailey! Come hang out!" His jovial tone and the way he sweeps his arm through the air suggest that this probably isn't his first drink of the night. Miles kicks out a chair for me, and I sit. He turns to the other guy at the table and shouts in his ear. "This is Hailey! She's a friend of the *Avalons*." He says the family's name with an air of tremendous importance that makes me cringe, but the other guy raises his eyebrows, apparently impressed. "And this is Dante," Miles continues, clapping his hand on the guy's shoulder. "He's the *Sentinel*'s *ah-maaazing* new style reporter."

Dante laughs. "You're being very kind."

"It's true," Miles counters. He leans over to me conspiratorially. "Dante let me call in this dinner jacket so I could 'write a review,' right, Dante?" Miles makes air quotes with his fingers. "It's nice, right? Normally, it's like three thousand dollars, but I got it for free. All I have to do is write some dumb story about how much I love it."

"What would happen if you didn't actually love it?" I ask.

Miles looks at Dante, who smirks and pats the back of Miles's hand. "We can always find *something* positive to say about any product we try. Luckily, this jacket is *genuinely* so chic." Dante laughs lightly.

Forcing a smile at their questionable ethics, I turn to Miles. "Hey, um, do you mind if I borrow Emmeline's phone to send myself those photos you took?"

"Oh yeah. Sure." He reaches into his jacket, pulls out the phone, and unlocks it. "What's your number?"

"Uh . . . d'you mind if I see the photos first?" I hold out my hand, praying he'll turn over the phone. If he doesn't, I'm going to have to find a way to pickpocket him later, and that is *way* less appealing than Miles handing the phone over willingly.

"Sure. I took a few. Send yourself whatever you want." He shrugs, passes it to me, and picks up his drink again.

Now there's another problem. I need time—and, ideally, privacy—to go through Emmeline's emails. For all I know, the editor-in-chief could walk up behind me at any moment and catch me scrolling through her inbox. I stare blankly at the awkward picture of me and Emmeline as I consider my options. Then I have an idea.

"Ugh, the service is so bad in this spot, for some reason. Can I try taking it somewhere else to see if it's any better? I won't go far—and I won't be long."

Miles furrows his brow at me.

"Sorry," I add. "Emmeline Gilbane is just . . . my hero."

Dante punches Miles playfully in the arm. "That's the most wholesome shit I've ever heard. Let her take the phone. We'd just be sitting here the whole time, anyway."

Miles sighs. "Fine. But you have to bring me another dirty martini on your way back."

"Done," I promise. *Thank God.* I leap to my feet, clutching the phone to my heart. It's mine—at least for a few minutes. I weave my way to the nearest spiral staircase—the one that leads to the North Lounge, where I was seated when I first came to Sunday Service. Up here, I'll be able to look through the phone in private. Settling into the deepest, darkest corner of the balcony, I remember my initial impression of the restaurant: you could be anyone here. And anyone could get away with anything.

It's a good thing I peeped Emmeline's passcode, because her screen has gone black in the time it took me to get up here. I tap the numbers, and it works. I'm in.

I've never had so much adrenaline coursing through me all at once. I can *feel* how close I am to the answer. I open Emmeline's email app and toggle to her work address. With a deep breath, I type Leah's name into the search bar.

CHAPTER 23

There are dozens of results. Most are emails from Leah last summer, with the enthusiastic subject lines of a journalism intern desperate to please her boss.

> Should I cover this party? Sounds interesting!

> First draft is ready!

> Revisions back to you—your notes were so helpful!

But it's the email thread at the very top of the list that catches my eye. According to the time stamp, the messages were sent the day before Leah died, not long after my sister texted Emmeline about the assault. The thread appears to include Leah, Emmeline, and . . . Rex Avalon? The subject line is "problem."

My heart thuds like a jackhammer. Did Leah decide to tell

Rex what Duke had done at the Haven? But then I remember what Leah wrote in her internship log: that she'd been accidentally included on emails that weren't meant for her eyes. I tap the thread to see the messages for myself, and the more I read, the farther my jaw drops.

Subject: problem

From: Emmeline Gilbane
To: Rex Avalon; Leah Falk

Hi Rex,

We have a problem. I'd normally go to Gracie, but given her closeness to the issue, I wanted to come to you. I understand that last night, Sylvie invited Leah to cover an event at the Haven where one of your GM's kids was DJing. You know I'm happy to send my reporters to as many of your events as you'd like, but this morning, Leah texted me to say that a source behaved inappropriately with her. I think we can both guess who it was, and that she didn't specify his name because she knows of the *Sentinel*'s close relationship with your family. I will gladly continue maintaining my side of our arrangement, however, I'm sure neither of us wants any assault allegations on our hands. Will you have a word with your team?

Thanks.
Emmeline

Subject: problem

From: Rex Avalon
To: Emmeline Gilbane; Leah Falk

I'm dealing with too many problems to worry about my grandson's extracurricular activities. I'll tell Gracie to butter the girl up with a press trip so she forgets it ever happened. Maybe the Maldives property.

Subject: problem

From: Leah Falk
To: Emmeline Gilbane; Rex Avalon

Was I supposed to be included on this?

Subject: problem

From: Emmeline Gilbane
To: Rex Avalon; Leah Falk

Leah, please disregard the previous messages. You were not meant to be included. My apologies.

Subject: problem

From: Rex Avalon
To: Emmeline Gilbane; Leah Falk

I should have mentioned above that I have no idea what "arrangement" you're referring to, Emmeline. Leah, I'm very sorry to hear what happened last night, and will ensure that it doesn't happen again.

Subject: problem

From: Rex Avalon
To: Emmeline Gilbane

YOU INCLUDED HER?

Subject: problem

From: Emmeline Gilbane
To: Rex Avalon

It was an accident. I'm so sorry.

Subject: problem

From: Rex Avalon
To: Emmeline Gilbane

Call me ASAP.

Oh my God. Oh . . . my . . . God. This has to be it: the story Leah wanted to pitch to the *New York Times*'s social justice section, and that she wanted me to help her report. According to these emails, there was an "arrangement" wherein the *Sentinel* promised to send its reporters to the Avalons' events. And when that "arrangement" provided the backdrop for Duke to assault Leah, Rex Avalon, founder and CEO of the Avalon Hospitality Group, suggested they sweep it all under the rug by "buttering" my sister up with a press trip to the Maldives. This wasn't your run-of-the-mill scoop: it was a bombshell—the kind of story that could bring down a whole business empire. Especially since Leah couldn't have been the only woman to experience this kind of manipulation, and my sister must have realized that, too. Duke admitted it when he assaulted her—when, as Leah tried to resist him, he growled, *Other girls don't say no.* How many other wide-eyed aspiring journalists have been preyed upon by the Avalons and their inner circle—people like Tommy Sunday?

The pieces of Leah's last days are finally coming together to reveal a horrifying picture. The Avalons are pros at covering up their wrongdoings, as Duke made clear when he crashed his BMW. But when Emmeline accidentally included Leah on these emails, the Avalons got themselves caught in the act—and that was something they couldn't cover up.

Not unless they could silence Leah forever.

I need to get this evidence into my own hands. I glance at the time on Emmeline's phone, wondering how long I've been up here. I stand and dart to the railing, where I peer down at Miles's table. He's still sitting there, talking and laughing with Dante. Phew. I sit back down. Should I forward the email thread to myself, and then delete the evidence from the Sent folder, or would Emmeline still have a way of finding out what I did? Maybe screenshots would be safer.

"What are you looking at?" someone asks.

My heart rockets into my throat, and I drop Emmeline's phone. It bounces on the carpet, and lands face up at Duke's feet.

CHAPTER 24

I reach for the phone, but I'm not fast enough. Duke drags it away with the toe of his shoe and smiles mischievously. "Uh-uh, no more phone time. You've barely hung out with me all night."

"I-I'm sorry," I stammer, casting around for an explanation. "I had to send an important message, and I couldn't focus down there."

"An important message? Who are you texting right now, the president?" Then, to my horror, he squats and plucks the phone off the carpet. Standing up again, he towers over me, his muscular body filling the narrow space. The light casts sinister shadows beneath his eyes as he reads what's on the screen. As his eyes dart back and forth, Duke's mischievous smile becomes a look of shock. "Wait. How did you get this?" He flips the phone over, seemingly noticing the unfamiliar phone case for the first time. "Whose phone is this? What's going on?"

I can't tell if he's angry or scared or both. All I know is that I need to get that phone back.

"That's mine." I reach for it, but he jerks it away easily. I'm no match for him physically, and we both know that.

"No, it isn't," he snaps. "What the fuck are you doing with this?"

"It's none of your business, okay? Please, just give it back." I'm finally getting close to the truth, and I'm not about to lose my strongest piece of evidence. I stand up and roll my shoulders back. "Duke, please—*oof.*"

He shoves me hard. With a cry of pain that nobody below us can hear, my back collides with the wall, and I slump down onto the banquette. That's when sharp, cold fear slices through me. Nobody knows we're up here, and it's too dark for anyone to see us.

"I think it *is* my fucking business when my family's involved." He cracks his knuckles and shakes his head. "I saw you looking over the railing a second ago, and I knew you were up to something shady. You've been acting weird all night." Shit. Duke must have spotted me when I went to the railing to check on Miles. Why did I have to do that? Why didn't I just take the screenshots?

Pushing down my rising panic, I lunge for the phone again, but Duke shoves me harder into the wall.

"*Oof.*"

The impact knocks the air from my lungs, and I keel over, gasping. While I struggle to catch my breath, Duke crouches in front of me, seizes the back of my hair, and yanks my head up. I can't push down my panic any longer. If I don't get out of here, with or without the phone, Duke could seriously hurt me. He could kill me. And then he'd call his lawyer and cover it up. Make it look like some kind of accident.

"I'll ask you again," he growls. "What the fuck are you doing reading those emails?"

My scalp sears with pain where he pulls on my hair, my neck aching from the unnatural angle. I try to wriggle my body off the bench, but he grabs my upper arm with the hand that's holding the phone, pinning me firmly in place.

He shakes me. "Are you going to answer me, or what?"

Both his hands squeeze tighter. The pain is almost unbearable. There's no world where I can fight back, or even run away from him. My voice is my only available weapon. "I know what you did to Leah Falk."

"You don't know shit."

"She was an intern at the *Sentinel* last summer. She started covering your family's parties. You were into her. She went along with it because she felt like she had to."

"Went along with it? She was into me too."

I believed the same story when Duke first mentioned the forehead kisses, but now that I've read Leah's internship log, I know the truth. "She wasn't into you. She was scared to say no to you because she worked for your family's personal propaganda machine, and your mom promised to help her in her career."

"You don't know what the fuck you're talking about."

"Yes, I do." I know it all too well, what it's like to fake an attraction to Duke because you feel like you have to. Leah was desperate to get her career journey back on track after a wild first year of college; I was desperate for answers about her death. We both cringed at Duke's touch but let it happen all the same. I need him to see that. "You remember when Leah told you how much she liked it when you kissed her forehead?" I ask him.

"How the fuck do you know that?"

"She was trying to take it slow—to let you think you were getting somewhere with her, without her having to *actually* kiss you." I want to cry just thinking about my sister in that situation, doing the math in her head, adding up how much she was willing to compromise, how much she was willing to lose. "She thought you were a creep. And she was right. I know what you did to her in the bathroom at the Haven. You decided you were getting what you wanted, whether she liked it or not. The next morning, she reported you to her boss. Emmeline emailed your grandpa to tell him what happened, but she accidentally copied Leah on the email. Leah saw your grandpa's response about sweeping it all under the rug. Your family was screwed, so *one of you* killed her." I don't know that last part for certain, but Jocelyn's reaction to my questions about Leah sure made it seem correct.

The longer I've talked, the tighter Duke has gripped my hair. My eyes water from the pain. When he speaks, his voice is low, dangerous. "How do you know all that?"

"Did you kill her, Duke?"

"Shut up. I asked how you knew all that."

"And *I* asked if you killed her. Did you give her the oxy, Duke? I'll tell you if you tell me."

"I'm not playing another one of your stupid games, Hailey." He yanks me so hard that I want to cry out, but I feel my sister here with me, and that helps me fight through the pain.

"My name isn't Hailey, you asshole."

"What?"

"You didn't hear me? I said my name—isn't—Hailey."

"What the hell is it, then?"

"It's Noa. Noa Falk."

"Falk? Like—"

"Leah Falk's sister? Yeah."

The revelation makes him loosen his grip on my hair and my arm—only by a little, but it's all the window I need. I draw my head back, preparing to strike. Just like Leah did in the bathroom that night, I swing my head forward as hard as I can, my skull colliding hard with Duke's nose.

He howls in pain. His body recoils; he crashes into the railing behind him. I'm free. I launch myself to my feet, but not before scooping Emmeline's phone off the ground. Now I'm the one towering over Duke, who's slumped against the railing, his hands cupping his nose. Blood streams down his chin. Sniveling, he looks pathetic.

"Is it broken?" he moans. "What did you do?"

I know I need to get the hell away from him, but I can't resist a parting shot. "I taught you a lesson," I fire back at him. "Don't fuck with the Falk sisters."

CHAPTER 25

I don't look back as I race to the spiral staircase. At the bottom, I forward myself the email thread. Who cares if she sees the evidence? Now that Duke knows my identity, the jig is up. I toss Emmeline's phone on the nearest table, next to a crumpled cocktail napkin swaddling a half-eaten latke with caviar on top. I hate this place. I hate these people. But I still need to know who killed Leah, and I don't have long to figure it out—just the window of time between now and whenever Duke finds his family and tells them who I really am.

Tick, tick, tick.

With each passing second, the curtain gets lower and lower on my access to the Avalons. I scan the packed room, but I don't see anyone I recognize in the crowd. That's when a flash of orange catches my eye.

Sylvie and Jocelyn are making their way toward the exit with flutes of champagne in their hands. I pull out my phone, open the Voice Notes app, and preemptively hit the Record button.

This might be the last chance I'll have to interview these people, and I'm going to make the most of it. I'm going to tell the story Leah died trying to report—and more. Because the Avalons didn't just try to cover up a sexual assault allegation. They killed my sister to keep the truth from getting out.

In the early stages of an investigative reporting project, you want to be vague about your angle. Your sources will reveal more when they don't know what you're looking for. It isn't until the end, when you've built up a rock-solid body of evidence, that you go in hard—that you needle them for exactly what you need to know. I've seen the internship log, and I've seen the emails. Now I'm ready to get my answers.

I follow Sylvie and Jocelyn out the door. They're lingering halfway down the steps. Sylvie leans against the railing with a cigarette in one hand and her champagne glass in the other. Jocelyn stands in front of her, sipping her drink. Sylvie has the same bored look that she did when I met her. Back then, I challenged her to tic-tac-toe. Tonight, I'm going to shock her in a different way.

"Hey, Sylvie."

The two girls peer up at me. Sylvie blows out a mouthful of smoke. "There you are. Duke was looking for you."

"I know. He found me."

Jocelyn crosses her arms. She looks uneasy.

Sylvie takes another drag and exhales. "What's up?"

"There's something I have to ask you."

"You seem stressed." Sylvie holds out her glass. "Want some champagne?"

"No. I want to know what happened to Leah Falk."

Jocelyn squeezes her eyes shut and hikes her shoulders up

to her ears. She looks like she's trying to force her body to evaporate on the spot.

Sylvie looks confused. "Leah Falk? The *Sentinel* reporter?"

"That's the one."

"She's that girl Duke was seeing last summer," she replies coolly. "We've talked about her. She's the one who died by suicide—an overdose."

I let out a sarcastic laugh. "Yeah, see, that's what I thought, too. But isn't it weird that she didn't leave a note? Or have any history of suicidal thoughts? Or a prescription for oxycodone?"

Sylvie takes another drag of her cigarette, but her arm is stiff, the movement unnatural. "I don't know. Why are you asking me?"

"Because it's *also* weird," I walk down a step, "that two days before she died, your brother sexually assaulted her. And one day before she died, she found out that the *Sentinel* and your family have a little 'agreement' to guarantee you good press and cover up any *bad* press—and that your grandfather had a plan to silence her by 'buttering her up' with a press trip to the fucking Maldives."

Sylvie's confused expression starts to look more like Jocelyn's, a crack in her cool façade giving way to an underlying fear. She lets out a shaky giggle. "Hailey, what the hell? I literally have no idea what you're talking about."

"Really? No idea?" I take another step toward her. "That's not what it sounds like in the recording I found of you and Leah talking hours before she died. You were here, at Sunday Service. You were getting frustrated because, according to you, she was only supposed to 'ask nice stuff.' Then you asked if Leah was still upset because of what happened at the Haven. You even said you'd talk to your mom about it. So, yeah: I think you know a whole lot more than you're admitting."

As I'm speaking, Sylvie lowers her arm and drops her cigarette. She grinds it out under the toe of her high heel. Narrowing her eyes, she takes a step toward me. "Why do you care so much about Leah? What are you, some kind of stalker?"

"No, I'm not a stalker."

"Then how do you know all that stuff?"

"Are you saying it's *true,* Sylvie?" I squeeze my phone, grateful to be recording her every word.

"No, I'm not saying it's true. Jesus!" Sylvie crosses her arms, shrinking into herself. She shoots a look at Jocelyn. "Let's go back inside." Sidestepping me, she marches up to the door, but when she glances back over her shoulder, she stops—because Jocelyn hasn't followed her. She's still standing there with her arms crossed, looking like she's going to be sick. "What are you doing, Jocelyn?" Sylvie hisses.

But Jocelyn doesn't move. Her eyes dart back and forth between me and Sylvie.

Sylvie glares at her friend. "What the fuck, Joc? We barely know this girl. Come on."

Jocelyn still doesn't move.

"Jocelyn and I know each other better than you realize, Sylvie. You've tried to use us both: Jocelyn as your little ... servant, and me as your future puppet at the *Sentinel.* Your family used Leah the same way. And when she found out what you were up to, *one of you* killed her. And I think it was you, Sylvie."

Sylvie's nostrils flare as she glares at Jocelyn, like a dragon surveying the prey she's about to burn alive. "What the fuck did you tell her?" she snaps at Jocelyn.

Now that Sylvie's made her a target, Jocelyn crumbles. Holding her palms up in defense, she races up the steps to join Sylvie at the door. "I swear I don't know what she's talking about," Jocelyn insists. Redness creeps up her neck and into her cheeks.

"Yeah right," Sylvie spits.

"I didn't say you killed anyone!"

"She didn't," I confirm. "I figured it out on my own, Sylvie."

"Jesus Christ." Sylvie rolls her eyes and curses under her breath. She looks down at me. "What makes you think I had anything to do with Leah's overdose?"

"Because you had a shit-ton of oxy last summer! You told me so yourself, in Montauk." I move closer, slotting clues together with every step. "Duke told me you want to follow in your mom's footsteps and do PR for the company. I think you knew about the assault, and you found out about the emails Leah saw, and you decided it was a chance to prove how good of an Avalon employee you could be."

Sylvie sputters at me for a second. Then she rounds on Jocelyn again. "This is all your fault. I can't believe you, going around and spreading lies about my family to random strangers." She flings her arm in my direction.

Tears spring to Jocelyn's eyes. "Please don't be mad, Sylvie."

"'Please don't be mad'? Oh, I'm mad, Jocelyn." She waves her arm at me again. "I don't know who the fuck this girl is, but she's going around saying I *killed* someone."

"Because you *did*." There's a triumphant note in my voice, but I still need to get a recording of her confession.

"Shut up!" she yells at me, before rounding back on Jocelyn. "How could you do this, after everything I've done for you? You're just a random person from Wyoming." *Wisconsin*, I say to myself. "I gave you a whole *life*. I brought you to parties and restaurants. I introduced you to people. I flew you around in first class. What the hell did I do to deserve *this*?"

Jocelyn's glassy eyes plead with me. It's the same desperate look she gave me when I asked how Leah died, like a person scared into silence. I can see what happened to Jocelyn, clear as day. A New York City transplant from a farm in the Midwest, she fell under the Avalons' spell, electrified by the opportunities a friendship with Sylvie could bring her: the dinners at fancy restaurants, the parties with $460 bottles of champagne, the shopping trips to Paris, and most importantly for an aspiring chef, the connections to power players in the restaurant industry. It's no wonder that when Jocelyn found out her new BFF killed Leah, she chose to stay silent and protect the status quo instead of speaking up and losing everything.

"I'm so done with you," Sylvie tells Jocelyn.

Jocelyn drops to her knees. "Sylvie, please . . ."

"I'm serious."

Jocelyn turns to me, the look in her eyes frantic. "*Sylvie didn't kill Leah!* She didn't do it—I promise. I know who did."

Wait, what? I was so sure Jocelyn reacted that way because she didn't want to rat out Sylvie. "Who was it?" I take a step toward Jocelyn. "Who killed Leah?"

Sylvie stares down her nose at Jocelyn's trembling body. "Tell her it wasn't anyone in my family," she demands.

Jocelyn doesn't say anything; she just cries harder.

"*Stop crying and tell her,*" Sylvie orders.

I walk to the top of the steps and drop to my knees next to Jocelyn. "Tell me who did it, Jocelyn. Please. You don't have to keep protecting the Avalons. You don't need them. You got that Josephine Desjardins externship all on your own. Think of how good that felt. Think of how freeing it is not to be indebted to anyone." I rest my hand on her shoulder. I want her to think about us smelling tomatoes in the grocery store and celebrating her birthday on the beach: real pure moments, when she had fun for the sake of having fun and nothing more. My own words reverberate inside of me as I speak them to Jocelyn. I think of making rice bowls in the loft, and hanging with Zayn at Sweet Bean, and watching Killian play *The Sims,* and kissing Ivy on the roof. "Look at yourself, Jocelyn. It's killing you to keep the truth in. Are these people and their parties and their private jets really worth it to you? Are they worth sacrificing your values?"

Jocelyn gives a heaving sob.

"For the record, she doesn't owe you anything either," Sylvie snaps at me. "Who even *are* you?"

There's a loud thud. The church door swings open, and out spills Duke, a wad of paper towel pressed to his face. Blood from his nose spatters the top of his shirt, tie, and dinner jacket. Gracie and Rex follow closely behind. Rex's face is the color of roast beef. "What the hell is going on here?" he roars.

"Don't talk to her," Duke shouts at Sylvie. "She's not who you think she is."

"Who is she?!" Sylvie shrieks.

Tick, tick, tick, boom.

My time is up.

Might as well end this on my own terms.

CHAPTER 26

"I'm Noa Falk. Leah Falk was my sister."

Sylvie drops her champagne flute, and it shatters on the concrete. I jump back to avoid the shrapnel, pulling Jocelyn with me. "What the fuck?" Sylvie cries.

"She's been spying on us this whole time!" Duke exclaims from under the paper towel.

"You're a psychopath!" Sylvie yells at me.

"I just care about my sister!" I shout back, and I know, at my core, that it's true. "Don't tell me you wouldn't do the same for Duke. You would. You *did*. You killed Leah."

"*She didn't do it!*" Jocelyn screams.

My stomach sinks. I thought I could convince Jocelyn to finally divulge the truth, but apparently, she's still siding with the Avalons.

She steps toward the people who've given her so much:

dinners, parties, trips, job opportunities. Things she never could have imagined when she moved here from the Midwest.

But then Jocelyn says, "*She* did."

And points at Gracie.

CHAPTER 27

Gracie sheds her sweet demeanor like a snakeskin. She narrows her eyes at Jocelyn. "What are you accusing me of?" she hisses.

"Of poisoning Leah Falk," Jocelyn says. "I saw you. When she was in the bathroom, you went over to her bag and pulled out her water bottle. You took out a baggie of crushed pills and dumped it all in."

Oh my God—the water bottle Janie said she tripped over after she found Leah's body. Leah must have chugged the water, full of dissolved pills, when she got home from the party. Then she died on the floor. Alone. My vision goes white with rage. It was Gracie. Gracie, who was kind to my sister. Who earned Leah's trust. Who let Leah believe she cared about her career. All so that her family and their business could succeed. And as soon as my sister posed a threat to that success, Gracie did whatever she could to silence her.

The next thing I know, I'm running at Gracie. Jocelyn grabs me and holds me back. "Don't!" she screams.

"Don't you dare touch me," Gracie snaps.

"She trusted you!" I scream, my voice ragged. "You told her you cared about her—you fucking liar!"

"I highly suggest that both of you leave the premises before I call the police and charge *you*"—Gracie narrows her eyes at me—"with assault on my son." I've seen enough of the Avalons to know they would win that fight. I stand there, helplessly, as Gracie turns to the rest of her family. "Let's go inside. Duke, we need to get you cleaned up."

The Avalons go back inside Sunday Service, leaving Jocelyn and me outside on the steps. The shards of Sylvie's champagne glass lie at our feet. I hit Stop on my Voice Notes app.

"You recorded that?" Jocelyn asks.

"Yeah, but it was useless," I mutter. "She didn't confess."

As the full weight of the situation settles on my shoulders, I start to feel dizzy and lightheaded. I'm a rabbit in an open field with hawks circling overhead, searching for their next meal. I stumble and clutch the railing.

"Are you okay?" Jocelyn asks.

"We're both in serious trouble, Joc. Gracie killed Leah for knowing way less than we do. What if she comes for us too? How are we supposed to protect ourselves?"

Jocelyn grabs my wrist. "There's something I have to show you."

CHAPTER 28

"But first, let's get the hell away from here," Jocelyn says.

She's right. The Avalons are out for our blood. "I know where we should go." I start to pull her down the steps.

"Where?"

"Somewhere safe. Come on."

I can't stop looking over my shoulder as I lead her down the street and around the corner. With every car that approaches from behind, I'm convinced the Avalons' henchmen are going to jump out, throw bags over our heads, and whisk us away to our doom. The tension doesn't ease until we race down the steps to the subway station, tap through the turnstile, and make our way to the platform. I've never been so relieved to be engulfed by sweltering subway heat and a dense crowd of commuters. The train arrives within seconds of us getting there, and we cram ourselves into the nearest car. I text Zayn to let them know what happened, and that we're on our way.

We're surrounded by too many random strangers to talk

about what just happened, but as our train hurtles downtown, we communicate through locked eyes and squeezing each other's hands. At Union Square, we switch to the L, and before we know it, we're in Brooklyn.

"Is this where you live?" Jocelyn asks as we climb the stairs in Bushwick. Her tone isn't judgmental—just curious.

"It's where my best friend lives. I've been staying with them for the past couple of weeks."

Jocelyn shakes her head. "It's so weird. I literally don't know who you are, but I feel like I know you better than any of the Avalons."

I hold out my hand. "I'm Noa. I'm actually eighteen, I'm from New Jersey, and I'm starting at NYU in the fall."

Jocelyn shakes my hand. We both giggle in spite of everything we just went through. Whatever happens from here, at least we'll have our new friendship to buoy us.

I press the buzzer for 4A, and the door unlocks. *I'm home.* The smell of spices warming me from the inside out, I lead Jocelyn up the rickety stairs to the loft.

"Noa." Zayn bursts through the door as we reach the final landing, Ivy and Killian close behind. The three of them wrap me tightly in a group hug. Ivy's hand wiggles its way to mine, and she holds on, tight, like she has no plans of ever letting go.

"Everyone, this is Jocelyn," I tell my roommates. "And she's a hero. Joc, this is Zayn, Ivy, and Killian."

"You wanna come inside?" Zayn asks.

"Please," I answer.

"I still have to show you something super important," Jocelyn reminds me.

We go inside and gather around the island, where Jocelyn

takes out her phone. But before she taps the screen, she looks down and takes a deep breath.

"What's wrong?" I ask.

"I'm so ashamed that I've had this for so long, and I haven't said anything or shown anyone. But, whatever. At least I'm doing it now." She sniffs and looks up again. "Noa, I know you didn't get a confession, but I have evidence."

My jaw drops. "Evidence of what?"

"Of Gracie putting the pills in Leah's water bottle. When I saw her grab the bottle and open the cap, I got this bad feeling in my stomach. I was too scared to say anything, but I figured I should do *something*. So . . . I took a video. I'm not sure how good the quality is, but . . ."

She pulls up the video and hits Play. The footage is dark, but there's just enough candlelight in Sunday Service to make out Gracie pulling a plastic baggie from her purse. She glances once, twice, over her shoulders. Then she unscrews the cap and dumps the powder into Leah's water, shattering my sister's trust and ending her life as easily as if she were adding another smoked olive to her martini.

ONE YEAR LATER

COURT TV

LEGAL MATTERS WITH SUE-ELLEN ROSENTHAL

<u>Sue-Ellen Rosenthal:</u> It's the murder trial everyone's talking about. Closing arguments were presented today in the Gracie Avalon murder trial, and we're awaiting the return of the jury to find out if the Manhattan socialite will be found guilty in the death of twenty-year-old newspaper reporter Leah Falk. Here with me is former New York State Supreme Court judge, now Court TV lead legal analyst, Joe Washington. Joe, I want to start with: how long do we expect the jury to deliberate this verdict?

<u>JOE WASHINGTON:</u> Sue, it's tough to say. The jury will have a lot to go over in this case, but I

feel, as a viewer, that the prosecution delivered a very strong argument.

SUE-ELLEN: What effect do you think the prosecution's presentation of the video had on the jury?

JOE: If I were a member of the jury, to have a video presented of the defendant putting the pills in the victim's water bottle, that would be quite damning indeed. I would have found that to be very convincing.

SUE-ELLEN: Give me your prediction on when we might see the jury return.

JOE: I've seen juries come back in as little as two hours with a guilty verdict, but I've also seen juries deliberate for three or four days. We never truly know what the jury is discussing behind closed doors.

SUE-ELLEN: That's the drama of it all. Now, Joe, joining us next to talk about the case is Noelle Rice, social justice editor at the New York Times, who recently published a chilling exposé on the twisted relationship between the Avalon family and the newspaper the victim worked for, the Gotham Sentinel. Noelle, thank you so much for joining us.

CHAPTER 29

When I open the door of the loft, I smell smoke.

"Oh my God!"

Panic seizes my body. I drop my newspaper on the ground and race into the smoke, screaming Zayn's, Ivy's, and Killian's names. My first thought is that someone set the place on fire—that amid these wild courtroom proceedings, maybe the Avalons or one of their supporters decided to strike back at me by targeting my best friends and my girlfriend.

"*Oof!*" I collide with someone as they round the corner from the kitchen into the corridor.

It's Ivy. She grabs me by the shoulders. "Don't worry—everyone's okay! It's just a burnt cake!"

It takes a second for her words to sink in, and for the panic to begin subsiding. I've been supremely on edge since the trial began, and I don't see that changing until I know whether the jury finds Gracie Avalon guilty of killing my sister. It doesn't help that I've had to see Duke again, and deal with the traumatic memories of him shoving me into the wall at Sunday Service. Duke didn't look at me once today; neither did Rex or Sylvie, their chins held high as they watched the proceedings. They've all stood by Gracie's side for the duration of the trial. I suspect they still believe, deep down, that the Avalon family is untouchable, and that it won't be long before they're back to sipping champagne and looking down on the world from their ninetieth-story penthouse. And who knows? Depending on what the jury decides, their belief could turn out to be true. The jury didn't finish deliberating today, which is frustrating, but I'll take more waiting over an acquittal.

Ivy kisses me softly on the mouth, and that helps my heart rate get closer down to normal. She and Zayn were there for the proceedings today. Afterward, they came back to the loft while I grabbed something to eat with my parents before they drove back to the suburbs. Killian's shown up to the courtroom, too—and so has Jocelyn, when she's been able to get time off from the restaurant. It's meant everything to have them all there with me and my family, standing shoulder to shoulder against the Avalons.

"What's going on?" I ask Ivy.

"Killian tried to bake something for you tonight."

"Killian knows how to bake?" The most I've ever seen him do in the kitchen is chop veggies for other people's recipes, and even then, he needs close supervision.

"No, he does not." Ivy gestures around at the smoke-filled corridor. *"Clearly."*

Out of nowhere, I start laughing. It's a laugh that starts in my belly and bubbles up through my chest. And the next thing I know, I'm slumped against the wall, shoulders heaving. Have I lost my grip on reality? Maybe. But given what I went through at the courthouse today—not to mention everything that's happened in the past year—I'm going easy on myself.

By the time Jocelyn and I left the *Sentinel*'s fiftieth anniversary party, Gracie knew that *we* knew she'd killed Leah—and that meant both of our lives were on the line. After all, Gracie had murdered my sister for knowing less. We had to do everything we could to protect ourselves from the Avalons' inevitable attempts to silence us.

So we decided to silence them first. We copied the incriminating video onto a thumb drive and brought it in to the police station. Gracie was arrested the next day. Still, I knew better than to trust the criminal justice system to punish a powerful person like Gracie Avalon. So I also reached out to Noelle Rice at the *New York Times*. She'd been interested in learning more about Leah's pitch the summer before. I told her I had even more to add. Then I waited to see if she would respond.

As for Emmeline Gilbane, she was fired by the owners of the *Sentinel* when details of Gracie's arrest came to light. She deactivated all her social media profiles, skittering away from the public eye the way a cockroach does when you flick on the light.

Gracie's trial wouldn't begin for another eight months, but in the meantime, I had a semester to start at NYU. Zayn, Ivy, and Killian helped me move into my dorm in Greenwich Village, on the condition that I would come back for miso mushroom rice bowl nights at *least* once a week.

At first, as I stand there cackling in the corridor, Ivy looks at me like she can't make sense of what she's seeing. Then she presses her fingers to her lips, suppressing a laugh of her own. It comes out as a snort, and for some reason, that makes me laugh even harder, which in turn has the same effect on Ivy. She slumps against the wall too, and by the time the smoke in the hallway diffuses, we're both wiping tears from our eyes.

In the kitchen, Killian sits at the island with polka-dot oven mitts pressed to his temples. He looks traumatized. In front of him sits what could only be described as a smoldering black brick in a loaf pan. Zayn stands at the foot of a ladder propped against the wall, evidently having been tasked with shutting off the smoke alarm.

I walk over, pat Killian's shoulder, and nod at the black brick. "I'm scared to ask what that was supposed to be."

"Banana bread." He shakes his head. "The recipe was supposed to be easy."

"What happened?"

"For what it's worth, I think you got the recipe right," Ivy says encouragingly.

"Setting the oven timer is where it all went wrong," Zayn chimes in.

"It was supposed to bake for sixty-five minutes," Killian says. "I assumed it worked like a microwave, where you punch in the minutes *and* seconds. I pressed six-five-zero-zero."

"He set the timer for sixty-five hundred minutes," Zayn explains.

"Then I started playing *The Sims*." Killian looks at me sternly. "You know how sucked in I get when I play *The Sims*. I looked at the clock and realized it had been in there for three and a half hours." He sighs. "I was trying to do something nice to take your mind off all the other shit."

"Hey, it's the thought that counts," I assure him. "I appreciate it."

"We're still going to have a fun, relaxing night," Ivy promises me.

"Maybe there's something else we can make for dessert," Zayn suggests.

"Uh, I used up all the flour and sugar we had left," Killian says apologetically.

"I think I have an idea." I go to the pantry and look inside. "Yes! This is totally going to work." I pull out a jar of peanut butter, the leftover Hershey bars from the night we made s'mores on the stovetop, the jumbo bags of M&M's and Reese's Pieces that Zayn uses to de-stress at the end of a work shift, and lastly, a box of saltine crackers.

Zayn shrugs. "Snacks work."

"No, no, it's better than that. Trust me." I set it all down on the island.

"When Leah and I were growing up, our parents were super strict about not letting us eat dessert. This is what we'd secretly make in my bedroom sometimes." The memory tugs at my heartstrings, but not in a bad way. While I melted the peanut butter and the chocolate bars I brought home from the school vending machine in a glass bowl placed on the radiator, Leah sat on the floor and anxiously crushed the vending-machine M&M's, her ear to the door, listening for our parents' footsteps. She was terrified to break the rules—until she finally took a bite of our finished concoction, and the sweet-and-salty bliss made her stress disappear. "We can do it properly now, seeing as we actually have a kitchen." I get out two baking sheets and line them with wax paper. Then I grab a glass bowl, a rubber spatula, and the mortar and pestle. "Okay." I clap my hands. "We're making candy-coated saltines."

I break up the Hershey bars and throw them into the glass bowl with a heap of peanut butter. "Will you melt these together?" I ask Killian, smirking. "I hear you're better with the microwave than you are with the oven."

While Zayn and Ivy laugh, Killian nods sagely. "I earned that," he says before marching over to the microwave.

I open the bags of M&M's and Reese's Pieces and sprinkle them into the mortar. I look at Zayn and Ivy. "Can one of you crush these?"

"That sounds strangely satisfying," Zayn admits, picking up the pestle.

"Now we just have to lay these out on the trays." I pull out two sleeves of saltines, handing one to Ivy.

"You got it."

The brushing of our hands still gives me butterflies, even though it's been six months since we officially became girlfriends. In April, she brought me home to Connecticut to meet her parents. It was the first time she'd introduced her parents to a partner of any gender. Over dinner, her dad—a sweet, well-meaning man, but whose friends are mostly straight dudes in the suburbs—asked, "So, Ivy: If you and Noa are dating, does that mean you've officially chosen girls?"

Ivy and I smiled at each other before she responded. "It means I chose *Noa*," she told her dad. "Being bi doesn't mean you're waiting to make some 'final choice' about the gender you're into."

"It means you contain multitudes . . . all the time . . . and that's okay," I added.

Ivy nodded. Under the table, she squeezed my hand.

At some point, I'd like to bring Ivy home to New Jersey, but

I'm not quite sure when that'll be. On the recommendation of my therapist—shout-out to my old friend Millie Santiago for the referral—I've been taking some space from Dad while he works through his own shit. Mom finally convinced him to talk to someone—by stepping up and threatening to divorce him if he didn't, because she couldn't deal with his aggression anymore. Mom and I are getting closer. She's come to visit me in the city a few times. Hopefully, someday, I can get there with Dad—but whatever happens, I'll always have La Forêt.

Killian impresses everyone by not setting the peanut butter and chocolate mixture on fire. When he takes it out of the microwave, I stir it around until it's smooth, and then we all work together to dunk the crackers, lay them back out on the trays, and sprinkle them with the crushed candies. Fifteen minutes later, they're dry and hardened.

"Okay, these actually look gourmet," Zayn says.

Killian claps me on the back. "Thanks for saving the day."

I smile to myself. "You can thank me *and* Leah."

The sudden sound of the buzzer makes me jump a foot in the air.

"Sorry. I'm still so on edge," I say. "Do you know who's at the door? We should make sure it isn't—"

"I know who it is!" Zayn says as they skip over to the intercom. "I invited a special guest."

"You did? Who?"

Ivy and Killian smirk at each other.

A few minutes later, I hear the door open, and footsteps make their way down the corridor. A blond girl with a messy bun wanders into the kitchen. She wrinkles her nose and sniffs the air. "Is something burning?" Jocelyn asks.

"Something *was*," Killian says while I hurry over to hug my friend. She's been crushing it in the culinary world, earning herself a full-time job offer from Josephine Desjardins. Her eyes have permanent bags from the long hours she spends in the kitchen, but they still sparkle whenever she talks about her work. Work that she got on her own, without having to give the Avalons anything in return.

"Aren't you supposed to be at the restaurant tonight?" I ask.

"A colleague offered to cover for me when I told them what was up, and Josephine understood, too." Jocelyn holds up the big paper bag in her hand. "She even sent me home with baked goods."

Zayn presses their palms together in prayer. "The universe is looking out for us."

I hope so. There's no telling what tomorrow holds: whether the jury will finish its deliberations, and if it does, whether Gracie will be found guilty. The news stories keep saying how compelling that video of Gracie poisoning Leah's water bottle is, but still, you never know for sure.

As Jocelyn, Zayn, and Killian gather supplies to hang out on the roof, Ivy comes up behind me, slides her arms around my waist, and rests her chin on my shoulder. "I love you," she says in my ear.

She kisses my cheek, and I close my eyes, letting the warmth wash over me. "I love you too," I whisper back.

There's a world where I emerged from my experience with the Avalons terrified to trust anyone again. But because I have Ivy—and Zayn, and Killian, and Jocelyn—I know what real love feels like. It's a love that fills me up—a love that doesn't make me calculate how much I'm willing to give away. I hope that Leah, wherever she is, knows what real love feels like, too. Because she has me.

"Everyone ready?" Zayn asks.

"Ready!" Ivy and I answer in unison.

I lead the way down the corridor, but stop when I see what's lying by the door. I can't believe I forgot it there—the newspaper I was carrying when I came in. It's a copy of the *New York Times*.

Not a copy—*the* copy. The one with the feature I worked on with Noelle Rice for the better part of a year, using reporting that my sister knowingly and unknowingly began during her internship at the *Sentinel:* the interview with Sylvie, where she told my sister she was only supposed to ask nice questions; the interview with Tommy, where he all but pressured my sister into going on a date with him. There was also the material I got my hands on last summer, like Leah's internship log, and the screenshots of the emails from Emmeline and Rex. All of it made it into the final piece, which ran on the front page. Grinning, I read the words we wrote—together.

WICKED DARLINGS

Sexual exploitation. Lies. Murder. This is the story of how the corrupt relationship between a Manhattan dynasty and the newspaper that idolized them led to unspeakable horrors.

BY NOA FALK AND LEAH FALK

ACKNOWLEDGMENTS

My first thank-you goes to Eileen, who told me over matchas on a rainy day that I should write this book. I went home, slept on it, woke up, and feverishly typed up a pitch for *Wicked Darlings*.

Danielle Burby, thank you for believing in the idea. Thank you for always supporting me—not just as an agent, but as a friend during my own experience as a budding journalist in New York City.

Wendy Loggia, thank you for taking a chance on that feverishly typed-up pitch. Your trust in me means the world (as does your love for Jocelyn). To Wendy and Ali Romig: thank you for guiding me through some serious rewrites with your insightful notes. I'm so proud of this book, and I couldn't have written it without your brilliant minds showing me the way.

Thank you to the wonderful team at Random House Children's Books who got this book to the finish line and beyond. Publicist Kathy Dunn; managing editor Tamar Schwartz; copyeditor Colleen Fellingham; production manager CJ Han; and interior designer Kenneth Crossland: I am so grateful for the creativity and care you've put into this book.

Dad, I'm so glad we were hiking a mountain in Arizona together when the offer for *Wicked Darlings* came in. It was only fitting that I got to celebrate a new book with my Hype-Man-in-Chief. Mom, thank you for your loving support through the marathon of writing this book—including those Florida and Toronto visits when I needed to sleep about forty-seven hours a day. I love you both so much.

Tim, thank you for everything, including your expert consultation on Duke crashing the X5 and the Avalons' ensuing cover-up. Whenever I'm stuck, your love powers me through. You are forever my rock at the bottom of the river.

Finally, thank you, reader, for coming on this adventure with me.

ABOUT THE AUTHOR

Jordyn Taylor is a former magazine editor and the award-winning author of the young adult novels *The Revenge Game, The Paper Girl of Paris,* and *Don't Breathe a Word.* She is also an adjunct professor of journalism at New York University's Arthur L. Carter Journalism Institute. Jordyn was born and raised in Toronto and now lives in New York.

jordynhtaylor.com